Unforgivable

Megan Hart

Chaos Publishing

ebook ISBN: 978-1-940078-71-7
print ISBN: 978-1-940078-72-4

Unforgivable

There is nothing crueler than the person who doesn’t want you enough to keep you, but who doesn’t love you enough to let you go.

Alice and Mick, hot young lovers with the whole world ahead of them...until it all went catastrophically awry.

It takes so little to lose so much.

When a not-so-chance meeting at an old friend's party brings them back together, Alice must decide if the pleasure is worth the pain that will surely follow. After all, people, and relationships, can't ever really change.

But if Alice does decide to let him back into her heart—and into her bed—will Mick be ready to show her the man that he's become…and take a chance on love? Can Alice ever trust him again?

Is it possible to forgive the unforgivable?

Unforgivable was previously published as a 3-part serial, Don't Deny Me. It has been revised and collected as a full-length novel featuring angst, woe, a frustrating but charming hero and a determined heroine who find their Happy Ever After together.

For those who had trouble finding the words

UNFORGIVABLE

A Second Chance, Will He Won't He Romance

MEGAN HART

Alice to Mick

This is how it works, at the end of things. You stop finding reasons to talk. You make excuses to avoid each other, or worse, to fight. All the funny quirks and flaws you used to find endearing and charming, the bits and pieces that made you fall in love so hard and fast, they all start to curl your lip. In the beginning, you never want to leave, and in the end, all you do is struggle to stay.

And eventually, you stop struggling.

—Alice to Mick

Chapter 1

Alice Clark hadn't been to Bernie's place in about ten years, but nothing outrageous had changed. The slim saplings planted in perfect formation in the backyard to be used as bases for the softball and kickball games had turned into thick-branched shade trees. The garden had been expanded. The furniture in the living room had been rearranged but contained the same comfy, overstuffed chairs and sofas with plenty of tables for the placing of drinks. The floor-to-ceiling shelves still overflowed with books. The kitchen had been updated with new appliances, but the center island around which they'd always all gathered was the same, as were the wine and spice racks and the scent of something delicious simmering on the huge six-burner stove.

"Hello, beautiful girl." Bernie greeted her with a kiss on the cheek and a lingering hug. He handed her a glass of red wine and pointed to the platter of meats and cheeses on the island. "Help yourself."

"What can I do?" As the first to arrive, Alice felt it was the question to ask even though it was well known that she didn't know a paring knife from a potato peeler and could burn water if given the chance.

"You can sit and drink wine and stay out of my way," Bernie told her. "Cookie's getting changed. She'll be out in a minute. Sit, Alice."

Alice sat and sipped the wine with a grateful sigh. She closed her eyes for a moment, relishing the thick, rich flavor. Bernie had exemplary taste in wines. Well, in everything, really. Including his taste in women, she thought as Cookie floated into the kitchen with a warm grin and open arms.

"Alice! So good to see you! It's been forever. I mean, literally, it feels like forever." Cookie hugged Alice hard and ran a hand down the length of her hair. She stepped back to look her in the face. "Your hair is so long!"

"That's what happens when you don't cut it." Alice laughed.

Cookie patted her own cropped cut. Her hair had gone completely silver in the past ten years, but it suited her. "I couldn't stand the upkeep for mine anymore. I went pixie a few years ago. What do you think?"

"It looks great." Alice looked to Bernie, who was busy chopping shallots at the counter. Though she'd been in regular contact with both of them, she hadn't seen either of them in a few years, and she hadn't been to their house in much longer than that. "You both look great. The house, everything. I can't believe it's been so long since I've been here."

Bernie glanced over his shoulder. "You're here now. That's what counts. The others are coming along later. And on Sunday, the picnic is going to be epic. Cookie told me we didn't have to invite every single person we ever knew, but I told her that of course we did."

"But only the ones we love the best are invited to stay

over! We're so glad you decided to come share our celebration with us," Cookie said. "It wouldn't be the same without you here."

"It's like old times," Bernie added.

Old times, Alice thought with another sip of wine. Some of them good. Most of them, actually. It was just that the bad times tended to overshadow all the other memories.

"I'm sorry," she said abruptly.

Cookie, who'd been delicately loading a thin slice of crusty bread with a layer of shaved ham and brie, looked at her. "For what?"

"Alice means because it's been so long since she came for the weekend." Bernie flourished the knife and pushed the chopped shallots into a sizzling pan. The smell was immediate and glorious, and he added a splash of white wine.

The best part of having good friends was how easy it was to slip back into that friendship, no matter how long it had been since you'd seen each other. And how you forgave each other for that distance. Impulsively, Alice hugged Cookie again.

"Thank you for inviting me," she said. "Over and over again, until finally I stopped being stupid and agreed to come."

Cookie looked solemn. "We wanted our twenty-year anniversary to include everyone who's been an important part of our lives. That's you, Alice. And others, of course. But I'd have understood if you felt like you couldn't come. . . . You'll be all right. Won't you? I mean, it's been years. And we wouldn't have invited both of you if we thought it was going to be . . . painful."

Oh, it would be painful, Alice was sure of that. There was no way around the past, no forgetting how it had felt to love and lose and hate and grieve. But it would be the pain of memory, bittersweet and easily borne.

"It's been a long time," she said simply in way of response, and sipped wine.

Cookie hugged her again, holding her close and pressing her cheek to Alice's. When she pulled away, her deep green eyes glimmered with a sheen of surprising tears. Her voice thick, she laughed. "It's just so good to see you, Alice. Truly. We're so, so happy you're here."

"Me, too. Are you sure I can't help with anything?" Alice lifted her wineglass toward Bernie, who glowered and waved her off.

"Go pick some flowers from the garden for the table," he told her. "You're the one who always had the eye for arranging them."

Alice laughed and finished the last of her wine. "You're trying to chase me out of the kitchen, huh?"

"You know how he gets." Cookie gave her husband a fond look. She poured more wine into Alice's glass and handed her a piece of bread piled with meat and cheese. "But you'd better do as he says, or else he'll get grumpy and dinner will be late."

Alice took the wine and the food, biting into it with a groan of delight. "Can't have that," she said around the mouthful. "I'm starving."

"Everyone else should be here soon. Go, take a walk. Relax." Cookie smiled.

"I can take a hint." Swallowing the last of the bread, Alice took a long sip of wine and got off the bar stool. The drink had gone to her head a little, the long drive and no lunch making it easier for the wine to work.

She slipped out the French doors onto the back deck, for a moment overlooking the sloping yard and the trees beyond before carefully navigating the stairs in the way of someone who's just tipsy enough to fear falling. At the bottom she drained her glass and set it on the railing so she wouldn't forget to bring it back inside with her, and then she took the winding stone path toward the flower garden.

Bernie reigned in the kitchen, but the yard was Cookie's domain. They had a gardener who came to deal with the vast expanse of soft green grass, but the flower garden had always been Cookie's love project. Laid out to imitate a formal English garden but with what she liked to call her own "modern sensibilities," it featured several raised vegetable beds among the meandering paths, but most of it was thickly planted plots of flowers. Brilliantly hued wildflowers tangled in overgrown beds, while exquisitely pruned and tended roses in their first spring bloom bordered them. Tinkling fountains and birdbaths along with bird feeders, statuary, shaded benches for sitting and enjoying it all . . . the garden was amazing, and Alice admired the time and talent Cookie had invested in it.

Pulling a pair of gloves and shears from a small cupboard shed near the front of the garden, along with a pretty wicker basket looped with ribbon, Alice felt like the heroine of a Jane Austen novel—minus the floppy hat and empire-waist gown, of course. Her teal maxi dress was romantic enough, she guessed, if you could forget the fact it was made of clinging T-shirt fabric. Then again, she'd read once that Victorian women had sometimes wet the fabric of their gowns to get it to mold to their bodies and become transparent, so maybe her sundress wasn't so out of place for a romance heroine, after all.

Except she wasn't.

Not a heroine, not a romance. She was here for the weekend to see old friends, she reminded herself as she headed for a patch of bright purple and red flowers with feathery green stems. And if one of those old friends had once been more to her, so what? Time had passed, Alice reminded herself. They were both adults. There was no reason for either of them to be anything but pleasant. Maybe even cordial. She'd gotten over Mick McManus a long time ago, Alice thought.

And then, of course, she saw him.

Mick to Alice

The night we met, I didn't want to talk to you. I'd have had to make an effort. Find some small talk, some chatter, and you were so vibrant and bright I knew instinctively that there was no way I could possibly live up to that. Not just then, not with my own shit going on, stuff that now I can't even recall as being important but sure seemed heavy at the time. I needed air, so I went out to the deck with a beer I didn't even want to drink, and I settled myself into the shadows like some kind of brooding hero from a gothic novel. Thinking if nobody saw me, nobody would make me talk.

And then out you came, through the French doors, the hem of your dress swirling just above your knees. That green dress, the one without sleeves. You wore it every week that summer, because I told you it was my favorite. I liked it best because it's what you were wearing the first time I saw you.

—Mick to Alice

Chapter 2

It hadn't been a secret or anything. Alice being here this weekend. Bernie had made sure Mick knew all about it ahead of time, and he'd assured Mick that Alice knew, too. So there wouldn't be anything awkward or weird about it. It had been something like ten years, after all. More than time enough for old, bad feelings to fade.

So why, then, had Mick taken so much extra time deciding what to wear? To shave or not? Should he use product in his hair, shorter now than how he'd worn it then, and noticeably (at least to him) thinner?

Because it still mattered, of course. A decade had passed, but a century could've gone by and he'd still be trying to make sure he looked his best when there was a chance of running into an ex-girlfriend. And not just some random girl he'd dated once or twice, either. *Alice* was going to be at this party.

He'd seen her once in the past ten years. Three summers ago, Mick had gone down to Baltimore with some friends to celebrate a bachelor party. They'd hit a few of Fell's Point's multiple pubs, then made their drunken way over to the Power Plant Live, a club complex a few miles away. Some of the guys had suggested they keep walking until they hit the Hustler club a couple of blocks away, but Remy, the guy getting married, had a fiancée who liked to keep his balls in the palm of her hand. She'd made it very clear she didn't want him getting a face full of tits and pussy. Mick could've told her a strip joint was a safer bet—at least there the girls definitely weren't angling to go home with anyone. Remy, however, was balls-deep in love with his girl, so instead of the titty club they'd gone to a country rock bar with a mechanical bull and a surprisingly great '80s cover band that blew the audience away. Alice, in a green dress much like she'd been wearing the first time Mick met her, had been in the center of a group of muscular guys in black T-shirts. All of them dancing and laughing, two of them making her a sandwich for a few minutes before giving her up to dancing again with her girlfriends.

He'd known it was her in an instant, and not only because of that dress. Her hair had fallen to her shoulders, longer than the ear-length cut she'd worn when they'd been together, but it was the same glowing dark auburn it had always been. Her eyes, the same pale gray. The pattern of freckles on her shoulders was the same, a small cluster on the right one that he'd always pretended to connect-the-dots with. And that smile, the way she let her head tip back as she spun, the way she danced, unfettered and free . . . that was all the Alice he remembered. *His* Alice.

He hadn't said a word or tried to approach her. Not even after all that time, six or seven years' worth of it between them by that point. It wasn't the time or place for that, not even with the four shots of whiskey topped off with a few beers rolling around in his gut. He'd never been drunk enough to call her after she'd told him she never wanted to see or hear from him again, and that night had been no exception.

He'd regretted it, though. Worse than the hangover the next day. Mick had wished he'd been bold enough to at least say hello. After everything they'd been to each other, surely it had been a mistake to let a chance to talk to her escape him.

He'd make up for it tonight, he decided as he pushed open the French doors and headed for the garden. Cookie had told him Alice was down there—"Not," she said, "that I'm telling you to go down there to see her, or anything. But in case you maybe wanted to say hello before everyone else gets here."

It was exactly what he wanted. That first greeting between them, after so much time and all that had happened, shouldn't be in front of a crowd, where both of them would have to pretend they were happy to see each other. Unless they actually were. He thought he was going to be very happy to see Alice again, but there was always the chance she didn't feel that way, even if she had agreed to come despite knowing he'd be here.

What would she see when she looked at him? The idiot boy he'd been, or the man he'd worked hard to become? Maybe a little of both, Mick hoped as he paused at the bottom of the stairs to look at the wineglass on the railing, imprinted with the faint smudge of lipstick. For a moment he stupidly almost lifted it to his mouth. To put his lips where hers had been, a pale substitute for a kiss.

He was so fucked.

It was very likely Alice was going to eat him alive.

Chew him up, spit out the bones. And he'd deserve it, wouldn't he? For a moment, he thought of turning back. Being a coward, the way he'd been so many years ago. But no. He was here. So was she. The time had come to stop running away from the past.

Alice to Mick

In the beginning, there was always that awkward moment when we first saw each other after being apart. We might've spent hours talking on the phone, hours, even, in bed together. But those beginning months, every time in those first few moments, I couldn't bring myself to look at you. My eyes would skate away, and heat would flood me—even though at the same time, I was usually trying hard not to shake. You'd lean to kiss me, and I would fight and sometimes fail to keep myself from turning my head so your lips would land on my cheek and not my mouth. Because I wanted you too much, you see. When you kissed me hello or good-bye or any time in between, the lightest brush of lip on lip, a casual embrace, I wanted to open for you. Let you sink deep inside. It was all I could do not to leap into your arms, suffocate you with my desire. I was afraid to show you how much I wanted you, because somehow I thought that would make it more real.

And in the end, all I did was waste all those first times when I could've been looking at you.

—Alice to Mick

Chapter 3

Flowers whispered in the breeze, and Alice paused for a moment to contemplate which she wanted to kill. The pink roses were gorgeous, soft and velvety petals with bright green leaves. The red blooms, on the other hand, would blend better with the wildflowers she'd already gathered in her basket. What Cookie needed in her garden was purple roses, Alice thought, stroking one flower while she shifted the basket over her arm. Did such a thing even exist?

"Alice."

She didn't move. Didn't turn. Didn't blink or gasp or sigh, though every muscle in her body tensed at the sound of her name. She knew that voice at once, though it had been so, so long since she'd heard it any place but in dreams.

"Cookie told me you were here."

Of course he'd found her on purpose. Of course, she thought with a small and throbbing *thump-thump* of her heart that she could not pretend she didn't feel. Lifting her chin, putting on a smile, Alice turned.

"Mick." Alice smiled, one hand reaching for his automatically. Out of politeness, she told herself. Not because she wanted to touch him.

He surprised her when instead of taking it to shake, he drew her close for a hug. Nothing too unusual in that—their group had always been affectionate embracers, hugging on greetings and good-byes and randomly in between. She'd already been squeezed and cuddled a dozen times today by Bernie and Cookie alone, and would expect more to come from the other guests as they arrived. Still, when Mick's body pressed to hers, Alice found herself melting into his touch as though the years had never passed and nothing bad had ever happened to them.

It lasted a few seconds, just long enough for her to feel the softness of his breath against her ear and the light press of his fingertips at the small of her back before they were both breaking apart from each other. She with a small, hitching breath. Mick with an embarrassed cough.

"It's good to see you," he said. "You look . . . good."

Her brows went up. "That's the best you can do after all this time?"

It had been a gamble, guessing he'd respond the way he would've back then, but he must not have changed all that much because Mick laughed and took a step back to very clearly look her up and down before letting his gaze settle on hers.

"You look," he said, "fan-fucking-tastic."

"Better," Alice told him. "Much better."

Silence, a beat of it, then another. But not awkward. They'd had their share of those uncomfortable silences toward the end, struggling to find words that weren't angry or frustrated or disappointed. It wasn't like that now. More like they didn't have to say a word, she thought, and forced herself not to look away from him.

He'd hardly changed.

"You too," she added.

"Flowers?"

Alice gestured. "Yeah. Cookie asked me to get some. I can't decide between the red and the pink."

"Red."

She gave him a half smile. "You think so?"

"You think pink roses are a waste."

There it was, then. Proof he hadn't forgotten her. Hadn't unknown her. For a stupid second tears threatened, burning, and Alice blinked them away.

"These are pretty, though," she said.

Mick shook his head, moving closer to push aside the pink flowers and reveal the red bush planted next to it. "You're a red-rose kind of girl, Alice. Always were. Ouch, shit."

The thorns had pricked him, bringing blood. Mick stuck his thumb in his mouth with a wince. Alice couldn't hold back a laugh at his expression.

"That's why you should always wear gloves when you handle roses. They bite." She held up the shears. "Let me."

Two, three snips and she'd added a half dozen long stems of crimson-topped green to her basket. He'd been right, of course. The red ones blended perfectly with the other flowers, and though she might have grown less vehement about her feelings over the years about the usefulness of pale pink roses, she would never like them as much as red.

"Alice! Mick!" The shout turned both of them toward the house, where Dayna was waving at them from the deck. Mick raised a hand. Alice, after a moment, did, too. Dayna cupped her hands around her mouth to shout again. "Dinner's almost ready! And I can't wait to see both of you! Get your asses up here!"

Alice gave him a look. "We'd better do what she says.

You know she'll come down and drag us up by our ears if we don't."

"Can I get that for you?" Mick reached for the basket.

He didn't need to carry it for her, but she let him take it if only to feel the brush of his fingertips on her arm. She was still a little tipsy, though now it was hard to tell if it were still from the wine or Mick's proximity. He took her elbow when her toe caught on a tuft of tough grass that threatened to trip her.

"Careful," Mick murmured, and held onto her for a few seconds longer than was necessary to help keep her from falling.

When had she ever been careful when it came to him? There was no such thing, Alice thought, and that was what finally pushed her to put some distance between them. She had to get her head on straight. Just because they weren't at each other's throats didn't mean he was anything more than a stranger to her, really, after all this time. No matter what they'd been to each other before, before was not now.

Dayna had come down the stairs from the deck to greet them, and they were all caught up in the frenzy of greeting. Hugging, kissing, squealing, and in the midst of it, Mick slipped away to take the flowers inside.

"So," Dayna said, linking her arm through Alice's as they both went up the stairs, Alice pausing to snag her glass from the railing. "It's been forever since I've seen you. You look great. Your hair's gorgeous."

"It's been like, six months," Alice said. "I saw you at Jay's just after Christmas."

Dayna laughed. "Feels like forever. C'mon. Bernie's got something cooking that smells so good I want to die for it. And I think I heard Jay pulling in just before I came out to get you guys. Paul will be late. He always is."

"The old gang, back together," Bernie said a few

minutes later as Alice and Dayna returned to the now-crowded kitchen. He held a bottle of wine aloft. "Get pouring, everyone!"

Things got down to business. The party had started. Glasses were filled. Hors d'oeuvres consumed.

And through all of it, the noise and clamor and hilarity, Alice felt the weight of Mick's gaze on her, heavy as stone and hot as lava. She didn't allow herself more than a glance or two at him, though. More than that and she'd have been the one staring, and how hungry would her gaze have been?

He circled her, though. Oh, sure, he talked to Paul and Dayna and Jay, to Bernie and Cookie. But he circled back to Alice, standing close enough that his shoulder brushed hers just often enough not to be coincidence. And finally, at last, she couldn't feign any longer that she didn't know he wanted to talk to her and only her. She closed her eyes for a moment, battling with herself. She could walk away. She should.

"Hi," she said, turning toward him.

He had a beer in one hand. She a glass of wine. They stood in the same room they'd been in together many times, surrounded by the friends they'd both known forever. If she closed her eyes for a second, she might've been able to convince herself nothing at all had ever changed.

Other than everything.

There were conversations you could fall into naturally after having not seen someone for years. Job, kids, spouse? Alice didn't ask any of those questions. Neither did Mick.

He asked her if she'd read *that* book. Seen *that* movie. Had she tried *that* restaurant?

Yes, no, yes.

"And you," she said, when they'd all moved to the table

and she had a plate of Bernie's amazing pasta in front of her. "Have you been watching that show about zombie housewives?"

He had.

She smiled at him. He smiled, too. But then, even if it might've seemed for a moment or two that they were the only ones in the room, the truth was they were not alone. Bernie came to the table bearing a platter of grilled vegetables, and everyone oohed and ahhed, and Dayna raised her glass in a toast.

"To Bernie and Cookie, two people who really got it right."

They had. Alice watched them kiss, the light of love in their eyes undimmed even after twenty years. She wasn't the only one moved; Dayna had spoken with tears in her eyes and Jay snuffled audibly. She was glad she'd come, Alice thought without looking at Mick. Because this wasn't about her and Mick and the mess they'd made of things in the past. This weekend was about her friends.

Dinner, as always at Bernie's house, was delicious and decadent. Sitting across from Mick, Alice did her best to keep her attention on the conversations going on all around her, but it kept getting snagged by him. A word here or there. The way he shifted in his seat to reach for more salad, and she couldn't stop herself from admiring how broad his shoulders were in the blue button-down shirt.

She excused herself from the table. Thoroughly buzzed from a fourth glass of wine and the way Mick's foot had nudged her ankle too many times to be an accident, Alice shook her head in silent laughter as she made her way down the long corridor to the powder room. Light from the kitchen filtered in, but the hall itself was mostly dark. She put out a hand to guide her. Her fingertips skipped along the rough textured paint and brushed the rows of framed pictures on the wall.

Years of parties had been captured, imprisoned in cages of glass and wood. Captioned with the dates and Cookie's wry humor—"St. Pat's, the year we got more snow than a leprechaun has gold!" Alice was in many of these photos, her hair and clothes changing over the years more than she hoped her face had.

He was waiting for her when she came out of the bathroom. She knew the shape of him immediately, although the way the shadows fell, he might've been anyone. He didn't move when she took a step toward him, but he spoke.

"Hi," Mick said.

"Hi."

Did he reach for her, or did she take that last step to put herself up close, pressed along his body? It didn't matter. In the time it took for her heart to beat once, twice, three times, Alice was in Mick's arms.

The kiss fumbled at first. Faces turned the wrong way, teeth nudging the inside of her lip hard enough to sting, their noses bumping. An elbow in his side. He stepped on her foot. She pulled away, trying to breathe without gasping, and failing. Her fingers curled in the front of his shirt, and she tried to push him away but could not. She shouldn't be doing this. This was not the place, and this was most definitely not the man. Her fingertips stroked the back of his neck beneath the feathery edges of his hair, worn so much shorter than he had back in their days.

It was too late to run. His mouth found hers with better skill the second time. Tongues stroked. They breathed together. It was exactly the same as it had always been, yet infinitely, vastly different.

Alice broke the kiss again, this time to look into his

eyes. She let her fingertips trace the lines of his brows, then down the bristles on his jaw and finally to stroke a tender, inquisitive touch along his lower lip. His mouth parted when she did that. His eyes grew heavy lidded. Against her belly, the press of his cock grew hot and thick.

"What are we doing?" she whispered.

Any second, someone else would come stumbling down the dark hallway on the way to the bathroom and bump into them. Or worse, be smart enough to turn on the light switch at the other end of the hall and shove them into eye-stabbing brightness so they'd have to spin apart and fake an innocence nobody would be likely to believe.

"I'm kissing you."

He did it again. A little harder this time, urging her to sigh. His hand slipped into her hair, tangling his fingers and tugging tight while the other one slid farther down to cup her ass and pull her against him.

Ten years was long enough to change many things. Regimes could rise and fall. Movies could become media franchises. Cities could be built. People could change.

But this kiss didn't feel like ten years had passed. Yes, there were differences in the way he moved and touched her, in how he used his tongue. In the way he murmured into her mouth, her name at first and then, "I didn't forget how good you taste, oh shit, Alice, you taste so good." But it was all still Mick as she remembered him.

Breathing hard, Alice broke the kiss once more, this time to step back and put a hand on his chest to keep him from grabbing her immediately close. "Mick."

"Alice." His voice, rough and low and full of longing.

"What are we doing?" she asked him again.

He straightened. He took her hands, linking their fingers, pushing their palms together. "Whatever we want."

Mick to Alice

I never met a woman who made me feel the way you did. You could turn me upside down in a second with a laugh. Turn me inside out when you said my name, all sweet and soft, on the edge of a gasp or a moan. Nobody else ever made me want to punch a wall or break a glass. My dad always told me a man who shows his anger with his fists isn't much of a man, but damn, Alice, you had this way of making me lose my mind. You'd say you were being honest, and I guess you were, but your every word could be as barbed as an arrow, as honed and sharp as a sword, and you ran me through with them. You left me to bleed. And you didn't seem to take any joy in it, but you sure did manage to do it over and over and over again.

—Mick to Alice, unsent

Chapter 4

Mick could still taste her, even with the after-dinner coffee and chocolate mousse cake trying to replace her flavor. Kissing Alice had been like falling onto a soft bed after a week of camping on rocky ground. Like coming home.

Too bad they'd been interrupted by Paul. Or maybe it was for the best, Mick thought, watching her across the table as she sampled another of Bernie's desserts. The sight of her tongue licking along the tines of the fork sent an uncomfortable tingle straight to his crotch. The make out session had already left him with a semi-hard-on, and it was taking its good damn time in going away.

He caught her eye. Alice gave him a wicked, slow grin and took another long swipe of chocolate from the fork. She knew exactly what she was doing, the same way she always had. Time hadn't changed her very much at all, at least not in the obvious ways the years had affected most everyone else gathered around the table.

"Okay, teams," Cookie announced. "I put everyone's names into this hat, and you pull out the name of your partner. And I have prizes, of course!"

There'd always been prizes at Bernie and Cookie's parties, to go along with the board game marathons that inevitably ending up spiraling into good-natured chaos the more alcohol was consumed and the later the hours went. Tonight, Mick was awarded a hat shaped like a hotdog for his winning round at Balderdash. Alice, wearing a pair of sunglasses with a mustache attached, stood to pose for a picture with him, taken by Bernie. Then a selfie with her phone, their heads pressed together, both of them laughing like idiots.

"There's one for the fridge." It was what she'd always said about something she meant to keep.

"Send it to me," Mick said.

Alice paused. "I don't have your number."

"I'll give it to you."

"Mick, Alice, we're ready to go again," Paul called out. "Get over here!"

Taking his time, Mick recited his number to Alice so she could put it in her contacts. A moment later, his phone buzzed with an incoming text including the picture. "Gotcha."

"Do you?" Alice said with a lift of her brow and a toss of her head that set her dangling plastic mustache swinging.

Later, after the last of the wine had finally been drunk and the games disintegrated into laughter, when the kitchen mess had been tidied enough to make room for the breakfast cooking Bernie would be doing in a few hours, when everyone else had made their good-nights and headed for bed . . . when the house was quiet and still, Mick found her.

She was in the swing, as he knew she'd be. Big enough for two, hung from the branches of an enormous tree near the bottom of the yard and overlooking the chuckling stream that wound through Bernie and Cookie's property. Down past the garden, it was a favorite spot, much coveted and fought over by everyone who came to stay. Tonight, it was all theirs.

"Hi." He handed her a bottle of water and settled next to her without asking permission.

Alice moved over enough to give him space, but not so much that they weren't still touching hip to hip. Her shoulder brushed his as she cracked the top off the bottle and took a long drink. "Thanks."

They sat in silence for a few minutes. Every so often Mick pushed at the ground to get the swing gently rocking. The creek burbled and splashed, and somewhere, not so far away, an owl hooted softly. The wind sighed through the trees, bringing him the scent of her perfume.

"It's good to see you," she said finally.

Mick put an arm along the back of the swing to settle on her shoulders. "I wasn't sure you'd think that."

"Me neither, to be honest. Not until I *did* see you, and I realized it was going to be okay."

He turned a little toward her. "More than okay, I hope."

Alice said nothing. She didn't move away from him, but she didn't move closer, either. Her fingers toyed with the plastic bottle, tapping the sides.

His fingers brushed the back of her neck, beneath her hair.

She shivered.

Her lips parted, though if she actually spoke she did it so softly that the night breeze and rushing water ate her words. Mick let his finger trace a circle on her skin. Then a heart. When her back arched a little and she shifted, he stopped to let his hand gently cup the back of her neck.

"Mick . . ."

"I want to kiss you, Alice. Again."

She twisted to look at him. Her eyes glinted in a shaft of moonlight. "So kiss me, then."

Alice to Mick

Our first public kiss was an accident. During one of Bernie and Cookie's games, you and I were partners in some convoluted game of charades. Our word was love. I mimed a bride walking down the aisle; you drew hearts in the air with your fingers. But nobody could guess what we were trying to show, not until you took me in your arms and dipped me. You kissed me in an exaggerated, silent-movie kind of way, lots of wiggling around but no tongue. Somehow along the way, my arms went around you and I opened for you. Somehow, that kiss became real, right there in front of our friends, who were all screaming out guesses and none of them were right.

We lost the round, but I always thought we won.

—Alice to Mick

Chapter 5

The kiss in the hallway had been furtive and desperate. Lunging. Fierce.

This time, Mick kissed her gently and slow, urging her mouth to open with the subtle motion of his lips on hers. At the stroke of his tongue, Alice shivered and broke it. There wasn't much room on the swing for her to pull away. Instead, she put her face to the side of his neck and her arms around him. She let the scent of his skin envelop her, as much of an embrace as his arms.

There had been times when missing him had felt like someone had reached inside her and pulled out the part of her that remembered how to breathe. And times when she'd barely given the memories of him a second's worth of her time. Touching him now, having him touch her . . . a river of fire rushed all through her. And there was that pesky, pain-in-the-ass thing about fire. It burned. You could touch a hot stove a hundred times to make sure it would still burn you, and it always would.

Well, Alice thought. So would this.

"Mick . . ."

He kissed her again. Harder. One hand on the back of her neck, the other going to her hip, then her ribs just below her breast. She couldn't stop herself from arching a bit into that touch, doing her own urging with her body. It worked. Mick slid his hand up to cup her breast through the thin material of her dress. Her nipple went instantly erect when his thumb passed over it. She moaned.

"There's my girl," Mick whispered against her mouth.

His foot pushed against the ground to get the swing rocking again. The hand on her breast moved down between her legs, pushing her thighs apart slow, slow, slow, so that she had time to tell him to stop. And she thought about it, knowing this path they were taking was probably going to end up causing trouble, but in that moment no longer able to care.

Match to gasoline, that's what Mick had always been to her. Should, would, could—there were a hundred thousand heartbeats between now and the last time they'd kissed, but it didn't matter. She was touching that hot stove again with fingertips already scarred from the blisters.

He didn't have to move. The motion of the swing pressed his knuckles to her again and again, just enough pressure each time to build up the pleasure before easing off. When she gasped, he laughed against her lips before kissing her again.

It went on and on, every sensation weaving together. The breeze and far-off cries of night birds. The water splashing on the rocks. The creak of the chains against the tree's branch. Mick's low moan when she unbuckled his belt to free him. His sharp gasp when she slipped a hand inside to stroke his erection. The sound of his desire added a fresh layer to her own.

It had always been like this with him. Knowing how to move. Where to touch. How hard, how soft, how fast or slow. She was on the edge within minutes and stayed on it for an hour, as every so often he'd push the swing again to keep them going.

You're a fool, her mind said. Idiot. Resist, her heart urged. You're only going to regret it! Head and heart for once were in agreement, but it was another part of her anatomy altogether that kept her going. At last, unable to keep herself from it, Alice pulled her mouth from Mick's and bent to take his cock instead. The angle was awkward, the swing not the most comfortable seat, but just as Mick had used the rocking to arouse her, now Alice was able to do the same. All she had to do was take him inside her mouth while the swing moved him in and out.

He muttered her name. One hand fisted into her hair. The other stayed between her legs though he'd managed now to slide a finger underneath the edge of her panties—plain cotton. If she'd known this was going to happen, she'd have worn silk or lace. She should've known. She was so wet that one finger slipped inside her without friction.

Mick pushed. The swing rocked. His finger moved in and out of her in the same rhythm that her mouth moved on his cock. They were completely in sync.

He said her name again, like a warning this time. With another smile she bent back to him again as her climax rippled through her. Her body clutched at his fingers as she took him in deep. Not letting go. The sound of Mick's hoarse shout as he came sent another wave of orgasm washing over her.

Body aching from being contorted into positions that hadn't been painful when she'd been distracted by pleasure, Alice sat up. The taste of him lingered; she leaned to kiss him and he sucked gently on her tongue before pulling away to look into her eyes.

"Whoa," Mick said.

Alice laughed.

"I mean, that was . . . whoa."

She swatted him lightly, a little embarrassed but mostly pleased. "Stop."

He pulled her close to kiss her again. "Never."

It was something he'd have told her way back then, so Mick, so familiar, and yet suddenly so unwelcome because it reminded her of broken promises and betrayal. She didn't yet regret what had happened, but she figured that was on its way. She sat back. He did, too, maybe feeling the way she did or maybe just sensing her discomfort.

"It's late," Alice told him. "We should get inside."

Mick to Alice

Whenever I see any of them, I always think of you. I can't help it. I mean, I would never have met you if I hadn't been invited to Bernie's house. You and I became so much more, and now it looks like we've turned into something so much less . . . but that never stops me from remembering you when I'm hanging out with them. They've stopped asking me about you, though. I guess they learned not to, maybe by my expression or how I find a way to change the subject when your name comes up. The worst part of it is, they were your friends first. And because of me, you lost them. They'd never say it, but maybe you would, if you'd only still talk to me, Alice. But you never answer me, so I guess that means you plan to never speak to me again.

I'm sorry for that, to have taken something away from you that meant a lot. But mostly I'm sorry that whatever I did made you hate me so much you'd be willing to give up the people who love you more than I could.

—Mick to Alice, unsent

Chapter 6

"Morning." Paul had always been an early riser like Mick. "Coffee?"

Mick helped himself to a mug from the cupboard and held it out for the other man to fill. Bernie had put out some trays of pastries and breakfast breads last night, though later he'd be making an enormous brunch. At the moment, running on only two hours of sleep, Mick thought coffee was more than plenty.

"Looks like it's going to be a great day." Paul went to the French doors to look out. "Can't wait to hit the lake. You in?"

"Yeah. Probably." Mick sipped the sweet, rich coffee with a small sigh and leaned against the counter. "Sounds good."

Paul looked at him over his shoulder with a grin. "Need a little hair of the dog? I brought some Baileys."

Mick wasn't hungover, at least not from drinking too much. He was suffering from a severe case of Alice withdrawal, something no morning shot of liquor was going to fix. He imagined he could still taste her, smell her, feel her.

He'd dreamed of her in the brief and fitful sleep he'd managed after finally drifting off. Jumbled images of her smile, her body, scenes from the past along with things that had never happened.

"Nah, man. I'm good." He lifted the coffee. "Just tired."

Paul rolled his neck on his shoulders. "I hear you. We're all getting fucking old, man. Used to be we'd be up until dawn and still manage to spend the day doing all kinds of stuff. Now if I'm not in bed by ten, I pay for it all the next day."

"Nobody was in bed last night before ten." Mick looked over the breakfast tray, at last considering a bagel with cream cheese, but not quite up to the effort of actually toasting one.

"Nobody'll be out of bed before ten, either." Paul laughed. "Hey. It's good to see you, man. It's been what. A year? Two?"

"Denver. Two winters ago." A bunch of them had gotten together for a weekend ski trip, not quite as extravagant as a weekend at the lake house but still fun. They'd tried to meet up for drinks or dinner since then, but schedules hadn't worked out.

"That was a good time. This'll be a good time, too. I need it. Work's been hell."

The conversation turned to work and life and after another half hour Dayna wandered into the kitchen to give them both absentminded but affectionate hugs and kisses to the cheek. Jay, scrubbing sleep from his eyes, was next. Every time a new person came through the doorway, Mick braced himself for the sight of Alice, but it was never her.

She'd left. He knew it. She'd snuck off before dawn, desperate to get away and forget about him. He'd screwed up, pushed her too fast and too far.

And then, there she was. Not exactly radiant, her gorgeous dark red hair tied on top of her head in a bun messy enough to be truly slept on and not for affect. No makeup but the faintly purple shadows that had always plagued her with lack of sleep. Not pretty, but beautiful. Laughing, she didn't look at him as Paul handed her a mug of coffee and Dayna urged her toward one of the stools at the kitchen island.

"Still got it for her, huh?" Jay said this so quietly that nobody else could've heard him, but Mick still jumped slightly.

Guilty, he shrugged. "It's been years."

"Some things don't go away." Jay let his gaze drift to Paul for the barest moment before giving Mick a small, tight-lipped smile.

By the time Bernie came down to start the cooking, Mick had drunk enough coffee to finally feel like he might be able to keep his eyelids open without the use of toothpick props. Soon the smell of bacon and sausage filled the kitchen, along with omelets made with fresh-sliced ingredients they'd all pitched in to prepare. Someone had put on some music. Some people danced. Cookie broke out the Bloody Marys and mimosas.

"It's already halfway to shit-faced o'clock." Jay lifted his mug toward Mick, who'd escaped the bustle in the kitchen to the deck outside.

Mick had been avoiding the booze so far, though through the window he could see Alice sipping from a champagne glass of orange juice. "Booze and food and games. Hear we're going to the lake in a bit."

"Yeah." Jay leaned on the railing to look out over the yard. "It's gonna be great."

And it was, of course. It always was when this group of friends got together. Some had known each other since college. Others had been introduced through relationships that had come and gone. There'd been some blowups over the years, clashes of personality. Moments of sudden, uncomfortable silence. But for the most part, these people had been in Mick's life for so long he couldn't imagine life without them, no matter how infrequently they saw one another.

It had been that way with Alice, too, for too short a time, until one day he'd woken up and realized that was it. She was really gone. No more late-night phone conversations, no more early morning lovemaking. No more fingers linking while they walked, no more laughter. Alice had disappeared from his life.

Until now.

"Good morning," he said to her at last when he brought a handful of dishes to the dishwasher she was loading.

She straightened to take the plates from him, fitting them neatly into the racks with a small smile for him. "Hi."

"Sleep okay?"

"Great." Dishwasher full, Alice reached for the soap and added it to the dispenser while Mick stood there like an idiot. She shut the door and pushed the button to start the cycle, then looked at him.

Her expression, open and neutral and without hostility, nevertheless sank his heart. There was no glimmer in her eyes. Nothing to show that last night they'd fucked around on the swing, that she'd made him come with her mouth, that he'd gotten her off with his fingers. The memory stirred his cock even now, and he wished he wore more than the lightweight pajama bottoms.

"You going to the lake?" she asked.

"You?"

She nodded. Around them, their friends laughed and

talked, making it really easy for her to stay silent without making a big deal out of it. Mick swallowed more words, smiling instead and backing off.

Forty minutes later, spreading out the blanket on the nubbly, sandy shore of Crane Lake, Mick was already wishing he'd been smart and stayed back at the house. Gorgeous weather, bright sunshine, more wine, good friends . . . the perfect recipe for a great day, and yet all he wanted to do was stare at the only woman who'd ever broken him.

He was an asshole.

It didn't help that Alice wore an emerald green bikini, vintage-styled with a high-waisted bottom. She looked like a fifties movie starlet with her hair up, her toenails painted crimson. She tipped a bottle of cola to her lips as she laughed at something Dayna was saying, and in that moment, Mick wished he could snap a picture of her without looking like a creep. It was bad enough she caught him staring, her smile fading a little before she turned her gaze away.

A dip in the water didn't help him, either, and finally Mick gave up. "Hey, I'm heading back to the house for a nap."

Cookie looked concerned. "Are you okay?"

"The best place to nap is on a towel in the sand," put in Dayna as she stretched out with a sigh of pleasure.

Mick gathered his towel and shrugged back into his button-down. "Right, and wake up with a dick drawn in permanent marker on my face?"

Dayna gave him an exaggerated look of innocence. "That was one time!"

"Yeah, well, I'm gonna sleep in the dark and quiet, unmolested." Mick laughed and flipped Paul the bird when the other man made a rude gesture. "See you all later."

Behind him the laughter swelled and eased. The walk back to the house took only ten minutes or so along a path carpeted with pine needles. He passed the stream and the swing, forcing himself not to linger, and headed for the house. He had the basement room, the smallest guest space in the house, but even though the bathroom was also tiny, he'd always preferred it for the privacy. Just off the furnished rec room, it was apart from all the hustle and bustle of the house, and with only one small window, it could be made completely dark. And silent.

He smelled of sunscreen and the lake water, but the bed was tempting him so much he didn't even consider a shower. Instead, he shucked out of his trunks and shirt, kicking his sandals beneath a chair, and slipped naked into the soft, cool sheets. He was asleep in minutes.

Alice to Mick

I am drunk on the memory of your touch.

The taste and smell of your skin. The feeling of your breath on my face and your arms going around me, pulling me closer, and how you let your mouth drift along my cheek to kiss the corners of my eyes, because you said you like the lines there.

You said I was beautiful, and it made me want to cry. Not because I didn't believe you meant it, but because I did. There in that moment, I was as lovely as I might ever be.

I needed to leave, but could not make myself go. Stay, you asked me. A half hour more.

And I did.

—Alice to Mick

Chapter 7

Alice didn't make a big deal about heading back to the house. She waited fifteen minutes, giving Mick plenty of time to get there and everyone else the chance to pretend they weren't noticing that she was also leaving. It wasn't that she cared, exactly, if any of them thought she and Mick were hooking up. She just didn't want to have to talk about it.

Why she'd followed him was a question she couldn't quite answer. Last night's adventure on the swing had seemed inevitable at the time, after the kiss in the hallway. After the hours of lingering looks and casual touches. When had she ever been able to resist him? Even when she'd hated him, Alice had been unable to stop herself from wanting him. And she hadn't actively hated Mick for a long time.

She didn't hate him now, neither.

What she felt for him couldn't be described. Lust, of course. Longing. She'd been unable to stop thinking about kissing him. Touching. She'd worried the thoughts of fucking him the way she was prone to probe and fuss with a snagged nail or the rough edge of a tooth . . . poking something that should be smoothed away and forgotten.

She shouldn't have kissed him. Definitely should not have touched him. Yet here she was again, on a path to self-destruction that confused and exhilarated her. She could tell herself all she wanted that it had been a one-time thing, a mistake made from a little too much wine and a little too much time.

Yet here she was again, letting herself in through the sliding glass door to the basement, pausing to slip off her flip-flops. She pushed her sunglasses to the top of her head, blinking so her eyes could adjust to the dimness inside. She could just go upstairs, she told herself. Take a shower in the bathroom she and Dayna were sharing. Slip into her own bed and fall into a nap. She didn't *have* to do this.

Except, oh, how she wanted to.

She didn't knock. He hadn't locked the door, and she slipped into the dark room, her bare toes making only a whisper on the hardwood floor. The blinds on the single window had been drawn so only the tiniest crack of light shone through, but after a minute or so she was able to see well enough. The basement room was outfitted with a double bed, dresser, and overstuffed recliner, with a small flat-screen TV mounted on the wall, and she took all of this in before letting her gaze settle at last on the bed. The shape beneath the covers.

He breathed softly, in and out. Sleeping, she thought with some relief. She hadn't woken him. She could still back out. Save herself.

But of course, Alice didn't. For better or worse, they'd both jumped on this train last night, and she was still riding it. She moved toward the bed, careful not to make a sound. She didn't want to startle him awake. Instead, she gently drew back the covers to reveal inch after inch of his naked flesh, her throat closing at the sight. When she'd pulled the covers low enough to catch a glimpse of the hair low on his belly, her hands started to shake. She had to pause.

"Alice."

The sound of her name sent a whirl of emotions through her, so fierce she had to close her eyes against them. Mick's hand circled her wrist, keeping her hand from tugging the blankets any lower. She waited for him to ask her what the hell she thought she was doing. Maybe even to tell her to get out.

He pulled her closer, instead. Eyes still closed, hands still shaking, Alice slid into the bed next to him. They were entwined in a moment. His mouth on hers. His hands diving into her hair, tugging it out of the elastic so that it tumbled down all around them. She gasped at the press of his tongue in her mouth, and Mick drew the breath out of her.

When his lips left hers to move along her jaw, his teeth nibbling, Alice arched into that caress. She said his name. His fingers twitched, pulling her hair, tipping her head back so he could get to her throat. The press of his teeth there left her shivering, nipples tight. Her pussy throbbed, the sleek fabric of her bathing suit rubbing her clit until she squirmed.

Mick shifted, sliding his thigh between hers, then moving on top of her so that the thickness of his hard cock pressed against her. In the darkness she could only glimpse the barest hint of his features, but she didn't need to see his expression to imagine the heavy-lidded look of his desire. She could hear it in his groan. Feel it in the nip of his teeth on her throat, then the soft swipe of his tongue in the same spot. In the way he moved against her, his cock rubbing, rubbing like magic on her swollen clit as though the thin material of her bikini bottom existed only to create just . . . that . . . much . . . more . . . pleasure.

They rocked together. Moving in time. Over and over, Mick rolled his hips to slide his erection along her. Alice cried out, low, when his mouth moved lower to take her nipple between his lips. Sucking hard, then biting through the cloth. She wanted him to strip her naked and fuck her, but that would mean he'd have to stop what he was doing now, and the thought of that was unbearable.

"Oh, fuck, Alice, you feel so good." He kissed her, hard and bruising, and she didn't mind the pain.

"Harder," she whispered.

He moved. Faster. Harder. Her top came undone, and he buried his face between her breasts as one hand went beneath her ass to tip her closer against him.

So close. So. Fucking. Close.

She was coming, then, every nerve exploding in the pleasure of him hitting her just right, over and over. Her nails raked his back. Mick groaned and shook. In the next moment, his heat splattered on her belly and breasts; the sensation of it sent her over into another round of climax that left her spent and shuddering.

Mick propped himself on his hands, thrusting a last few times, this time in the slickness on her bare belly. His cock, so thick and hard and hot, fit perfectly against her, and she slipped a hand between them to cup him for a moment as he collapsed on her.

In the silence that followed, he nuzzled her neck. Then he rolled off her. Beneath her still-cupped palm, Alice felt the sticky sweetness he'd left behind, but she could not rouse herself to move.

She didn't have to. Without a word Mick got out of bed and went into the bathroom. The water ran in the sink. In another minute he was back with a warm wet cloth that he used to swipe along her skin. Carefully cleaning her up, then running his hands over her body to make sure he'd done the job right.

Mick's hand fit between her legs, the heel of it pressing her still swollen clit. "I think I made a mess of your bathing suit."

She rolled to face him, pushing a leg between his and fitting her face to the hollow of his neck and shoulder. "It can be washed."

Mick pulled the covers up over both of them, then settled back against her. His hand stroked her hair, over and over. He kissed the top of her head. She was going to fall asleep here, and that would be awkward.

"The others will be back soon," Mick said in a low voice.

"Yeah."

"We should get up. Shower or something. Maybe open a couple bottles of wine for dinner."

She tilted her head to look up at him, though she still could see nothing more than shadows. "You don't want them to know."

"Do you?"

"No. Yes. I don't care. No," she said again. "It might make them feel weird, you know?"

"To see us back together?"

She propped herself up on her elbow at that. She'd had no trouble picturing him before, but was unable to imagine his expression now. "We're . . ."

Not back together, she meant to say, but the sound of voices and laughter and footsteps on the deck overhead cut her off. She sat up. Both of them moved at the same time, and even in their rush to hide what they'd been doing, Alice couldn't help noticing how in sync they were. She went left, he went right, both got out of bed. She gathered her flip-flops and towel, wrapping it around her waist.

"Back stairs," Mick told her. "They're all going into the kitchen."

It was like the first time they'd been together, as furtive and giddy, and she bit back laughter as she started out the door. He grabbed her wrist to hold her still. Kissed her, licking at the corner of her mouth before swatting her ass lightly and opening the bedroom door for her.

Alice took the back steps two at a time, reaching the hallway just as she heard the lilt of Dayna calling her name. She jumped through the bedroom door, tossed her towel to the floor, and hurtled into the bathroom, where she leaped into the shower and turned on the water as she stripped out of her suit, all just as Dayna rapped on the door connecting the bathroom to her bedroom.

"Alice?"

"Hey." The water had not warmed up, and Alice bit her tongue to keep her teeth from chattering. "I'll be out in a few."

Dayna, who'd never had much of a problem with personal boundaries, peeked around the door. "No rush. How was your nap?"

"Very . . . refreshing." Alice scrubbed at her skin, washing away the last evidence of Mick's touch, and prayed he hadn't left any marks that couldn't be swirled down the drain.

Or maybe hoping he had, she thought as Dayna chattered away and Alice let her hands roam over all the places he'd so recently touched. She ducked her head beneath the spray, letting the frigid water pebble her skin into gooseflesh. She cupped her breasts briefly, then slid a hand between her legs. He was all over her. Everywhere.

Mick McManus was never going to be washed away.

Mick to Alice

I know I disappointed you. I know I let you down. I guess most guys are a little used to that feeling—we want to make you happy, but we don't know how to do it, and sometimes we're too stubborn to ask you exactly what you need from us. And sometimes, you have to admit it, you don't or won't tell us, or maybe you can't, so it's this clusterfuck of misinterpreted emotions and desires, and nobody ever wins. Someone's always angry or hurt. I knew it, at the time, that what I was doing couldn't end well. I couldn't seem to stop myself from hurting you. It doesn't make it right. I know that. All I can say is that when I look back on what happened, how it all ended, there were things I blamed you for, but never for telling me to fuck off.

—Mick to Alice, unsent

Chapter 8

"No, no, no." Dayna, laughing, shook her head and got up to demonstrate what she was talking about. She jerked one way, then the other. "It was like this. I mean, he danced like he'd been pithed."

Paul got up to join her, grabbing her by the hips to do a bump and grind. Moments after that, everyone was on their feet, gyrating. Booze helped, Mick thought as he took Dayna's outstretched hand and twirled her. Then Cookie's. And then, eventually, inevitably, Alice's.

She fit so right against him that though the time came almost at once for him to let her go so she could dance with another partner, he didn't do it. He couldn't stop himself from pulling her closer. Gripping her a little harder. It had only been a few hours since they'd been dry humping like a pair of teenagers, but smelling her now, soap and water and that subtle scent of Alice, his cock twitched all over again.

She must've seen something in his expression, because with a smirk and a toss of her hair Alice pushed him away to dance with Bernie, then Jay. Dayna moved into Mick's arms. For a moment she looked over at Alice and gave him a knowing smirk, but Mick pretended he didn't see it.

The dancing went on until Cookie collapsed onto the couch and with a breathless command said, "I need a break! This old lady is going to expire!"

More drinks, more food. Bernie ushered them all into the basement theater area to watch old home movies from back in the days "before cell phones and selfies." He'd transferred a bunch of footage from old VCR tapes and digital video to DVDs, and the group settled in to the plush leather recliners with popcorn and candy from the authentic movie theater display case Cookie had picked up at an auction. This was the life, Mick thought, only a little envious at the luxuries his friends had managed to accumulate. He ended up in the back row of the tiered seating, next to Cookie, who was controlling the light dimmer.

"Look how young I was," she murmured as Bernie hit play on a series of videos taken during what looked like an epic Fourth of July party.

Mick hadn't been at that party, which had happened before he met Jay, who'd been the one to start bringing him around. But Alice had. Her hair had been worn to her chin in a blunt bob when he'd met her, but in this video she wore it buzzed short around her ears, with some longer bangs on the top. Streaks of blond, some black tips.

"Oh, God," Alice said. "You caught me in my punk rock phase!"

She looked, Mick thought, gorgeous. He looked at her now, sitting two rows up from him. Silhouetted in the light from the screen. Laughing. Happy, he realized. He was seeing how she looked when she was happy. There in the movie, and there in front of him.

Had she ever looked like that when she was with him? Maybe in the very beginning, before it had all gone to shit.

But even then, her happiness had been overshadowed by the drama of their relationship. Whatever joy Mick had given her had been fleeting and probably eclipsed by the grief he'd caused her.

He'd spent a lot of years regretting the way things had ended with Alice, but until just now Mick had never truly realized how much he must have hurt her to take the light from her eyes in almost every memory he had of her. In the way they were still dark when she looked at him now, even when they were fucking around. Watching the Alice in that video, he saw her as she'd been before she met him. Vibrant. Alive. Free. A little wild, a little wacky, nothing close to the shuttered, chilly woman he'd once left sitting and waiting for him so long that she'd given up on him.

Watching her now, Mick saw not the woman she'd become, but the woman she must've always been . . . when she wasn't with him. It didn't sit well in his gut, seeing this. That somehow everything they'd been to each other had bruised and dimmed her. He'd known all this time that he'd been an asshole, that he'd been the reason for their breakup, that if he'd been a little less selfish and scared or a little more willing to take a risk, he and Alice might've had a longer run. Or at the very least, managed to part as friends instead of shattering so violently there'd been no way of ever putting anything back together. But what he hadn't known, or maybe just refused to admit, was that no matter how much he told himself that time healed all wounds, what he'd done to Alice had changed her intrinsically. Irrevocably.

Unforgivably.

Alice to Mick

There are levels to the experience of making love. There's the act itself. Being caught up in the moment. Pleasure. Comfort. Moving together, mouth to mouth, breathing in and breathing out. The language of moans and sighs tell the story of every touch and tease.

Then there's what happens after. The next day, when you stop in the middle of a task, distracted by that faint bruise pressed into your flesh by your lover's touch. When you lose track of what you were thinking because all you can remember is how it felt to be naked, skin on skin. The sound of his voice when he said your name, and how he arched and writhed when you stroked him. How you tried to leave but had to go back to bed to kiss him good-bye once, twice, three times, and how he gathered your hair in his fist to tug you closer so that another hour passed before you could finally tear yourself away. How you can still smell him all over you.

The memories last longer than the time it took to make them.

—Alice to Mick

Chapter 9

Alice ought to have been embarrassed by those old videos. Her hair, her clothes, the extra bit of pudge around her middle she'd spent the last ten years working hard to take and keep off. Yet Alice didn't feel ashamed of any of it. The moments captured in these mini movies had, for the most part, been the highlights. It would've been easy to let herself pretend those happy moments had been the only ones.

For a second, she risked a glance back at Mick.

He wasn't looking at her, thank God. That would've been embarrassing, to be caught like that. Never mind that they'd spent the afternoon getting each other off, or that last night she'd gone down on him on the tree swing. Heaven forbid she meet his gaze, Alice chided herself. She made herself look at him again, this time letting her eyes linger. Hoping he *would* look at her.

He didn't. He kept his focus on the screen, or on Cookie beside him. He laughed at something the older woman said, leaning closer. Alice looked away, and after that, she didn't try again to catch his eye.

"Oh, the wedding," Cookie said from the back of the room. "Whoever told me that dress was a good idea, you ought to be kicked someplace soft!"

She'd worn a mermaid style gown with lots of flounces. Her blond hair in a sleek French twist. She was thinner now than she'd been back then, Bernie a little heavier, but the love they shared was obvious in every glance. The video clip wasn't long. Three, maybe five minutes, tops. No dialogue, just some faintly cheesy dubbed music that nevertheless had Alice's throat closing with emotion. Twenty years was a long time to love someone that much. She couldn't keep up an interest in a television series that lasted longer than about three seasons. Loving someone for a couple of decades seemed impossible.

At least that's what she told herself, not believing herself in that moment, not with knowing Mick was sitting in the back of the room. She'd fallen for him hard and fast, and the relationship itself hadn't lasted very long . . . but the feelings . . . oh, those had lasted, hadn't they? All these years later, and the mere sight of him had sent everything inside her swirling and tangling all over again. It wasn't love, Alice reminded herself as the wedding video ended. It might've tasted a little bit like it, but in the end, it was only desire.

The lights came up briefly while Bernie got up to switch the DVD. Cookie brought a fresh round of drinks and more snacks, and some people used the bathroom, but Alice kept to her seat. For the first time that weekend, she wished she had her phone in her pocket so she could pretend to be busy with something on it so she wouldn't have to talk.

"You want a refill, Alice?" Jay held out the cocktail pitcher.

She shook her head. Gave him a smile. Jay had been

one of her closest friends since college; he'd been the one to introduce her to Bernie. Jay had introduced Mick to their group, too, much later, because he and Mick sometimes worked on projects together. Everything was a chain, she thought. One link to another.

"You sure?" Jay gave her a smile and a nudge as Cookie flicked the lights and a new DVD menu appeared on the screen.

Alice lifted her glass, still three-quarters full. Though typically these weekends with Bernie and Cookie had always included a lot more drinking than she usually indulged in, tonight Alice wasn't feeling it. Maybe she'd had too much to drink last night. Or maybe what had made her feel so drunk and now a little hungover hadn't been the booze at all. She caught herself looking for Mick again, but stopped herself.

Jay didn't miss her glance. He looked, too, then back at her. He leaned close to squeeze her. "You okay?"

"Fine. Hey, the movie's starting." She moved over so he could squeeze into the chair beside her. "Sit with me."

Jay, expression solemn, linked his arm through hers and then tangled their fingers. Such a simple contact. Such a comfort. It was too much, though, because it made her want to burst into horrible, wrenching sobs that Alice held back only by the fiercest force of her will.

The universe, of course, had other plans for her. Bernie had been showing the movies in random order, and the one he'd chosen now opened with a familiar scene, similar to many of the other clips. The group of them in the kitchen, glasses and plates full. Lots of laughter. Music, dancing. Close-ups of funny faces.

But in this one, there was Mick.

His hair had been longer, and Alice had forgotten that he'd had a scruffy sort of beard the first time she'd met him. How could she have forgotten? Her breath caught as the camera tightened on his face.

"And here's our new best friend," Bernie said in the movie. "Michael McManus . . ."

"Mick," he said. "You can call me Mick."

There in the background, an open door, and Alice coming through it. She wore that green dress, the one she'd loved and worn so much it had finally fallen, literally, to pieces in the wash. Watching this now, Alice could not remember this moment, even as it unwound in front of her. She came through the door calling for a drink and succumbed to hugs and kisses from Jay and Cookie's niece Tanya. Alice waved at Bernie's camera. She looked at Mick and gave him a small, hesitant smile, and just as quickly looked away to focus on hugging Cookie.

There it was. The first moment she had ever met him. So quick it had been almost nonexistent. And ultimately nothing, right? A barely there greeting, the passing of her gaze over him, a stranger. Scarcely an acknowledgment at all.

Yet so much had come from it, that first glance. Meeting Mick had changed everything for her. And how many people had the moment of their first meeting captured that way? Alice wanted to ask Bernie to rewind it, replay. She wanted to be greedy with it, gorge herself on it.

That first moment when everything between them had yet to happen.

There was more to that movie. Glimpses of the party, Mick brooding in the background. Alice accepting a glass of wine and lifting it in a toast. And one heart-thudding shot of the two of them through the French doors. She'd gone outside to the deck, she remembered that. Tipsy on wine and laughter, she'd found Mick standing with a beer.

"I'm Alice," she'd said, and he'd tipped his bottle toward her.

"I know."

The movie didn't show that, of course. Just the shadow of them outside and Jay's voice asking, "Where did Mick and Alice get off to?" Bernie's answer in the swing of the camera, a few seconds' glimpse before the scene cut to a group shot of them playing a drinking game involving shot glasses and ping pong balls. Then it was over and the DVD returned to the menu screen. The lights came on. Jay squeezed her hand and used his other one to discreetly wipe away the tear Alice was mortified to discover had escaped the prison of her eye to slide down her cheek.

There were no more movies after that.

"I'm getting old," Bernie said as they all gathered up their plates and glasses to clean up the theater. "I want to stay up and party with all of you, but I think I'm going to head off to bed with my beautiful wife."

"That has nothing to do with being old," called out Paul. "That's just called being smart!"

Cookie laughed as Bernie hugged and kissed her. "I'd say it's called being lucky."

Bernie bowed at the collective *awww* that went around the room. "See you all in the morning."

Upstairs, Paul and Jay went onto the deck to smoke cigarettes of a dubious nature while Dayna mixed another pitcher of cocktails. She poured herself one and offered a glass to Alice, who accepted though she knew she didn't really want to drink it this late. Dayna pulled out a cheesecake from the fridge.

"Late-night snack?"

Alice winced. "Oh, my God. Wow. No!"

"You sure? Bernie made it, you know it's good." Dayna

grinned and sliced off a piece, then put it on a small plate. "Mick do you want . . . where's Mick?"

"I don't know. Maybe he went to bed." Alice eyed the cheesecake and put a hand on her stomach. "I can't believe I forgot how much we eat at Bernie's house. And drink. Damn, I'm gonna have to roll myself home."

Dayna licked the tines of her fork. "No kidding. If I make it home without busting the zipper on my jeans, I count myself lucky."

Alice pulled the cheesecake a little closer to cut herself a sliver. "I know I shouldn't eat this, but I'm going to anyway."

"What's life without inappropriately eaten cheesecake?" Dayna dragged the fork through her cheesecake, but didn't lick it this time. She gave Alice a long look, instead. "Pretty cool seeing those movies, huh? I'd forgotten some of that stuff. I guess we all *are* getting old."

"Bite your tongue," Alice said lightly.

"Lots of memories. And some regrets, no?"

Alice looked at the other woman. They'd met at Bernie's years ago, and since they were both girls often ended up sharing the bathroom. You learned a lot about someone else when you had to use the same shower. They both lived in Central Pennsylvania about forty minutes apart, and kept in touch through occasional texts or e-mails, but it wasn't as though they spent hours every week chatting on the phone or anything. They got together for lunch or dinner every so often, or met at Jay's. Alice liked her quite a bit. Dayna had a great sense of humor and a way of putting everyone around her at ease in a way Alice had always admired. But they'd never been particularly close.

"I try not to regret things," Alice said after it had

become impossible not to say anything without this becoming weird.

Dayna nodded. She drank, then went to the fridge for a large bottle of seltzer water. She poured them both glasses without asking Alice if she wanted one this time, and Alice took it to sip gratefully.

"Maybe you should go talk to him," Dayna said. "Maybe he's waiting for you."

Alice didn't pretend not to understand what Dayna meant. She rolled her eyes. "If he is, I'm sure it's not for the conversation."

Dayna laughed wryly. "Maybe not. Paul and Jay out there, they're talking about something dire. You can see it in the way they're standing."

Alice looked. "And Jay's smoking. I thought he gave that up. I guess he only does that with Paul, though to be honest, I thought he gave up Paul, too."

"Yeah. Me too. Did Jay say they were getting back together?" Dayna's tone was super casual, though her expression was anything but.

"No." Alice sipped more seltzer, letting it settle her stomach and gave the other woman a curious look. "I asked, but he claimed he was done with Paul, done with a capital D. You know they've been on and off forever. They get back together, then they split up, then the next thing I know, they're going away for some debauched weekend in the Bahamas or something. I try not to judge."

Dayna winced. "Paul can't stay away from him."

Alice looked again through the doors, uncomfortable at watching even from this distance. It felt intrusive, even voyeuristic. "That's how it is with some people."

"Yeah. Some people you can't shut the door on, even when you should."

Dayna's voice had gone raspy and rough. She gave

Alice a wobbly, watery sort of grin. From the deck a brief flare of raised voices turned both women's heads for a moment. Dayna didn't have to say a word, but suddenly, Alice understood a whole lot more than she had before.

"Even when you should," Alice said by way of agreement.

Dayna swallowed hard and lifted her chin. She took a deep breath, visibly getting herself together. "Stupid hearts, always gotta break."

If Alice saw Dayna only once every few months, she saw Paul even less often. She'd never been friends with him the way she'd been with any of the others, knowing him more through Jay's eyes than anything else. And it was hard to like Paul when she knew how much he'd hurt Jay, over and over. Jay might've been able to forgive him, but Alice had always found it harder. Now that she had this sudden insight into the reason for at least a few of the breakups, she liked him even less.

"Does Jay know?" Alice asked.

Dayna shook her head. "No. And I don't want him to know. Jay's my friend—"

Alice laughed sharply, unable to hold it back though it came out harsher than she'd intended.

Dayna flinched. "He is. Believe me, that makes it all so much harder, because Jay's my friend. But I love *him*."

The French doors opened. Paul whirled through them, Jay on his heels. Whatever had happened outside, both men were keeping it close to the vest. Jay gave Alice's shoulder a squeeze as he passed her. Paul, very carefully, Alice thought, didn't look at Dayna at all. Or maybe Alice was seeing things that weren't there because she knew something she hadn't before.

"I'm heading to bed," Jay said.

Paul nodded. "Me too. Night, everyone."

In the silence after the men had left the kitchen, Dayna let out a long, shuddering sigh. She dug back into the cheesecake with a vengeance, and gave Alice a look. "You want coffee? I'm making coffee."

At this hour, coffee would keep her up until dawn, but it seemed unkind to refuse or abandon Dayna so she could also go to bed. And she didn't want to, really, did she? Not to her own bed, anyway. Alice wanted to slip down those back stairs to Mick's basement room and crawl in beside him, to wake him if he were sleeping with her hands and tongue and lips. For the first time this weekend, she was smart enough not to give in.

"Sure," she said. "I'll drink some coffee."

While it brewed the women bustled with cleaning the kitchen. Not saying much, the revelation of Dayna and Paul hanging between them. With full mugs, each of them took a seat at the island and sipped in silence, until at last Dayna broke the mutual quiet.

"Does it ever go away?"

Alice blew on the coffee to cool it and give herself a chance to reply, uncertain what, exactly, Dayna was looking for. Comfort or validation. Maybe condemnation. Alice only had one answer. "I don't know what you mean."

"The wanting." Dayna added cream and sugar to her mug and stirred it, but didn't drink again. She shrugged and gave Alice a bleak look. "I mean . . . I wasn't going to come this weekend. Cookie had invited me months ago, and I figured if you could be here with Mick, I could stand to see Paul. I knew it was important. Twenty years, you know? I wanted to be here for them, but I also knew he'd be here. They'd both be here. And I didn't want to see them together."

"They're not together."

"I didn't want to see *him*," Dayna corrected herself.

"And know there was no way he'd look at me. Not the way he used to, like there was nothing else in the world that mattered but the sight of me. Or worse, what if he did look at me that way? What would I do then, when I know that even if he still wanted me, there was no way for it to happen?"

Alice had no answer for that.

"I would have to pretend everything was okay when it's not, because I look at him and my heart still breaks. So, I want to know. Does it go away? The wanting," Dayna asked.

Alice wrapped her hands around the mug, which was really too hot to hold, but something in the sting against her palms was somehow soothing. "No. I guess it doesn't."

"Shit." Dayna gave a shaky laugh. She went to the cupboard and pulled down the bottle of Baileys, adding a shot to her mug and offering it to Alice, who refused.

"So why did you come for the weekend, then? If you felt that way? And to be honest, Dayna, I'd never have guessed if you hadn't told me. I know Jay and Paul have had their ups and downs, but I would never have known you were involved with any of it."

"Thank God. If Jay knew it, I couldn't forgive myself. It only ever happened when they were split up, Alice. I swear it. I know Paul might find it impossible to commit to any one person, but I promise you, I was never with him if he was with Jay."

It made it easier to know, though Alice still wished she didn't. "I won't tell him. It would only hurt him, and I don't have any desire to hurt Jay for any reason."

"Me neither. Which is why I never said anything. Why I put on the smile and act like looking at Paul doesn't shred me open. I don't want Jay to know, but I don't want Paul to see it, either. I couldn't bear it, you know?" Dayna sipped her coffee with a wince. "If he knew how much it hurts me, that he still affects me so much. I decided to come because not seeing him seemed like a worse torture."

Alice laughed. "I almost didn't come, either. But so much time had passed, I thought it would be okay."

"And was it?" Dayna gave her a solid, knowing look.

Alice shook her head.

"Fuck," Dayna said. "We're both fucked, huh? Well, at least Mick looks at you like he wants to eat you alive."

"Does he?" Alice asked, startled and pleased, flushing at the thought.

"When you're not looking at him. Yes. He does. And it's been how long?"

"Something like ten years." Saying it out loud made it seem like so much longer.

"That's a long time," Dayna said.

Alice nodded. They both drank coffee. The clock ticked louder than the sound of their breathing, but the silence wasn't uncomfortable. Alice turned the mug around and around in front of her, contemplating how some time changed some things and left others completely the same.

"Do you still love him?" Dayna asked quietly.

Alice looked at her. "I don't know if I still do. But . . . I think I still could."

"So what do you do about that?"

"I don't know." Alice shook her head. "Things have changed. Or not. It's just a weekend, Dayna. You know things are always different when it's just a party. It doesn't mean they can last, or be real."

"Shit. Yes." Dayna sighed.

More silence. Alice yawned. Dayna smiled.

"To open doors." Dayna lifted her mug.

Alice clinked hers against it. "May we learn to close them."

Mick to Alice

I wanted to drink in the memories of you, absorb and consume them. I sat unmoving. Breathing, breathing, trying to keep myself covered in the way being with you felt. Trying to hold on tight to the memory of how it had been, that first time I saw you. It was like trying to grab a glass out of a sink full of soap. Slippery, sliding, and ultimately, the choice became hold too tight and shatter it in my fist, or drop it and watch it break all over the floor.

Everything about us had broken. The question was, could it ever be fixed? Or, like a glass you glue back together, would the cracks always mean we could never really be whole?

—Mick to Alice, unsent

Chapter 10

Mick wanted to be asleep, but when another hour passed and he did no more than toss fitfully, he swung his feet over the side of the bed. There was no hint of light around the edges of the window shade, and he didn't feel like checking his phone for the time. It could be any hour after midnight and before sunrise. It felt like 4:00 A.M., which had always been, in his opinion, the shittiest hour to be awake. There was no good reason not to be sleeping at four in the morning. It meant you were sick or having bad dreams or had been making bad decisions.

He'd made some very bad decisions.

There was no help for it now, though. He could blame it on being unable to stop himself. He could tell himself the sight of her had made him lose his mind just enough to put aside reason for the sake of lust. He could try to convince himself that he shouldn't be held responsible for what they'd done—booze, old times, nostalgia. But he couldn't make himself believe any of that.

The truth was, he'd wanted Alice the moment he saw her again. He could've, should've stayed away, been polite and distant. It would have been okay. But no, now he'd touched and felt and smelled her, tasted her, and how the hell was he supposed to go back to not knowing her anymore?

With a groan, Mick scrubbed at his face, running his fingers through his hair until it stood up like he'd been in a tornado. Resting his elbows on his knees, he pressed his face into his palms for a minute or so, thinking maybe the floor would tilt beneath his feet. But nope, he couldn't even blame his wakefulness on drinking too much. Shit.

Stretching, he figured it was better to get up than try to keep sleeping when it was obvious there wasn't going to be any rest for him tonight. Sunday morning was going to dawn whether he wanted it to or not. He might as well accept the fact he'd be up to greet it.

First, a shower. Cold, to keep himself from sinking into erotic reminiscences of the afternoon and Alice in his bed. It didn't help much. Sure, the frigid water goose-pebbled his skin, but all he had to do was flash back to the feeling of her underneath him, and his cock started twitching. He stroked a hand along it and bent his head into the spray with a groan. Another stroke. A shudder. Not even the fact that his teeth had begun to chatter could stop his cock from getting hard when he thought about Alice.

Mick stroked a little faster, feeling his balls tighten. He pressed his forehead to the wall of the shower, letting the water hit his back in stinging spray—the pain, fuck yeah, he could admit that it made this all a teasing torture. A little faster. A quick palm of the head, then all the way down. He gripped the shaft and fucked into his palm.

Imagining her.

They hadn't fucked for real in the past two days, but that didn't stop him from remembering how it had been in the past. He groaned again, his hand no good replacement for Alice. Her slick heat. The way her body tightened around him when she came. There'd been times when they'd spent hours in bed, when he'd moved inside her, mesmerized by the look in her eyes when she finally tipped over the edge. When he'd been buried balls-deep inside her as her orgasms rippled over her, and he'd felt every single spasm on his cock as he stayed still. His fingers couldn't replace the squeeze of her on him now, but damn, he was trying.

Faster. This wasn't going to be easy. Cold water, the fact he'd already come once in the past twenty-four hours and he was no longer a teenager . . . the fact his hand was his own and not hers . . . but closer, he was getting closer. He bent his knees a little, one hand on the shower wall, the other still working on his cock. He closed his eyes.

"Fuck me," he imagined Alice saying. Pleasure speared him. "Make me come," he heard her whisper, and everything inside him tensed. Over the edge, hard, his climax short and sharp and somewhat unsatisfying. A little fraught with guilt. He spattered the shower wall and gasped, shuddering. Blinking. His cock softened faster than usual as the cold water became impossible to ignore and he actually bit his tongue with the chattering. It hurt, too.

Rinsing himself and the shower of any evidence he'd just spent himself like a horny kid, Mick turned off the water and got out to towel off. A glimpse of himself in the mirror didn't make him feel any better. He looked puffy eyed and scruffy, his hair a mess. He sneered. Glowered. Ah, shit, there was no helping it, he looked like 4:00 A.M.

Wearing a pair of jeans and a button-down shirt he didn't bother to button, bare feet, hair still wet, face still bristly, Mick went upstairs to see if he could round up some coffee. Someone, God bless them, had made a pot that was still warm, and he filled a mug. Added sugar. Took a minute to smell the glory that was coffee. Then went out to the deck to watch the sun rise.

Alice, bundled in a fleece blanket, was in one of the lounge chairs, only her face peeking out.

"Hey," she said softly, not like she was surprised to see him at all. Almost as though she'd been waiting for him.

Mick set his mug onto the railing and leaned against it. "Haven't you been to bed yet?"

She shook her head. "Dayna made coffee about an hour ago, and I was dumb and drank some."

"Ah." He turned to look out over the yard and the sky above the tree line at the bottom of it. "Sun'll be up soon."

"That's what I'm waiting for." With a yawn, Alice stretched under the blanket. "If I make it."

"Want some more coffee? You might as well. It's going to be daylight soon."

"You don't have to—"

But he was already going inside to pour her a mug, adding the sugar and cream the way she liked it. Or she had liked it, back then. Uncertain, Mick brought out the mug and handed it to her.

She sipped. "Perfect."

"Oh, good."

"You still know," she said quietly.

Mick didn't answer. He faced the impending sunrise and drank his own coffee, thinking that action would make it easier to pretend as though he was trying to avoid talking to her on purpose. He'd never been able to fool her, though. Behind him, he heard the shift of her on the chair and the soft swish of the blanket as it fell away. He tensed, closing his eyes, waiting for her touch.

It didn't come.

The hint of her breath on the back of his neck teased him for a second, but Alice didn't touch him with anything else. She put her mug on the railing next to him and leaned on it. She shivered a little in the chilly morning air. The sky was starting to brighten enough that he could easily make out the curves and lines of her face even without the light from the kitchen.

"Why do I feel like you'd still know everything about me, Mick?"

He cleared his throat. "I wouldn't. How could I?"

"You know how to make my coffee. You know how to make me come," Alice whispered. Her arm brushed his sleeve. He didn't move.

He forced the words. "I never knew everything about you, Alice. Nobody ever knows everything about anyone."

"You knew enough. More than anyone else ever did before you, or has since." She went quiet.

Both of them watched the sky getting paler. She sipped her coffee. Mick had lost the taste for his.

"I've missed you," Alice said.

He'd missed her, too. For years, Mick had thought about Alice, wondering what she was doing. Who she was seeing. He'd seen her face on random women and in his dreams, always wishful thinking and never her, save that one lucky time a few years ago when he'd spotted her dancing with her friends. He'd been stupid, maybe, not to say something to her that night. He'd be stupid not to say something now.

But though his mouth worked, his tongue trying without success to push the words free of his lips and teeth, the only thing that came out of Mick's throat was a soft, hissing sigh.

"Well, I guess that's my answer," Alice said, and went inside the house.

He almost went after her, but as with so many other mistakes Mick had made, he waited too long. By the time he was able to get himself moving, Alice had gone inside her bedroom. Knocking would wake everyone up, if she deigned to answer. He almost did that, too, raising a hand to let his knuckles rest against the wood. Then his forehead. Straining for the sound of her inside, all he heard was the sound of his own breathing and the pound of his heart in his ears. His stomach, gone sour, sent a surge of bile into his throat.

"Alice," Mick whispered, knowing there was no way she could hear him.

There was no light beneath the door, nothing to indicate she was awake, though he had to imagine she hadn't simply tossed herself into bed and slept. What if, he thought suddenly, she wasn't in there at all, but in his room? She'd done that more than once. Left him upstairs only to be waiting for him in his bed, usually naked. It was too much to hope for, but Mick let himself hope for it.

Disappointment slapped him in the face when he found only the tangle of his sheets, his own drool-spotted pillow. He had missed her, that wasn't the problem. Admitting it, saying it aloud, that had been too hard. Why? Because he was stupid. There was no other real explanation, other than faced with the reality of seeing her, all he could think about was how much he didn't want to lose the fantasy. But faced with his empty bed, the empty room . . . empty fucking life, Mick thought as he sank onto the bed. Without Alice, everything was empty.

And later, he would tell her.

He woke to a roaring hunger and sprang out of bed to yank back the curtains. Daylight, bright enough to blind him for a minute. He'd slept in the clothes he'd put on early this morning after his shower. He didn't bother combing his hair or washing his face, though he did brush his teeth. That was just courtesy, he thought with a grin, already imagining Alice's kiss.

In the empty kitchen, he snagged a doughnut from among the detritus of breakfast and went out onto the deck to look for everyone else. He found only Cookie, her huge, flopping sunhat shading her eyes as she sat in the same lounger Alice had been using this morning. The fleece blanket, not needed in the afternoon heat, had been folded neatly across the end of the chair. She looked up from her book, her finger holding her place.

"Hi, sleepyhead."

"Morning." Mick, nearly dancing with excitement, bent to give her a kiss on the cheek.

"You missed brunch." She laughed and brushed away the sugar granules his kiss had left on her skin. "But I see you found something. There's plenty of leftovers in the fridge, if you want."

"I'm good." He bounced on the balls of his feet. "Where's everyone else? Lake?"

"Bernie and Jay went into town to get some propane for the grill, since my ridiculously prepared husband for once forgot something important. Paul and Dayna went to the lake. Everyone else should start getting here around three."

Mick turned. "And Alice, too?"

Cookie paused, then gave him a look of such sympathy that instantly, his stomach sank. "Oh, honey, Alice left early this morning. She said something came up at home, so she couldn't stay for the picnic."

"Did she . . . say what it was?"

"No." Cookie shook her head. "I'm sorry, Mick. We were all as surprised as you that she left."

But that was the problem, Mick thought. He wasn't surprised at all.

Alice to Mick

When I found out you were going to be there, my hands started to shake. The world spun, and I had to breathe deep. Deep. Deep. Everything shifted and changed, and I was sure, for a moment, I was going to pass out.

You were going to be there.

After all that time, the things we'd said and done and what had passed between us, and it was such a simple, casual comment. "He'll be there. You're okay with that, right?" I had to say yes, of course. Couldn't make it into anything important, make a big deal, cause a fuss.

Was it okay? It was more than okay. After all this time, I was going to see you again.

I had done my time waiting on you. Done my share of crying. And yes, I knew a part of me would always ache at the loss of you in my life, part would forever find a way to weep for missing you, some part of me would infinitely yearn for you the way a flower desires the kiss of a bee to help it to bloom . . . but it was no longer the biggest part of me. I closed the door to that room in my house of many. Ended that chapter in the novel of my life. I had said good-bye to you and meant it.

Yet there you were again.

And everything I thought I had known crumbled, shattered, scattered, splintered, broke.

—Alice to Mick

Chapter 11

Fool her once, shame on him. Fool her twice, shame on her. It was an old saying that made total sense.

Open doors should be closed, Alice told herself as she pulled her clean laundry from the dryer and piled it into the basket. The faint smell of sunscreen lingered on everything, normally a good smell but one that made her melancholy now. Her bathing suit tumbled out, tangled in a T-shirt. She pressed it to her face, breathing in the clean laundry smell, nothing of Mick left there at all.

Then she was crying. Sitting back on her heels in front of the laundry basket, gathering handfuls of her clothes, digging through the pile of everything she'd worn this weekend that had touched him. Smelling all of it. Holding everything to her face in a futile attempt at breathing in any small molecule of his scent, but she'd done too good a job. All she had was a basket full of clean clothes.

"Enough," Alice said loud enough to make her cat meow at her. "Enough, Alice. This is enough. No more of this. No more of him. Ten fucking years," she gasped out on a sob, the tears coming hot and fierce and fast enough to drown her. "You're over him."

That was the problem though, wasn't it? She'd never been over him. Not a day after they'd broken up. Not a week. A month, a year, five years, ten. Alice had never completely let him go, and she'd been an idiot to think seeing him again would've brought anything but grief.

She shouldn't have let him kiss her, touch her, make whatever love they'd made. She should have kept her distance and been pleasant and polite. Like Dayna had said about Paul, seeing him would surely have broken her heart, but at least it would've broken quietly, with only her to know about it.

"I missed you," she'd said, and he had said nothing.

Nothing!

Not one fucking word. The thought of it, that he could put his hands all over her, his tongue down her throat, his fingers inside her . . . God, it was too much. With a strangled, growling sob that scared the cat into running away, Alice got to her feet with the laundry basket and took it upstairs to her bed, where she tossed out the contents and began folding. *Snap, snap,* making creases in the fabric. She folded the fuck out of that laundry because to do anything less would be giving in again to the rising urge to fall onto her knees again and weep into her hands.

"Fuck him," she said aloud, lower this time. The words, bitter as bile, burned her tongue.

In her bathroom, Alice got out the bleach and scrub brush to attack her grout. The toilet and sink got their share of attention. Then the shower, where she used an old toothbrush to clean out the tracks in the shower door and around the drain, and where at last she turned on the hot water to rinse away the soap and bleach, and she got under the water herself, no longer able to hold back another round of sobs.

She hated him, she told herself, and knew it wasn't true. Shaking, Alice curled into a ball on the floor, grateful as always for the oversized shower. Perfect for a breakdown. With her forehead pressed into her palms and the hot water pounding onto her back, Alice could let the sounds of the shower drown out her hitching, desperate cries. She hated herself for letting him do this to her. Again.

"I missed you." Her voice echoed inside her head, and Mick's silence became as loud as the thud of a drum.

She stayed in the shower until the water ran cold, and then a few minutes more as some kind of self-punishment, until at last she couldn't stand it any longer and got out. Shivering, she wrapped herself in a towel and went into the bedroom to curl up among the piles of her clean clothes. She thought there'd be more tears, but apparently that well had gone at least temporarily and thankfully dry.

She rolled onto her back to stare at her ceiling. "Fuck him," she said, this time without heat. "Fuck me."

This was not how she'd planned to spend her weekend. Not doing laundry and cleaning tiles. She should be in her bikini, lathered with lotion and sunning herself on her beach towel next to the lake while her friends laughed beside her. She should be eating hotdogs and macaroni salad and drinking sangria and dancing to eighties pop tunes.

She'd let Mick make her give that up. She couldn't even blame him for stealing it from her, because she'd been the one to run. She'd made up an excuse about a vague emergency at home. Dayna had hugged her hard before she left, murmuring in her ear, "Call me if you need to talk."

She wouldn't, of course. Not to rehash this old news, this story that had ended long ago and hadn't needed this stupid epilogue. No, Alice thought as she forced herself to sit up and pull on some clothes rather than keep allowing herself to wallow. No more of this.

No more Mick.

No more memories.

No more regrets.

No more open doors.

Mick to Alice

How many times can a person say the same thing before it loses all meaning? How many different ways can I tell you I'm sorry before you believe me? I've tried my best with you, Alice, but you won't listen to me. I'm sorry for what I said or didn't say, or didn't do right. I'm sorry about how it all turned out, believe me, if I could go back and undo it, I would. But I can't. All I can do is tell you that I'm sorry, but unless you answer your phone, you'll never hear me say it.

I'm sending you this letter as one last chance to reach you, Alice. I know I made mistakes, but all I can do is try to apologize. That doesn't mean I'm willing to beg. If that's the sort of man you're looking for, you've got the wrong one.

—Mick to Alice

Chapter 12

He had Alice's phone number in his contacts list from when she'd texted him the photo of the two of them. He'd looked at it over and over. It was a picture of two people delirious with joy when they were together, he thought. Two people who were meant for each other.

He had her number, but it wasn't so easy for Mick to actually call her. The Alice he'd known ran hot with all her emotions, maybe especially fury. Not that he'd have blamed her for being angry at him. He'd fucked up by not telling her he missed her when she'd said it. Classic dumb-fuckery, on his part.

The old Mick would've gone after her right away, even knowing she was likely to be mad, without giving her time to settle down. He'd have poked at her, probably angry himself, or at least defensive. That had been the way they'd played that game, circling each other like hissing cats, each winding up the other until there was nothing for either of them to do but scratch.

He liked to think he'd grown up at least a little bit since then. At least that was what he told himself was the reason he waited two weeks after Bernie's party to finally call her number . . . that he was giving her time to work through her initial fury with him. Not that that he was terrified of actually having to talk to her.

"I was scared to call you before now," were the first words out of his mouth, and they were the truth. "I thought you'd curse me out, or maybe hang up on me."

"I still might." Alice's voice was chilly and distant.

He had no trouble imagining her expression.

"Alice, look. I just wanted to say I'm sorry."

Icicles clung to every up-and-down dip in the beat of her laughter. "For what?"

"For not . . . saying what I should've said to you." Shit. The words still clogged his throat.

Alice said nothing. The soft huff of her breathing tickled his eardrum through the distance. He waited, giving her time. To cut him with her words, if she was going to. Or to say she forgave him. He waited for a very long minute, counting off the seconds of silence before finally giving in.

"I'm sorry," he repeated.

She hadn't hung up him. That was something. Alice sighed. "It's not 'sorry' that I want to hear from you, Mick. Fuck's sake, I don't want you to be sorry. I want you to say you missed me, too."

"I did. I have. Shit, Alice, so much, you can't even believe it." He'd been sitting in his recliner, but got up now to pace.

"I have missed you every day. Some more than others. But every fucking day." Her breath hitched. There was a beat or two of silence in which he imagined her getting herself under control. "And all I wanted was for you to say it. And you didn't. You couldn't."

"No. I guess I couldn't."

"Why, Mick?" In the past she'd have already been calling him names, raising her voice, slinging barbs. If he were lucky, that was, and she hadn't disconnected and then refused to answer his call again. "Why couldn't you just tell me? Why is it so hard?"

"I don't know." He could peel away the layers of his existence to figure out the reasons, he supposed, and would still probably never know why. "It's a guy thing. It's hard for guys to talk about their feelings."

"That's no answer," Alice said harshly. "Not after all this time. And it's bullshit, because I've had lots of guys who didn't have a hard time telling me how they feel. There were times when you didn't, either. So fuck your excuse. And seeing you again . . . I just . . . how could you kiss me that way?"

Mick laughed, low and sad. "How could I *not* kiss you that way?"

"You could have not kissed me at all. You could've stayed on your own side of the table. You didn't have to kiss me. Or touch me."

Mick cringed at the sound of tears in her voice. "I did have to. There was no way I could've looked at you and stayed on my own side of the table, Alice."

If that didn't tell her how he felt, she wasn't listening very well.

"I'm sorry," Mick added.

"Don't be sorry!" she cried. "God dammit, Mick, don't you fucking dare tell me you're sorry for kissing me!"

He didn't answer right away. The silence spun out between them again. This would've been easier and harder in person, where he'd have been able to touch her the way she said he shouldn't want to.

"Look . . . I want to see you," he said. "Will you meet me?"

"For what? We already fucked around. You didn't get your fill?"

That stung. She could complain about him not being able to share his feelings, but she was totally missing what he was actually saying. "That's not why I want to see you, Alice."

"Great," she said sourly. "So you don't miss me and you don't want to fuck me, either. Thanks."

"That's not what I meant and you know it, so stop it."

Alice paused, then said, "I'm sorry."

"That might be the first time I ever heard you say that to me." Mick grinned.

Alice snorted softly. "Well . . . you might be right. In which case, I'm sorry again."

"I want to see you, Alice."

Again, she didn't answer him, but this time the silence felt filled with anticipation, not anxiety. She sighed. He imagined her rubbing the spot between her eyes, pinching the bridge of her nose between her thumb and ring fingers in that way she had when she was thinking hard about something.

"I'm not sure that's a good idea," she said at last. "Why should I see you?"

"Because I miss you." There. He'd said it, right out loud. How could she complain about that?

She laughed a little more warmly this time. "That's why you should see me, not the other way around."

"Because you miss me," Mick told her. "And you want to see me again."

Alice muttered something, a curse word, he was sure of it. She'd spoken so low he couldn't be sure exactly which of her favorite profanities she'd uttered. It sounded something like "bruised whores," which made him laugh uncertainly and ask her to repeat it.

"I said closed doors," Alice told him. "As in, doors that should be closed. As in us, this. All of this. Everything about it. Closed. Door."

"I don't get it."

"Never mind. It doesn't matter. I appreciate you calling me."

Shit, she was back to sounding chilly again. Distant. "Alice—"

"But I don't think it's a good idea for us to see each other. Thank you for apologizing. It wasn't necessary."

"Yes, it was."

She hesitated, and for a second, he had hope she'd change her mind. "Well. Thank you for it, then. And for telling me that you missed me."

"I *do* miss you." Easier this time. Like pressing ice to a bruise, eventually it numbed.

She cleared her throat. "Thanks. I appreciate that. A lot."

No, no, no. This was all going wrong. He'd just been about to get her to agree to see him in person, so he could make *sure* she understood what he was trying to say.

"Alice, please—"

"Good-bye, Mick."

"Alice!"

But it was too late. She'd disconnected. He'd lost her all over again.

Alice to Mick

How many times do I let you break me, before I decide I've had enough? We spin and spin so much we've created our own gravity. Like no matter how hard we try, neither of us can break away. We are in orbit. Caught. How many times do I let you break me?

I guess the only answer is, every time.

—Alice to Mick

Chapter 13

Dayna's call hadn't taken Alice by surprise, not after their conversation at Bernie and Cookie's. They'd agreed to meet for happy hour drinks at some place Alice wouldn't have normally gone to, but that Dayna had raved about. It had a tropical decor and fancy drinks that came in specialty glasses, which was about all it had to recommend it as far as Alice was concerned, but Dayna looked so happy to see her that it didn't matter about the creepy platoon of business guys ogling her as soon as she walked in.

"Hey. Good to see you." Dayna hugged her. "I got us a table over here."

Alice followed, careful not to make eye contact with any of the men circling the free buffet. "How's the food here?"

"Order from the menu, not that cesspool," Dayna advised. "The chicken fingers are all right, but not worth having to deal with the bad pickup lines."

Alice laughed as she took a seat at the highboy table. "Good to know. Thanks."

They ordered drinks and a platter of appetizers. They chitchatted for a few minutes, until Dayna finally took a long, deep breath. Alice waited, but Dayna didn't say anything.

"Paul," Alice said.

Dayna nodded.

"We might need more than one drink."

Dayna laughed, which was better than crying. "He said he can't give me what I want. That he can't go all in, whatever the hell that means."

The drinks came, along with the food, and Alice waited to answer until the server left. Then she lifted her glass. Clinked it to Dayna's.

"It just means he doesn't have any idea what else to say that won't make him sound like a giant douche bag." Alice sipped cold liquor and picked up a tortilla chip laden with refried beans and salsa. "I mean, did you tell him what it is, exactly, that you want?"

"I said I wanted *him*."

"And he can't give you him?"

"He can give me his dick," Dayna said sourly. "That, he seems able to manage."

Alice laughed, not meaning to make light of what was Dayna's obvious distress. But there was nothing but laughter to be had in a situation like this, because how else do you react to the absurdity of love? After a second or so, Dayna laughed, too.

"I told him I didn't need a marriage proposal. Just that if he was going to come over and fuck me on occasion that he should answer my texts once in a while, too. I didn't even say we had to be exclusive." Dayna paused to drink, looking thoughtful. "I mean, it wasn't so long ago that even the thought of someone else touching me was enough to make me want to puke, but funny how it happens that when someone keeps hurting you in the same way how easy letting go starts to get."

"No kidding. Mick called me." Alice dug into more food.

Dayna shook her head. "And?"

"And, nothing. He wanted to see me. I said no."

Dayna's jaw dropped. "You didn't!"

"I did." A strange sense of pride stung her for a second as Alice lifted her chin and shrugged. "There was just no good to come from that. Sure, we'd fuck around, I'd get off, he'd get off, but we'd be back to the same old shit as the first time around. Doors should close, remember?"

"Maybe, but . . . how did you manage to do it?" Dayna drained her glass as the server reappeared. "Two more, please."

Alice shrugged again. "I don't know, really. Just that seeing him that weekend was better and worse in a lot of ways than I'd expected, but . . . there is no more me and Mick. That's the thing. It ended for a good reason. I mean, what ended it was bad, but it was a good reason to end it."

The booze had started tickling her already. Words tangling on her tongue. Memories flooding in. All the feels, filling her up.

"Why did it end?"

Alice sat back. "You don't know?"

"Nope." Dayna shook her head and dug into the mozzarella sticks.

"There were lots of reasons, aren't there always more than one? But let's just say that when I needed him, he wasn't there." Alice paused. "Nobody talked about it?"

Dayna grinned. "What, you think we all gossiped about you?"

"Maybe." Alice thought about it. "Jay knows. I figured he'd have told Paul."

"Jay's your best friend, he doesn't talk out of school about you. And Paul and I didn't exactly have what you'd call a relationship based on sharing and communication," Dayna said.

This set them both off into more peals of laughter. More drinks appeared, perfect timing. Also a pair of business guys dressed in identical khakis and polo shirts, even their smiles matching. And somehow, though Alice would've said the very last thing on her agenda tonight was going to be getting picked up by a slick-talking salesman in town for a tech convention, she found herself doing just that.

His name was Bill. His friend, so clearly taken with Dayna that he could barely look away from her face, was Gary. The two of them were staying at the hotel attached to this bar, a fact they'd stated right up front, which made Alice laugh.

"I'm not going to your hotel," she told Bill. "You can buy me a drink, but that's it."

Bill grinned. Gary had lured Dayna away to the next table so Bill could take her seat. Whatever he was saying to her was making her laugh. Good for her. Alice lifted her brow at Bill.

"I'm serious."

"I know you are. I could tell that about you right away. Serious." Bill tipped his beer bottle at her and put on a solemn face. "Serious Alice."

Alice gave in to a laugh, but shook her head. She made a show of looking around the bar, then back at him. "There's a bar full of young, single women. You pick the one who's not interested in hooking up. I have to question your judgment."

"I might have poor judgment," Bill said, "but I have very, very good taste."

He got bonus points for being charming, she thought. Dayna seemed to be having a good time with Gary, the two of them leaning close. And Bill was a good-looking guy. Smart and funny, straightforward about what he was going for but, despite that, not actually too pushy. Another time, not so long ago, she would have given him her number. As it was, with the party at Bernie's still too painfully fresh, Alice couldn't muster any enthusiasm for the thought of hooking up. Or dating.

Because let's face it, Bill was no Mick. Nobody was Mick. Nobody ever would be. But hadn't she decided just a few nights ago that she was done with Mick McManus and his hold over her? Great sex aside, all the feels aside, no matter how sweet the berries tasted, if you knew they were poison, you left those bitches on the bush.

Which is why when Bill asked her if she wanted to dance, Alice put down her drink and took his hand.

Mick to Alice

These are the flowers I cut for you before you told me that pink roses were a waste of a flower. I put them in a vase anyway, because I cut them and what the heck do you do with flowers once they've been cut? You put them in a vase with water on the kitchen counter and hope your girlfriend doesn't sneeze herself into apoplexy over them before you can get her out of the house and take her to her favorite restaurant for a big steak dinner.

I'm sorry, baby, that I didn't know you hated pink roses.

Let me make it up to you.

—Mick to Alice

Chapter 14

"She likes big romantic gestures," Jay said. "You know. *Say Anything* type stuff. You're gonna have to be John Cusack holding up the boom box outside her window. And really, man, it sounds like you need to grovel a little bit. Maybe a lot."

Mick took a long draw on the beer Jay had handed him. The other man had been rightfully reluctant to let Mick come over, so Mick had already done some groveling. Jay was one of Alice's best and longest friends, though. If anyone knew how best to get her to listen to him, it would be Jay.

"I'll beg, if I have to."

Jay laughed. "Don't beg. She'd hate that."

"You sure?" Mick leaned against the granite counter in Jay's kitchen. The dude had some kind of kitchen, man. Mick looked around, thinking of his own place. He didn't even have matching glassware. "I thought women liked it when a man begged."

"Groveling is one thing, but not begging. Have some dignity." Jay rolled his eyes.

"I already apologized to her."

Jay cracked open a tub of dip and put it out on the table, along with some chips. At Mick's look, he shrugged. "I have someone coming over later. But you can have some, too."

"Oh, shit. Didn't mean to—"

"Relax. I'm not doing this for you. I'm doing it for Alice. Because that girl is crazy about you, no clue why, and she has been for a decade." Jay gave Mick a look. "The question is, are you going to fuck it all up again?"

"Not on purpose." Mick turned the bottle around in his hands.

"Well, thank God for that." Jay snorted and shook his head. "Look, man. I don't have anything against you."

"Other than I broke Alice's heart," Mick said.

Jay grinned. "Yeah. That. She's my girl."

"No," Mick said quietly. "She's *my* girl."

"If you hurt her again," Jay told him, "I will fuck you up. You got it?"

"Got it." Mick put the empty bottle in the sink and straightened. "I don't want to hurt her. Trust me. I've never met another woman like her. Beg, grovel, whatever I have to do to get her to give me another chance, I'll do it."

"Tell her that." Jay set out a small stack of fancy paper plates with matching napkins and gave Mick a glance over his shoulder. "Tell her you still love her. That you never stopped."

Mick winced.

Jay frowned. "Dude. C'mon."

"Dude," Mick mimicked. "You know how it is."

"How what is? Being crazy about someone you can't let go of? Yeah. I know."

That wasn't what he'd meant. "No. I mean about feelings and stuff. It's hard to say that stuff."

"Is it?" Jay narrowed his eyes. "Why?"

"What if she doesn't feel the same way?"

Jay stood and gave Mick a pitying look. "At least you told her the truth, then, right? You afraid of getting your wittle feelings hurt?"

"Who isn't?"

"You know the definition of bravery isn't being unafraid. It's being afraid and doing whatever that thing is that terrifies you anyway."

"You know the definition of crazy, right? Doing the same thing over and over again but expecting different results," Mick countered.

Jay nodded, not smiling. "Fair enough. I guess the question is, man, is you brave? Or is you crazy?"

"Both," Mick said. "I guess I'm hoping to be both."

"You'd better hurry, then," Jay said. "She told me last week she met some new guy, and she's going out to dinner with him tonight."

Alice to Mick

There is nothing crueler than the person who doesn't want you enough to keep you, but who doesn't love you enough to let you go.
—Alice to Mick

Chapter 15

Alice had stopped drinking two hours ago, which was good, because the way Bill had been nuzzling at her neck and running his hands up and down her back, a better lubricated Alice would've been more likely to succumb to the temptation of wiping away the memories of Mick with another man. Instead, she'd bid Bill good-bye on her doorstep, though she had allowed him to kiss her—not chastely, sure, but not making out, either. Now in her comfy pajama bottoms with a carton of ice cream in one hand, a spoon in the other, she was scrolling through the choices in her Interflix account. So she'd be fat, single, and a little lonely for a while, she thought. There was a lot to be said about being unafraid to be alone.

Dinner with Bill had been fine. Pleasant. He was charming and funny. He tipped well, something that was always important. Were they hitting it off? She supposed so, though nothing about the evening had been particularly memorable. It was nice to go out, though. Have food, some conversation. No pressure, really. No spark, either.

At the knock on her front door, Alice put down the ice

cream. Listening harder, certain she'd imagined it. Who the hell would be pounding on her front door at just past eleven on a Friday night?

A serial killer.

Alice, spoon in hand, went to the front door to peek out the curtains in the side panels, but all she could see was a shadow. Shit. Serial killers didn't knock, did they? What if it was some Ted Bundy type of guy pretending he'd been in a wreck and needed to use her phone? Or that he'd lost his puppy, they did that sort of thing too, didn't they, to fool people . . . ?

Her phone rang.

Alice screamed.

The phone, still tucked in her purse, which had been slung over the newel post, let out another few bleats and went silent as the call went to voice mail. It rang again a second or so later. Same ringtone, the standard one she'd assigned as default, which meant it wasn't someone she talked to often.

Bill, she thought with a hand over her still pounding heart. It was probably Bill. She dug out the phone, but it was too late. She'd missed this one, too.

Before she could check the voice mail or even swipe to see if she recognized the number, the person on the front porch pounded the door again.

"Alice! I know you're in there! Let me in!"

"Mick? What the hell?" In her hand, the phone rang again. She'd never put his picture in her contacts, but since he'd called her once before, his name and number did show up.

She should've blocked it.

"Answer your phone!" he shouted.

He was going to wake up all the neighbors. Alice swiped her screen, hissing, "Shhhhh!"

"Open your door."

"No way. Are you drunk?"

"Why not? You have someone in there? Let me in!"

"Be quiet," Alice said. "No, I don't have someone in here with me. Not that it's any of your business. Go away, it's late."

"I want to talk to you. Let me in, I want to see you."

She tweaked aside the curtain and made a face at him through the glass. Mick glowered and gestured for her to open the door. She gave him the finger.

"Alice. Please."

"Why should I let you in here? I told you I don't want to see you." She let the curtain fall shut, though through it she could still see his silhouette.

"I want to see you. Please. I have to. I have to talk to you. Are you sure you don't have anyone in there? Like the guy you were with earlier?"

She paused at that. "What the? Stalker! Are you creeping on me?"

"Jay told me."

"What were you doing talking to Jay?"

Silence. She could hear his breathing, but didn't give in to the temptation to tweak aside the curtain again. She sat on the stairs, though, in full sight of the door in case he did something insane like try to break in.

"I wanted him to tell me how to get you to give me another chance."

Alice narrowed her eyes. "What did he say?"

"Let me in, Alice. Please." Mick's voice softened. "Just listen to me. If you don't like what I have to say, you never have to listen to me ever again. I'll leave you alone, walk out the door. Never bother you. I promise."

"Never talk to me again?"

Mick sighed. "Yeah."

"Never . . . see me again? Not even at Bernie's?"

"If I do, I'll stay on my own side of the table and treat you like my dear, sainted aunt. I swear to you. I'll never touch you again. Just . . . let me in. Please." His voice hitched.

The thought of that, never seeing or talking to him again, or worse, seeing him but knowing he had no plans to touch her . . . Alice got to her feet. Phone still pressed to her ear, she opened the front door. Mick stepped through it, kicking it closed behind him. He took her phone out of her hand, ignoring her startled protest, and shoved it into his pocket.

He took her in his arms.

He kissed her, long and deep and slow and hard, until gasping, they broke apart.

"Alice," Mick said, "there's never been another woman like you in my life. I've wanted you since the first time you turned around and looked at me, and I've wanted you all this time, and I think I will want you for the rest of my life, if you'll only give me the chance to prove it to you. Please, Alice. Let me prove it to you."

BEFORE

Chapter 16

Alice Clark had no idea how many angels could dance on the head of a pin, but she did know she couldn't squeeze even a single one into her weekend bag. She'd be lucky if the bag's zipper didn't bust open. A weekend at Crane Lake in the summer meant bikini, sunscreen, flip-flops, nightgown, and a couple of cute dresses. A book or four. Minimal toiletries. But at the last minute she'd shoved a pair of jeans and some socks along with an oversized sweatshirt into the bag, which was the tiniest bit too small to hold everything she wanted to bring. Last year she'd been caught chilly when a summer storm hit, and Alice believed in being prepared.

She didn't know much about angels, but heaven must've been smiling on her because she managed to zip the bag and get it into the trunk of her car without incident. She even made it to work on time. The rest of the day, though, went quickly to crap.

"I'll be there," she promised Jay, phone cradled to her shoulder while she typed as fast as she could. "Have the wine ready."

"As if I wouldn't? Why didn't you take today off?" Jay's voice sounded muffled for a second. "You're going to get there late, and you'll have to take the crappy bedroom."

Alice snorted soft laughter and rolled her eyes. "What, you won't let me share with you this time?"

She'd been half joking, but Jay's silence gave her pause. She stopped working and twirled in her chair. The last trip to Bernie's, she and Jay had shared the loft room he always snagged because it had a small, private balcony where he could go to smoke. The double bed had been too small for two, especially if they weren't lovers, which she and Jay of course had never been. She didn't want to share a room with him, but the fact he wasn't offering meant something important.

"Jay!"

"I . . . invited someone along."

"Yeah, you told me you had a new friend. Mick, you said his name was."

Another beat of silence. "No, another friend. He's . . . special."

Jay hadn't had a boyfriend in about eight months. His last breakup had been bad, right around the same time as hers. They'd both vowed off men for a while.

"What's his name?"

"Paul."

"Not the guy from the club!"

"The guy from the club," Jay admitted. "I know. It's trashy. But . . ."

"It can't be that trashy if you're bringing him to Bernie's for the weekend. Unless you're trying to get rid of him, thinking we'll scare him away." She grinned.

Jay laughed. "You might anyway."

"We'll be extra super nice to him. You know that."

"Yeah. That's what might scare him away." Jay made

another muffled noise. "Hey, gotta run. Bernie and Cookie just got back from the grocery store and I promised I'd help with the marinade. Or something, I thought it was marinade but who knows, I might've agreed to anything. Get here! I miss the hell out of you."

"Me too. I'll be there by dinner time." She made kissy noises into the phone and hung up, then spun her chair another time or two, thinking of the weekend ahead.

Nothing but sunshine, booze, food, and relaxing. She was so ready for it. Work had been brutal over the past month or so, somehow made more indignantly awful because the weather had been so stinking hot. Not even the end of June yet, and already there'd been heat warnings all over the place. She couldn't wait to get to the lake house.

She'd meant to leave work at noon and be on the road by one, get to Bernie's place in Northern Virginia by three or four at the latest, but she ought to have known better. Getting out on a Friday was never easy, especially not when she was taking Monday off. Everyone in the world had the same idea about avoiding traffic of course, and she'd needed to stop for gas and an extra-large coffee to pep her up since she'd been up until past midnight packing and taking care of all the stuff she always managed to wait until the last minute to do. Now here she was on the road on a Friday afternoon and hitting all the traffic on 83 South toward Baltimore—and yep, there was an accident that closed the road, diverting traffic to the alternate route.

For six hours.

By the time she was able to finally get off the rural highway and back onto the state route, Alice had gone through every CD in her car a few times over. She'd stopped for gas and to use the bathroom as well as stock up on some road trip snacks, since at this point, making it to Bernie's house by dinnertime was so not happening. Thank

God for her sleeveless summer dress, because she'd had to drive with her windows down to keep her engine from overheating. By the time she finally pulled into Bernie's driveway, Alice felt frazzled.

"I'm here!" she cried when she opened the door, flinging it wide and stumbling through it on legs numb from sitting so long, her bag heavy enough to keep her off balance. Graceless, awkward, uncoordinated, she didn't care how she looked as she let go of the bag and tripped into Bernie's living room. "Who's bringing me a drink?"

Too late, she saw the video camera. Bernie waved at her, and she waved back, self-conscious but only a little. She was among friends, after all.

And some strangers, Alice realized as the man talking to Bernie turned and gave her a half smile. It couldn't be Paul, she knew that at once. Jay had described his new flame as blond and blue-eyed, a Viking. This guy had thick black hair and eyes of piercing, vivid blue beneath dark, knitted brows. Mick, then—Jay's other friend—unless Bernie had invited some other new stranger for the weekend.

"That's Mick McManus," Jay confirmed ten minutes later while Alice dumped her stuff in her room. "Irish as Guinness and *Lord of the Dance*."

Alice unzipped her bag and shook the three dresses she'd packed to get the wrinkles out, then hung them in the closet, debating if she needed to change her clothes after the horrendous trip. "How'd you meet him?"

"We worked on a project together last year. He's one of the few guys from Herston Tech I can handle for more than an hour at a time."

"I thought you could handle most guys for more than an hour at a time," Alice teased.

Jay made a face and lounged on the bed while she dug

through her bag to lay out the rest of her stuff. "Anyway, we've managed a couple projects together since then, and sometimes we'll have drinks after work, and then I just ended up inviting him here. You know Bernie and Cookie love to meet new people."

"And he's straight?"

"So straight," Jay said.

Alice went into the Jack-and-Jill bathroom she was sharing with Cookie's niece Tanya and ran some cool water on a washcloth she used on her face and the back of her neck. A quick swipe under her arms. After a second's hesitation, she grabbed her makeup bag and swiped on some powder. A little gloss. From the bedroom, Jay made a *woo-woo* noise.

Alice poked her head out of the bathroom. "Shut up."

"I thought you were swearing off guys." Jay grinned.

"What? I'm just trying to look like I didn't spend six hours on a three-hour car ride." Alice shrugged and smoothed on a touch of mascara, eyeing her reflection. Her hair was a mess, but not in a bad way. And she didn't look like she'd made a huge effort at primping. She came out of the bathroom. "Hey, do I smell bad?"

Jay chortled but took an obligatory sniff. "Like spring flowers and gas station chicken."

"You can be such an ass." She punched his shoulder, and he grabbed her wrist to tug her down next to him.

"Missed you." He hugged her.

Alice squeezed him. "That's the problem with being adults, right? Gotta work, pay bills, do responsible things."

"Yeah." Jay sighed against her neck and flopped back onto the bed, arms out, to stare at the ceiling. "Shit, Alice. What am I gonna do about Paul?"

She poked his side and got up to put her bag away in the closet. "Where is he, by the way?"

"Later than you, and he's not stuck in traffic. Maybe he's not coming. Maybe," Jay said dourly, "he's blowing me off. Again."

That sounded bad. "Again? Don't tell me you settle for that."

Jay gave her a look. Alice sighed. Shook her head.

Jay sat up. "He's worked his cock magic all over me, Alice."

"Oh, lordy." She raised both brows, but not in judgment. "That bad? Or good, whichever."

"He's . . ." Jay's voice trailed away, not quite dreamy but definitely a little starry eyed. "Just . . . so . . ."

"I get it. I get it." Alice held up her hands. "And you know I'll be there with you every step, even if it means picking you up after you fall. That's our deal."

Jay looked solemn and held out his hand. "Pinkies."

"Always." Alice linked her pinky with his, both of them curling their fingers tight. "You know it."

Chapter 17

Mick didn't believe in regret, but he was sort of wishing he hadn't let Jay talk him into coming along this weekend. It was always a little weird being a houseguest anyway, and being a guest in the house of someone he didn't even know was just that much stranger. Not that Bernie or his wife, Cookie, had made Mick feel anything but welcomed or comfortable. He just wasn't really used to being the odd guy out, the one without the inside jokes.

He was flat out grumpy, that was the problem. No good to anyone but the devil himself, his grandmother might've said with a shake of her finger, before sending him to his room to sulk it out. He sent himself outside to the deck instead, a bottle of beer that should've been good enough to change his mood in one hand. He'd finish it up, then make his early night excuses and hit the sack. Sleep would help the bad mood. It usually did.

And if it didn't, he admitted, he was an asshole who didn't deserve to be here. This place was amazing. When Jay had described his buddy Bernie's place, Mick had imagined a rustic cabin in the woods. As it turned out, the house was amazing, a log structure, sure, but built into a hill with a finished walkout basement and a huge deck overlooking a vast, sweeping yard and garden. The kitchen, top-of-the-line gourmet. The guest rooms, even the tiny basement room Mick had been assigned, were well-appointed and totally set up to make everyone staying there feel like they were at a resort. Only a dick would stay in a bad mood, Mick told himself as he took a long swallow of beer and tried to force himself to stop being a dick.

Behind him, the French doors opened, letting out a waft of good cooking smells and laughter. He half turned, preparing to make small talk, but stopped when he saw who it was. Alice, whom he'd met only briefly forty minutes ago when she arrived. The redhead in the green dress.

The gorgeous redhead, Mick amended, watching her as she leaned on the railing to look out into the yard. She wore her hair, red, yes, but the darkest shade, cut just to her chin and swept to one side, tucked behind her ear to reveal a pointed chin. Heart-shaped face, Mick thought, knowing he was staring but unable to look away. She caught his gaze and gave him a smile.

"Hey. I'm Alice, and you're—"

"Mick McManus."

She lifted her glass of wine toward him. "Jay brought you."

"Um . . . yeah. He mentioned you, said you were friends since college?"

Alice turned to rest her elbows on the railing, cocking one leg so the hem of her green dress hitched a little higher on her thigh. "Yep. And you guys work together sometimes."

"Yeah."

Mick drank some beer. Alice drank some wine. Neither of them said much of anything. Just drank and looked at each other until he wondered if maybe he had spilled sauce on his shirt during dinner or something.

"So," she said, "are you always this much of a scintillating conversationalist, or is it just me?"

Incredibly, Mick laughed. Grumpy, out of place and out of sorts, lack-of-sleep mood and all, to anyone else his reaction would've been a scowl. But not to her.

"Sorry," he said through a chortle. "I'm in a bad mood."

Alice burst into laughter, too. "Are you?"

"Yeah." He laughed a little harder, not sure what was so funny about it other than it felt so freaking good to laugh with her that he didn't want to stop.

She was that kind of girl, he thought, watching her tip her head back in peals of bright and shining giggles that completely charmed him. The kind that made you never want to stop. At that thought, he took a couple of steps closer.

She noticed. Eyes gleaming. Her tongue dipped to touch the center of her bottom lip for a second or so, long enough to catch his attention but not keep it from going back to her eyes. Not blue, though he'd have thought so. Gray, pale gray with a dark ring around the iris. Maybe it was the light. It didn't matter, really. He was caught in them.

"So," she said in a low voice. She hadn't moved. One hand still curled loosely around a wineglass that was now almost empty.

Mick smiled. "So."

They stared again for a moment or so until her chin lifted. She took a long, slow sip of wine, finishing the glass.

He watched her throat work as she swallowed, and his own went dry.

"You could get me another drink," Alice told him. "If you wanted to."

Yeah. He wanted to. "White?"

"Yeah. I'll come in with you. It's a little chilly out here." She handed him her empty glass and rubbed at her arms with a little shiver but a smile that heated him up. She brushed past him in a way that only a jackass would have thought was accidental. A glance over her shoulder had his eyes making those little hearts like in the cartoons.

He followed her inside.

They weren't alone in there, which wasn't as nice as it had been out there on the deck, but his mood had improved immensely. Mick put his empty bottle in the bin and poured Alice a fresh glass of wine. Her fingers brushed his when she took it. Her eyes—and they were indeed pale gray, as he'd guessed, held his. She smiled and sipped, and there was nobody else in the room. Not for him.

Somehow after that the inside jokes didn't bother him. Not that he felt like he had to be the life of the party or anything—it was enough to sit next to Alice on the couch and feel the heat of her hip on his, the occasional brush of her shoulder. The drift of her fingers on his knee every so often when she reached to put down or pick up her glass. The group had moved conversation to a rowdy game of Bullshit, so cards were flying and people were shouting and laughing. It was easy enough to let her touch him like it was an accident, though every now and then the way her gaze snagged his convinced him that it was anything but.

The hours crept past midnight before he knew it. At nearly one in the morning, someone new arrived to a chorus of friendly catcalls and admonishments—Paul, his name was. Jay had invited him the same way he'd invited

Mick. Or not quite the same, Mick thought as he watched Jay embrace the other man. They didn't kiss or anything, but there was more to that greeting than casual friendship.

Alice saw it, too, and she murmured, "Finally."

Mick looked at her. She shrugged, the two of them still sitting on the couch while everyone else had moved to take empty plates and glasses to the kitchen, or to say hello to Paul. It would be obvious in a few seconds that she ought to move away from him now that there was more room on the couch, but for the moment, they still pressed thigh to thigh. She half turned toward him with a small smile.

"It's late," Alice said. "Probably bedtime, huh?"

If it was an invitation, he lacked just enough confidence to act on it. She squeezed his shoulder as she got up, but it could've been meaningless. Mick watched her say hello to Paul and get a kiss and hug from Jay, he watched her say good night without looking his way or sending any other signals, and when she'd disappeared down the hallway, he finally found the incentive to get off the couch himself.

In his basement room, Mick fell asleep thinking of Alice's laughter, but he fell asleep alone.

Chapter 18

A full day at the lake, followed by dinner and a bonfire, with S'mores, campfire songs, and hilarity . . . it would've been enough to send anyone off into slumberland. Yet Alice hummed with the unreleased tension of the hours and hours of not-quite flirting she and Mick had been doing since last night on the deck. It was making her crazy.

She hadn't meant anything the night before, heading outside where he'd been brooding with a beer. She'd only meant to get some air and say hi to Jay's friend. Okay, so the new guy was easy on the eyes, nothing wrong with that, right? But it wasn't the thick dark hair falling over those crystalline eyes or the quirk of his smile or the broad shoulders or amazing forearms that had gotten her so tangled up inside. At least it wasn't *only* those things. It had been the simple way he made sure she always had a fresh drink. The almost sly way he'd let his eyes slip to hers when someone told a joke, as though he'd been waiting for her reaction alone, as though nobody else's mattered.

She'd been snared.

No other way to describe it. The question was, would

she do something about it? Watching him now from across the fire, Alice thought she would.

She'd never been the kind of girl to sit back and let the world come to her. She went after scholarships and relationships and whatever else she wanted, usually with a practiced determination and practicality that had served her well enough through the years. Sure, she'd been disappointed in her pursuits a few times, but that was part of going after what you wanted—you had to be prepared to lose.

Somehow, Alice didn't think she was going to lose. Not with the way Mick's gaze kept slipping back to capture hers, no matter where she stood, or how he made sure to somehow be wherever she was. Not in an obvious way, nothing anyone else might see, because while Mick was pursuing Alice, she was making it extremely easy for him to do it.

When the fire had burned to coals and there were more yawns than laughs going around the circle, Alice gathered up as much trash as she could and paused next to Mick. "Hey. Help me carry this up to the house?"

Jay and Paul had both disappeared an hour before. Bernie and Cookie were snuggled together, and Tanya had fallen asleep in a lawn chair. Alice, with Mick a step or two behind, carried the garbage to the oversized can at the base of the deck steps and dumped it in. It was darker up here, the light from the fire an orange haze at the bottom of the garden and the house itself lit only dimly from a few lights in the living room. Under the deck, sliding glass doors led into the finished basement . . . and the room where Mick was sleeping.

"Wanna play some pool?" Alice asked.

Mick laughed softly. "Are you any good?"

"Terrible. But that's what makes it so much fun."

There was a beat or two of silence, in which she was sure he'd reach for her. He had to, didn't he? After eyefucking her all night long, surely he'd move a little closer. Lean in. Put his hands on her hips.

Instead, Mick backed away. "Sure. I'll play."

Alice followed him inside, calculating how many steps between the sliding doors and the hallway to his bedroom. Imagining herself stripping out of her dress and letting it fall to the floor, walking in just her bra and panties to his room with no more than a glance over her shoulder and a crook of her finger. He'd follow, she was sure of that. Yet something stopped her. . . . Anticipation was delicious, after all.

"You can rack," she told him, and went to the glass-front fridge Bernie had salvaged from a convenience store being remodeled. "You want a soda?"

"I'll be up all night." Mick grinned.

Alice smiled back and lifted her brow. "And?"

"Sure. I'll have one." Mick grabbed two cues from the wall rack and handed her one, taking the can of cola from her. "You want stripes or solids?"

"Stripes." Alice took a drink and set the can down, then put some chalk on her cue. She was truly terrible at pool, that part hadn't been a lie. But bending over the table and shaking her ass to keep him distracted? *That* she was good at.

They played for about five minutes before the sound of shouts from upstairs made her pause. Mick hadn't heard them; he was in the middle of a joke when she held up her hand to hush him. To give him credit, he did at once, looking concerned.

"You okay?"

"I heard something." She went to the bottom of the

front staircase, head tilted to listen. "I thought it sounded like Jay."

Mick put his cue down and stood beside her. "I don't hear anything."

She didn't either, now, just the huff of their breathing. The heat of him brushed her bare arm. When she turned her face, his mouth was there. The kiss felt like an accident, or at least like something they could pretend wasn't on purpose. His lips urged hers to open. He pushed her back against the wall, his hands on her hips.

Everything else was forgotten then. The pool game, Jay's shout, the late hour. Alice wound her arms around Mick's neck. She opened for him, hips tilting forward. He slipped a hand beneath the back of her knee so he could press against her center. She let out a long sigh against his lips.

"I've been wanting to do this all night," he murmured. "God, Alice, you taste so good."

She pushed her fingers into the thickness of his hair, tugging. "Less talking. More kissing."

"Yes, ma'am." He laughed and went back to the job of kissing her.

They kissed for a long time. No urgency. Lips and tongues moving. Teeth clashing every so often. He nibbled at her jaw and throat, pausing when she arched and shivered to do it again, a little harder that time. His hands moved over her body, no place terribly intimate, just belly and hips and sides, until she couldn't stand it any longer and took his hand to cup her breast.

"Ah," Mick said into her ear. "Okay, then."

From upstairs came the shuffle of feet in the kitchen, but nobody came downstairs. The lights went out, casting the stairwell into dimness. Mick turned them both so he sat on the lower steps, Alice straddling his lap. He rocked her against him. His hands roamed her back, digging in just hard enough to make her moan into his open mouth.

It had been some long months since the last time Alice had kissed anyone, and then it had been nothing like this. Mick's mouth and hands on her, his kissing, were all magic. She didn't want any of it to end, not even to take him to the bedroom, strip him down, and fuck him until neither of them could walk.

Alice wanted to kiss Mick forever.

He shifted beneath her. The press of his cock hit her just right through the barrier of his soft khaki shorts and her dress, tangled around her thighs. She let out another low moan, swallowed by his mouth. His hand came up to fist in her hair, his fingers digging gently into the base of her skull and tugging her head back so he could get at her throat. The top slopes of her breasts revealed by the dress's scoop neck. A little lower, his nibbling lips found her erect nipples, hard enough to poke through her bra and the dress.

"Yes," Alice whispered. "That."

With a low chuckle, Mick pulled her neckline down to gain further access to her bare flesh. Her bandeau bra, lightweight nylon, slipped easily down. For a second, just a second, Alice hesitated. She arched into the slide of his tongue along her skin, the tug of his lips on her nipples, but common sense, her stupid brain, did tell her to slow down. Before she could pull away, though, he did.

Mick kissed her mouth as he let her neckline return to its original place. Then he buried his face against her neck, holding her close. They sat that way in silence, breathing in unison. Under the press of her lips on his neck, Alice felt the beat of Mick's heart slowing in time with her own.

She waited to feel rejected—she'd been half naked, her tits in his mouth, after all. He hadn't even tried to get his fingers in her panties, not that she was sure she'd have let him. But all Alice felt just then with Mick's arms around her was a strange sense of contentment.

She lost track of the time they sat there, just that it was long enough for her to need to stretch. They moved at the same time, disengaging. Uncoupling. She stood and shook her foot, which had started to fall asleep. Mick got up, one hand on the stair railing, and cracked his neck.

"It's late," Alice said.

Mick smiled. "Yeah."

He reached for her, and she stepped back into his arms. Her head fit neatly under his chin, something she wasn't expecting. His hand ran down her back, pausing just above her ass, and though she totally would not have minded had he taken a little squeeze, Mick stopped there. Alice discovered she liked that even better.

"Good night, Alice," he said into her ear.

She let her lips brush along his cheek as she stepped away from him to climb the stairs, looking back over her shoulder. "Good night, Mick."

Chapter 19

Good night, Alice.

Good night, Mick.

It had become their ritual. Each logged into their laptops and tucked into bed for an instant message conversation that always meant to be a few minutes or so but almost always lasted for hours. Sometimes they talked on the phone, too, but the distance between them and expensive cell phone minutes meant IM was easier. On the rare nights they didn't manage to connect for even a quick chat, without that *Good night,* Mick found it hard to fall asleep.

They'd met a month ago, but it seemed a helluva lot longer. Sometimes, Mick felt like he'd known Alice Clark forever. Sometimes, he felt like forever wouldn't be long enough.

With an hour and a half drive between them, dating Alice wasn't convenient, but that only made the time they'd managed to spend together even better. They'd seen each other three times since Bernie's party. Dinner, movies, one night they'd gone bowling. She'd kicked his ass, and her victory dance had been so cute he could hardly stand it.

He was falling for her. Hard. It was like the universe had taken a look at Mick's secret checklist of everything he'd always wanted in a woman—sense of humor, smart, passionate, considerate. Beautiful. Damn, she was so beautiful it hurt his heart. And thickened his dick.

It was getting hard right now, as a matter of fact. He'd been dating a few different girls when he went to Bernie's, but since meeting Alice, Mick had stopped returning their calls and messages. Less drama that way, he figured. It wasn't like he had anything serious with any of them, anyway. Easier to simply let it fade.

Thinking of her now, the memory of her mouth sent a surge of desire flooding him. That girl kissed like a fucking dream. She could do things with her lips and tongue Mick had never even dreamed of, and that was a fact. He could still remember the taste of her perfect pink nipples, though. The way she'd moaned when he sucked them. Shit, his cock was straining at the front of his sweatpants now.

Mick slipped a hand into his waistband and found his hard-on. Two nights ago they'd had a steamy phone conversation, full of teasing and innuendo, but it hadn't quite made it into phone sex. The same with a few of their instant message sessions, which tended to be even more frank on the subjects of sex and love, maybe because it was easier to be honest about what you liked when you could feel at least a little anonymous. He knew a lot about what turned Alice on, and off, just like he knew how she voted, her views on religion, hell, even what size shoes she wore. But so far, though they'd danced around it, he had yet to get her off . . . or hear her getting off. At the moment, he couldn't be sure which would be hotter.

Cock hard in his fist, Mick stroked a little faster as he pushed his sweatpants down to his thighs. Closing his eyes, he pushed his hips upward, sliding his dick through curled fingers.

"Fuck," Mick breathed, pumping. "Alice."

She was making him crazy, and she wasn't even there. Giving in to the desire rushing through him, toes curling with it, Mick stroked his cock to the thought of making Alice just as crazy. Of kissing her mouth and the curve of her jaw. Slope of her neck, throat, shoulder, tits . . . ah, shit, her nipples again. Down her belly, over hip. He thought of the noises she would make when he nibbled her there, and how she would gasp and sigh and moan his name when he let his mouth drift over her belly. Lower. To her thighs. Inside, the sweetness there, then a little higher, to that heat—

He let out another long, slow groan and palmed the head of his cock. Fingers sliding down, gripping the base. Up again, his other hand cupping his balls to stroke a thumb along the seam between nuts and ass. His hips pumped. Feet flat on the bed to give himself purchase. Harder, a little harder and faster.

He wanted to taste her so fucking bad.

Mick rolled onto his belly to thrust that way. In moments he was shuddering and spent, the pleasure leaving him gasping her name. In the aftermath he flopped onto his back to catch his breath. Blinking into the darkness. Wishing she were with him . . . and not just so he could've been making her moan his name, feeling her touch him instead of his own hand. No, he thought as dreams stole him away at last. He just wanted Alice with him there when he fell asleep so she'd be there with him when he woke up, too.

Chapter 20

"It's going to happen this weekend." Jay shook his head at the dress Alice held up. "Ugh, no. That one makes you look like you're someone's favorite babysitter."

With a grimace, Alice looked at it, then at him. "That's a bad thing?"

"If it's not, it ought to be." Jay lolled on her bed, no help at all.

Alice put the dress aside and picked another. This summer had been hotter than Satan's asshole, and all she could manage to wear was dresses. Anything else was simply too freaking much. She waved it on the hanger. "This one?"

"Just bring a bathing suit and a sarong. It's not like you need to look nice for anyone—hey!" Jay ducked away from her swatting hand. Laughing, he kicked out at her. "Wow. Bitch."

"Asshole," she said without anger, and tossed the dress into her bag. "And how are you so sure it's going to happen this weekend, anyway? Is he giving you hints, or what?"

Jay scowled. "No. Getting anything out of Paul is like

pulling teeth, one at a time. Without gas. Like tying each one to a doorknob and slamming the door."

"I get it. Gross." Alice eyed him as she tucked her favorite bikini into the bag and added some pretty lacy panties and matching bras she tried to be casual about. Eagle Eyes saw it anyway.

"Spill it," Jay demanded, sitting up straight.

Alice gave him an innocent blink. "I thought we were talking about you and Paul and how you were sure this was the weekend he was going to finally ask you to move in with him."

"Oh my *gawwwwwd.* Mick? Not Mick!" Jay had always been able to see right through her. He got up to grab Alice by the upper arms so she had no choice but to face him. "How long has this been going on?"

"Nothing's going on. Nothing much. I mean . . ." Alice coughed, incapable of lying to him. They'd been friends for too long. "We've been sort of seeing each other since the last party at Bernie's, when we met."

Jay raised an eyebrow and squeezed her gently before letting go. He crossed his arms. "Uh-huh. And you didn't tell me because . . . ?"

"Because it's really been . . . nothing." This didn't quite feel like a lie.

"It doesn't look like nothing. Alice, you should know better than to think you could keep something like that from me. Why would you, anyway? Shit, I tell you everything." Jay frowned and took a peek in her weekend bag, then looked at her. "I'd go with the pale blue panties with the flowers, not those."

"I didn't ask you!" With a swat and a laugh, Alice pushed him out of the way to get back to packing. She paused. "I like him, Jay. A lot."

Jay laughed. "Well, there's a recipe for disaster, right there. Liking a guy. Who does that?"

"Right, I'm stupid." Alice shook her head and moved to the dresser to pull out a camisole she knew she'd never wear but was going to pack anyway, just in case. She tossed it into the bag, then sat on the edge of the bed to look at Jay. "So stupid."

"Yeah. Me too." Jay flopped onto the bed, bouncing her.

Alice curled up next to him, both their heads on the same pillow. Staring at the ceiling, she reached for his hand to link their fingers and squeeze. They stayed that way in silence for a bit, until finally Jay turned to push his face into her shoulder. Alice stroked his hair.

"I'm totally in love with him," Jay told her.

"I know you are, honey."

"He makes me crazy."

Alice laughed. "I know that, too."

Jay pushed up to look at her face. "You don't think he's right for me."

"I never said that." Alice twisted to face him. "I barely know him, to be honest. You haven't brought him around a whole lot. I really haven't had a chance to get to know him."

"You shouldn't have moved so far away." Jay frowned.

"Oh, my God, Jay. An hour! I moved an hour away from you, and it was for a really good job!" Alice poked him, then tickled him until he squirmed away from her.

He caught her hands, holding her still. "I miss you."

"I miss you, too," Alice said. "Always. Of course."

Jay settled back against the pillows with a heavy sigh. "He mentioned last week that it was a pain to always have to bring his stuff in a bag to my place. The week before that, he bought me a toothbrush when we were out, because I forgot mine."

"How . . . sweet."

Jay laughed, but there was a hint of anxiety below the humor. "He hates my apartment. Says it's too small and dark, too 'vintage.' His place is all bright and modern, much bigger . . . very spare. But there's a lot more room in it. He'd never suggest he move into my place. Maybe I should get a new place. Something with a better kitchen."

"But you think he's going to ask you to move in with him." Alice thought about this. She'd never lived with a guy other than Jay, and that didn't count. She'd had a few serious relationships, some that had definitely been in the "sleeping over" stage, but never any that had moved beyond that. She couldn't quite imagine it, actually. Sharing her space with someone else on a permanent basis.

"Yes. I mean . . . I hope so. I think so."

"Why this weekend?"

Jay rolled onto his side to look at her. "Because Paul talks a lot about how important things should be accompanied by the right mood and stuff like that. And he freaking loves it at Bernie's house. Once he told me it was the perfect place for a marriage proposal . . . oh. Shit. Shit, Alice!"

Neither of them said anything for a minute or so.

"He couldn't," Jay said finally.

"No. I guess he couldn't." Alice frowned at the unfairness of that. "Not that."

Jay sat up and pulled his knees close to his chest, linking his fingers. "But moving in together. He could ask me to do that. I mean, when he asked me to be his boyfriend, he had a singing waiter bring me a bouquet of roses with a watch in a box attached. He said it was 'time' for us to 'bloom.'"

"He didn't!" Alice burst into laughter. "Wow. That's . . ."

Jay shot her a sour look, and she sobered. "It's romantic!"

"It's romantic." She nodded. "And cheesy. But romantic, it's romantic! Hey, you're sure he's going to show up, right? I hate to say it, but . . ."

Jay made a face. "You think he'll blow me off?"

Paul had done it before. Lots of times. "I don't care if you ride down with me, you know that, but I'm worried he won't show and you'll be stuck without a ride home."

"He'll show. He has to," Jay said. "This is the weekend he's asking me to move in with him. I know it."

"I hope it's everything you're hoping for, Jay. That's all."

Jay grinned. "Me too."

Alice shoved down the contents of her bag to make more room. Couldn't. Took out a pair of sneakers she knew she wouldn't wear and tossed them into the closet. She tried again to zip the bag, but couldn't, and gave up with a sigh.

"I'm nervous," she admitted.

"About seeing Mick?" Jay gently pushed her aside and started unpacking the bag, laying out everything in neat piles and refolding things that had become crumpled. "Look, I told you this before. You roll things, makes more room."

"Yes. About Mick." Alice leaned against the dresser to watch him. Jay had paid his way through college by working as a flight attendant. He knew more about how to pack a week's worth of clothes into a weekend bag than she ever could.

He glanced at her. "Why?"

"Because. We've talked almost every day and stuff, but this will be the first time I've seen him for longer than a few hours since the last time at Bernie's." She paused, trying to put her thoughts into words. "I don't want to act like we're a couple, if we're not. And we haven't talked about it. I mean, we aren't sharing a room or anything like that."

"Have you slept with him yet?" Jay tightly rolled a sundress and tucked it in the bag.

Heat flooded her at the memory of Mick's hands and mouth on her. "No."

"You think you will this weekend?"

She didn't answer that, not right away, because the truth was Alice had no idea if she and Mick were going to have sex. They hadn't talked about it, not specifically anyway, though of course she assumed he wanted to get into her panties as much as she wanted him in there. And it wasn't like she believed in holding out for some reason, like putting a time stamp on when it was acceptable to finally get into bed together. It hadn't happened yet because she and Mick lived far enough apart to have made their few face-to-face dates tricky enough to organize. They'd ended up meeting halfway, which meant a couple heavy duty kissing sessions in the backseat of his car, and there'd been the smoking hot make-out session on the stairs at Bernie's. . . .

"Earth to Alice." Jay sounded annoyed. "Hello!"

Alice gave him an apologetic smile. "I don't know. First times should be special, you know?"

"I've known you for a long time. It would not be your first time."

"You know what I mean," Alice told him. "The first time for us. I'm not sure I want to do it in Bernie's guest bedroom with everyone around. It should be . . . you know. Special. What?"

Jay had given her such a stunned look, Alice was confused.

"Oh. My. God," he said. "You are totally fucked, Alice. You know that, right? Utterly and completely fucked."

"Why?" she cried, heart and stomach both twisting.

"You're in love with Mick!"

"No." Alice shook her head firmly. "No way. It's too soon for that."

"Soon or not," Jay said, "you'd better put on your crash gear, baby, because if you aren't yet, you're about to fall for that guy. Super hard."

Chapter 21

"Mick! Welcome." Cookie, Bernie's wife, beamed and gestured for him to come inside. "We're so glad you could join us."

He kissed her cheek and handed her the basket of breads and cheeses he'd picked up on the way from one of the farmers' markets. Normally shopping in a place like that gave Mick hives, but somehow a case of light beer and some tortilla chips just didn't seem like the right thing to bring to this kind of party. How he'd even managed to become a part of this crowd, he had no idea, but he was glad he had, because of Alice.

"Jay and Alice are driving together and they're on their way. Paul called to say he'd be here in half an hour. Dayna is coming, too. You haven't met her yet. She's a friend of mine from work. Tanya unfortunately won't make it, she's actually moved to Ohio to take a new job. But that makes room for new friends!" Cookie peeked into the basket and made a sound of appreciation. "Oh, this looks wonderful. You didn't have to, Mick."

"Of course I did. My mom told me never to go to a

party without taking something for the hostess." Mick followed her inside and carefully closed the door behind him, then waited for an awkward second. "So . . . should I put . . ."

Cookie, halfway up the stairs to the living room, turned. "Oh! Do you mind the rumpus room bedroom? You had it last time, and I know some people don't care for it, but—"

"No, that's great, actually." Mick looked toward the stairs to the lower level. "Let the wild rumpus start, right?"

Cookie laughed. "Get settled, and then come upstairs. I'm going to slice this bread and we can have wine. You drink wine, don't you, Mick?"

"I'll drink whatever you have," he told her honestly, and took his things into the small basement room he'd used the last time. He tossed his bag on the bed, thinking he'd unpack it later, if at all, but for a second he sat. Testing the mattress. Thinking about Alice and if this was where they'd finally make good on all those subtle promises they'd been making to each other over the past couple of months.

The thought stirred him up, so he forced himself to stand. In the small attached bathroom, Mick splashed his face with cool water. For good measure, he brushed his teeth. They hadn't talked about how they were going to handle sharing what they'd been up to with the rest of the weekend crowd, but he was sure that if he had the chance to kiss Alice, he was going to take it.

Upstairs in the kitchen, Mick took a glass of wine and plate of bread, cheese, and mustard, along with some small sausages Cookie had cut. Bernie offered him a cigar, too. Mick wasn't much of a smoker, but when in Rome, he supposed.

"Living like kings," Bernie said.

"And queens," Cookie added archly. "But smoke outside."

On the deck, Mick tried not to pace or act antsy, though as forty minutes and then almost an hour passed without Alice's arrival, he was starting to go a little nuts. Paul showed up laden with bottles of wine with labels the names of which Mick couldn't even pronounce.

"How's it going?" Paul leaned against the railing, a glass of wine in his hand. He held out his hand for Mick's cigar.

After a second, Mick gave it to him. He watched the other man take a long puff and then look over the cigar with an assessing eye. He waved it away when Paul offered to hand it back, though. "You keep it."

"Not into cigars?"

Not into sharing them with other dudes he barely knew, Mick thought, but shrugged an answer, instead. He sipped his wine and listened for the sound of tires crunching on the gravel. The French doors opened behind them, and he was already turning at the sound of a new female voice, but it wasn't Alice. A pretty blonde in a flowy sundress stood there.

"Hi. I'm Dayna. Cookie sent me out here to meet you . . . Mick?" She pointed at him. "And Paul?"

Paul straightened. "Well, hey, now. Hi."

Dayna laughed and shook her head, her blond ponytail swinging. She stepped carefully out onto the deck, her feet bare. She'd painted her toenails red, Mick noticed. Everything about her seemed designed to make a man notice.

She shook Paul's hand, then turned to Mick. "Hi."

He shook it, but didn't let their hands linger too long against each other. Dayna wasn't used to men who didn't linger. Mick saw that at once in the slightly confused look she gave him, but her expression turned knowing in the next second when the doors opened again. She turned to follow Mick with her gaze, but everything about his concentration had turned to Alice.

"Hi," Alice said with a small wave.

And though he'd imagined himself sweeping her into his arms and kissing her breathless, in the moment, Mick found himself paralyzed by her obvious hesitation. She hadn't been that way with him the times they'd met up over the past few weeks, so seeing her cut her gaze first to Paul and then Dayna and finally Jay, who'd come onto the deck after her, Mick didn't move. Alice had taken a step or two toward him, but suddenly everyone was there on the deck, all of them shaking hands or hugging or being introduced, and the chance to kiss her had been lost.

Chapter 22

So much for bothering with the lacy panties, Alice thought as she unpacked her bag into the dresser and hung up the dresses Jay had rolled for her in the closet. She and Mick had barely said more than a few words to each other, much less had any chance for him to get a glance at what she wore beneath her dress. Despite what she'd told Jay, she had been half hoping tonight would be the night they finally got down to it.

"Oh, well," she muttered. "Tomorrow is another day."

"*Gone with the Wind*?"

Alice turned at the sound of Dayna's voice. The other woman stood in the doorway to the bathroom between the rooms each of them was using. Alice laughed. "Something like that."

Dayna smiled. "So, I'm going to take a quick shower. Unless you need to get in here, first?"

"Nope, I'm good." Alice stretched a little and eyed the bed. She wasn't even close to tired, and considering it was nearly two in the morning, that was saying something.

When Dayna closed the bathroom door and the water

started running, Alice quietly closed her dresser drawer. She paced for a moment or so. It didn't seem likely that Dayna would try to come into Alice's bedroom again, but just in case, Alice locked the door from her bedroom into the shared bath. She turned off her light. She slipped into the hall, listening for any sounds of other wakeful weekenders, but there was nothing but the soft bubble from Bernie's fish tank in the living room. With her heart thumping so loud she'd have been incapable of hearing anything else anyway, Alice closed the door behind her and tiptoed into the living room.

Someone had left a light on in the kitchen, and she prepared to make an excuse about needing a drink of water, but the words died before they ever escaped her lips at the sight of Mick standing at the counter. He turned when she came in. She didn't imagine the light in his eyes at the sight of her.

And then he was moving across the room toward her, that light turned to a look of determination. She was in his arms before she knew it. His mouth on hers. Backed up against the edge of the counter, Alice let out a muffled *meep* of surprise that became a sigh when Mick's tongue swept inside her mouth. Her arms went around his neck, pulling him closer.

"Hi," Mick whispered into her mouth. "I wanted to do this all night."

Alice shifted so the counter wasn't digging into her, but didn't let him pull away. "Why didn't you?"

"Wasn't sure you wanted me to."

"And now?" Smiling against his lips, Alice nudged a knee between his legs.

Mick groaned a little and slid his hands to grip her hips. "I should've kissed you right away."

"Yeah, you should have," she told him. "You always should."

Mick nipped at her chin, then nuzzled against her neck. He tipped her head back to get at her throat, sending shivers all through her. "You could've kissed me, you know."

Alice slapped at him playfully. "What, me? What kind of girl do you think I am?"

"A super sexy one." Mick's tongue traced a pattern on her skin.

Her nipples had gone hard at the first press of his teeth on her flesh, but at this gentle touch, they felt as though they could cut glass. Between her legs, heat pooled. The lace of her panties pressed her impertinently every time she moved—and she couldn't bring herself to care, even though she could feel herself getting wet enough to soak them.

She murmured his name. He laughed against her neck and pushed himself against her, then went still. They stayed that way for a long moment. Alice timed their breathing, in and out, until it synced. She didn't want to move.

Mick's fingers squeezed her hips, then drifted a little lower to her thighs. Helplessly, Alice arched. She wanted his mouth on her neck again. His hands on every other place. And Mick obliged as though she'd spoken aloud, commanding him, though all she'd done was sigh. One of his hands went to the small of her back. The other inched up the hem of her dress.

Alice shuddered. Her nails dug into his shoulders. When he nibbled again on her throat, her entire body jerked.

She wanted him. Truth was, she'd wanted him since

almost the first moment she'd seen him, even though he'd been sullen and grouchy at the time. The wanting, Alice knew from experience, often went away the longer she knew a guy. Little things like the sound of him chewing or how he answered the phone or his views on which way the toilet paper roll should be hung could destroy any semblance of lust. With Mick though, nothing had worn away the edges of her desire to make them soft. Instead, everything about him had honed the wanting to a razor's edge, and it sliced her open now. Made her raw with hunger for him.

The shuffle of feet behind him moved them apart from each other like they'd been attached to uncoiling springs. It would've been too late to hide what they'd been doing if Jay had been paying attention, but the look on his face said he was too wrapped up in his own drama to have noticed what he'd walked in on. He saw them, of course, and since he'd already talked with Alice about her and Mick he might easily have guessed, but clearly he wasn't in the mood to care.

"Hey," Alice said, pushing Mick gently to the side. "What's up? You okay?"

"Didn't feel good." Jay went to the fridge and pulled out a pitcher of water. He filled a glass and drank it without looking at either one of them.

Alice looked at Mick, who shrugged. She looked at Jay, whose shoulders had slumped. Friendship or fucking, she thought, wishing she and Mick had gone to his bedroom ten minutes ago. With a sigh, she squeezed Mick's shoulder.

"Want to talk about it?" she asked Jay.

Mick took a step back from her, eyes on hers, mouth quirked on one side. "I'm going to head to bed. 'Night."

Jay turned as Mick left, so Alice didn't watch him go.

She looked at her friend, his face pale. Circles below his eyes.

"You look like shit. Are you going to puke?"

"No. Feel like it, though." Jay lowered his voice and looked at the glass of water in his hand. He poured it down the sink and rinsed the glass, then put it in the drainer. His shoulders slumped again.

Shit. He might actually be crying. Alice put her arm around his shoulders. "Talk to me, Jay. Is it Paul?"

Jay nodded.

Double shit, she thought, but waited for her friend to speak. He didn't at first. They stood in the kitchen in silence, until finally he turned to face her.

"He's not going to ask me to move in with him." The words clearly stuck in his throat, but he forced them out. He even managed to give her a wobbly smile. "I'm not even sure he's not going to break up with me at the end of the weekend. I think he's just holding off because he's here with me."

"Gross, Jay. Why would he do that?"

"So he doesn't make it awkward." Jay grimaced. "Because Bernie's my friend, not his."

Alice petted his shoulder. "It *should* be awkward for him, then. If he's going to be a jerk."

"He's kind of always a jerk," Jay said with an embarrassed laugh. "That's part of his charm."

Alice sighed and gave him another hug, but ended up laughing along with him. She squeezed him. "Is it worth me telling you to dump him?"

"You've known me longer than that." Jay leaned into her embrace. "But I don't want to wait for him to break it off with me, either. The rest of my weekend is kind of ruined, anyway. Can we get out of here?"

Alice hesitated. It was Saturday morning by this point,

but she hadn't planned on leaving until Sunday night. She'd been looking forward to another two days and one more night to spend with Mick.

"Please," Jay said.

And, with a sigh, Alice agreed.

Chapter 23

Mick waited until lunch time to ask Bernie where Alice was. He thought maybe she'd slept in, or gone off to town with Cookie. Something, anything other than that she'd up and lit out without bothering to tell him she was going. But when noon ticked around and still no Alice appeared, he had to know.

"Jay wasn't feeling well, so she took him home." Bernie offered a bottle of beer, but Mick shook his head. "She left me and Cookie a note. Sorry, I should've mentioned it earlier."

"Nothing serious, I hope." Dayna had a platter of deli meat and cheese in both hands. She'd been on the way to putting it on the dining room table, but paused at Bernie's explanation.

Paul, who'd been setting the table with flatware, put in, "He had a case of the vapors."

Dayna laughed. Mick didn't. Bernie smiled briefly, but without much humor. Cookie came out of the pantry with some bags of chips, and lunch carried on without more on the subject. If Paul felt the loss of his boyfriend at the table, he didn't show it. He spent his time charming Dayna and Cookie with stories about his world travels. They didn't talk about Jay at all, nor about Alice.

She hadn't left Mick a note explaining her late-night escape. She hadn't left him a message, either, though the cell service out here was spotty enough that even if she had, he wouldn't get it until he was closer to home. He checked his phone anyway, dialing in to his voicemail just in case there was something there. Nothing.

And nothing all day, though he tried not to think about it too much. Still, he felt her absence too keenly to ignore it. At the lake, during dinner, the games they played after. He thumbed a text or two to her, but suspected they didn't reach her. Either that, or she wasn't answering him, and the thought of that was worse than the fact she'd ducked out without telling him.

Sunday morning, Mick made his excuses about wanting to avoid traffic and a heavy workweek ahead, and got on the road by 9:00 A.M. Bernie's place was two and a half hours from his place, but only an hour and a half or so from Alice's. He'd never been to her house, but she'd sent him a funny card in the mail a week or so ago. They'd been doing that, sending each other notes and cards. He'd had flowers delivered to her, too. He remembered the address.

It wasn't until he was pulling into her driveway that it occurred to him he should have called first, in case she were still in bed. Or not home. Or had snuck out of Bernie's house without telling him because she never wanted to see him again. But it was too late, he'd been impulsive and now here he was. He had two choices—get out of the car and knock on her door and tell her there was no way he could last another day without being inside her. Or, he could be responsible and respectable and not a creepy stalker sex freak and go home.

Mick got out of the car.

Chapter 24

Alice had been up since dawn, too wired and anxious to sleep any longer. She and Jay hadn't gotten home until six yesterday morning, and she'd managed to keep herself awake all day so she didn't throw off her sleep schedule . . . well, sort of. She'd been a zombie all day long, mustering little more energy than it took to watch old movies and read before she crashed at just past 7:00 P.M.

She'd slept hard, but fitfully. She'd dreamed of Mick. His hands, teeth, tongue, lips. His cock, hard against her. She'd woken in a sweat, the covers tangled, her body singing from the dream but aching from the lack of release.

He hadn't called her.

She had left in a rush at Jay's insistence, but she'd made sure to leave a note for Bernie. Surely Mick would've asked why she'd left. He might even have worried, a little. Jay was his friend, too. If he were really worried, wouldn't he have at least called once?

She hadn't been shy about calling or even texting him occasionally in the past few weeks, but for some reason her fingers now refused to punch in his number. She didn't want to interrupt him having fun, she told herself, but the real reason was more complicated than that. Stupid head, she thought now with a jaw-cracking yawn. Making trouble for the body.

At the knock on her front door, Alice frowned. It wasn't even noon on a Sunday, and even if she hadn't had a terrible two days without enough sleep, shouldn't there be some unspoken rule that nobody was allowed to come over without warning on a Sunday morning? She almost didn't answer, that was how annoyed she was, but as soon as she peeked through the curtains covering the side transom window, her heart thudded. Skipped. Her stomach leaped.

"Mick," she said as she opened the door. "What the . . how did . . ."

"I didn't want to be there if you weren't." He stepped through the door and took her in his arms. "I'm going to kiss you, Alice. And then I'm going to take you upstairs . . . your bedroom is upstairs, right?"

"Oh, yeah. Absolutely." She grinned.

He kissed her. Slow. Sweet. But determined, no doubt about that. His tongue stroked hers, and Alice shivered with delight. She backed up one step, their mouths still lingering, and he followed. Step by step, laughing and kissing, shedding their clothes. By the time they got to the top of the stairs, Alice had stripped out of her pajama top and Mick was down to boxers.

She couldn't get enough of him. Her hands were all over him, roaming. Feeling, discovering. Enjoying. In her bed, Alice rolled them both so she was on top, straddling him. When Mick made to grab her hips, she shook her head and gave him a wicked grin.

"Nope." Pinning his wrists above his head, she let his mouth get close enough to her breasts to feel the heat of his breath—but not to actually get his lips on her skin. "Patience."

Mick groaned, but didn't try to get away. "I've been patient."

"Shh." Alice nuzzled the side of his neck and added a nibble of his earlobe.

His erection pressed her through the soft fabric of her pajama bottoms, and she rocked against it. But slow. She wanted to go fast, writhing and grinding, but this was the first time.

She wanted it to be special.

She found his mouth. She didn't keep his hands pinned, but he kept them there anyway while their lips and tongues worked. Still so slowly that it was driving her out of her mind, Alice rubbed her pussy along Mick's thick, hard cock. When the head of it peeked out from the top of his boxers, she nearly lost her mind . . . but she didn't move any faster.

She sat up, her thighs squeezing his. She watched his face, his eyes closed, mouth open. He'd gripped the spindles of her headboard, and though she'd never have said she was a dominatrix sort of girl, the way he'd succumbed to her commands was absolutely flipping her switch. When she stroked her hand along his length, gripping him through his boxers and not actually touching flesh, his mouth tightened.

So beautiful, she thought with something like wonder, lost in the sight of how her touch was affecting him. She did it again, sliding her hand along his length, this time letting the tips of her fingers tickle the bare flesh peeking from his waistband. His mouth opened at that. Hips bucked. His cock leaped under her touch, and her pussy clenched.

Alice moved in small, tight circles, nudging her clit

against the base of his cock. She let her head fall back a little, letting the pleasure build and build as she kept the pace excruciatingly slow. It seemed impossible, but she was going to come from this alone. She hadn't planned it that way, but now she was getting so close, she couldn't stop.

She opened her eyes to look at him, her breath catching in her throat. Her hands ran up his flat, taut belly, nails scratching. He bucked and groaned, at last letting go of the headboard to grab her hips. Their eyes met. Held.

Mick's tongue slipped out to stroke along his bottom lip. Alice moved, desire flooding her. She said something, maybe his name or maybe a string of nonsense syllables; the sound was low and guttural and full of aching need. She couldn't look away from him, not even as the pleasure overtook her and the edges of her vision went a little red and hazy.

She cried out as her orgasm rolled over her in slow, cresting waves that left her shaking and breathless. She rocked against him once more, thighs squeezing. Her hands had gone to cover his, holding his hands tight to her hips as she shuddered. When the pleasure faded, she fell forward to capture his mouth with hers.

"Drawer," she said against his lips. "Condom. Must have you inside me. Now!"

Somehow, she rolled and he moved and the clothes came off and he had the condom on, and then, oh, God, yes, he was poised between her legs with the tip of his cock nudging her entrance, and all Alice could do was sigh. But instead of pushing inside her, Mick waited. He gave her a slow, knowing grin.

"Patience," he told her.

She wanted to scream in frustration, but she laughed instead, and that was one of the sexiest things that had ever happened to her. Her post-orgasm glow hadn't erased her arousal, not even a little bit, but somehow giggling made it all so much hotter. She'd never laughed in bed before, not that she could remember. But then nothing with Mick had been like anything she'd ever done or had with anyone before.

He rubbed the head of his cock against her clit, his face tight with concentration. It wasn't the act itself that set her off, but his expression. A man determined to get her off again, even though she'd just come spectacularly from rubbing herself on him . . . Alice was lost. Consumed. Ignited.

"Wanna see you come again," Mick breathed.

Alice arched, pushing her clit against him. She was so wet he slid against her as easily as the turning gears of oil-coated clockwork. She hadn't thought she'd come again, not so soon, but already her orgasm was building at the slow and steady rubbing of him against her. She cried his name, shaking, and at the point of her climax Mick slid inside her.

Ecstasy slammed through her at the penetration. His cock slid deep. He kissed her, hard enough to bruise and bring the tang of blood, and Alice didn't care. Her nails raked his back, and then he was fucking her so hard the entire bed slammed against the wall. She came again, or hadn't yet stopped, she could no longer be sure. All that mattered was the feeling of him inside her, on top of her, covering her. Devouring.

His teeth found her throat in that way he had that made her lose her fucking mind. He said her name in a hoarse, desperate voice. Alice looked at him. She ran her hands along his tight biceps, then his chest. At the pinch of her fingers on his nipples, Mick lost it. He came with a shout and thrust inside her so hard she was sure they were going to break the bed.

Then, quiet.

The weight of him should've been too much, but she took a strange comfort in it and in the smell of them both —sweat and sex and heat and passion, an indescribable perfume she wished, in that moment, that she could bottle. She gathered him close and listened to the sound of his breathing slow. He pushed off her after a few heartbeats and kissed her. Then again.

She broke the kiss to take his face in her hands, looking into his eyes. "I can't believe you came here."

"When I woke up and you were gone, nothing else really mattered except seeing you again," Mick said, and looked immediately ill at ease, as though his own words had surprised him.

Alice was smart enough not to let him linger on the revelation. Instead, she shoved him until he rolled off her, then got up to pull on a pair of panties and a T-shirt from the drawer. She looked at him over her shoulder.

"Food," she told him with a smile. "I'm starving. Want some eggs and bacon?"

"You are the perfect woman, you know that?" Mick had been taking care of the condom, but he looked at her now with a half smile and a blaze of heat in his gaze.

She would never have claimed perfection, but the way he looked at her made her believe him. Or at least believe he meant it. And that, Alice thought as she took him downstairs to feed him and kiss him some more, was better than actually being perfect.

Chapter 25

Sunday dinner with Mom's roast chicken and all the trimmings had been a McManus family tradition since before Mick's birth. He hadn't been to church in years except for a few weddings and a couple of funerals, not even at Christmas or Easter, but that didn't usually stop him from heading over to his parents' house around two o'clock to be fed. He'd watch some TV with Pop, argue with his older brothers Jack and Jimmy, get a lecture or two from his younger sister Mary who thought that being married with three kids somehow gave her the responsibility of making sure everyone else was as crazy as she was.

Mick had never brought a girl around before.

Somehow, this morning, waking up in Alice's bed with the smell and taste of her still all over him, inviting her along to Sunday dinner had seemed the most normal thing in the world. Especially since he'd spent the last four Sundays waking up in her bed, usually making love to her before making his retreat early enough in the morning to head home and grab a quick shower before heading to his parents' house. She'd never complained or questioned.

Never pouted like lots of the other girls he'd dated would have. Which was exactly why this morning after spending a nice thirty minutes with his mouth between her legs, Mick had asked her to come along. It had seemed like a good idea at the time, but now that they were in the driveway, he was second-guessing.

"You okay?" Alice gave him a sideways glance. She'd unbuckled her seat belt but hadn't yet made a move to open the door. She leaned forward to peek through the windshield at the house. "Should I be more nervous?"

Mick tapped the steering wheel to the beat of a song only in his head. "No. Of course not."

"Should you be less nervous?" she teased, and leaned across the seat to kiss him.

Bam, just like that, she'd managed to make him want to laugh and toss her in the backseat all at the same time. Five words and she'd figured him out exactly. When she tried to pull away from the kiss, Mick held her closer for a second.

"Are you afraid they won't like me?" she whispered against his mouth, then pulled away enough to search his gaze.

"No."

"Are you afraid I won't like them?"

"Maybe," Mick admitted.

Alice smiled and swiped her fingertip across each of his eyebrows. "How bad can they be?"

It wasn't that they were bad, exactly. "I've never really brought anyone around before. That's all."

Alice's grin disappeared as her eyebrows went up. "Oh. Shit."

Mick laughed. This girl, he thought. This girl was amazing.

"Well, no pressure on me, then," she continued, sitting

back and smoothing her skirt. "Not like I have to be extra special or anything."

Mick pulled her close for a lingering kiss that threatened to turn into a full-on make-out session if he wasn't careful. That's how it was with them. Always on, always hot, always making him want more, more, more. He settled for a nibble of her jaw and a nuzzle against her neck, making her shiver. Her nipples would be tight and hard, too, he thought, and almost reached for her before he caught himself. He did have to shift a little in his seat to accommodate the sudden tightness in his crotch.

"We could run away," she said seriously, tipping her head back as he let his teeth graze her throat. "Join a circus or something. I'll sell popcorn. You can be the guy who cleans up after the elephants."

"How come I have to be the guy who cleans up after the elephants?"

Alice giggled softly. Her fingers curled in the front of his shirt. She kissed his mouth. "Because you don't like popcorn."

It was true, though how Alice knew that, Mick couldn't guess. It was one more thing to add to the long, long list of magical things about her. He kissed her mouth, but this time she put a hand on his chest to hold him back.

She shook her head and looked stern. "Nope. Inside. We're doing this."

"You were just talking about running away to the circus," he protested, but she cut him off with a fingertip to his lips.

"You're the one who didn't want to go inside," Alice said. "This is for your own good. Me. You. Your family. I'll try not to make them hate me—"

"They aren't going to hate you, Alice." Mick snorted softly. "All right. Let's do this."

He shouldn't have worried, he realized about five minutes into the visit. Even Mary, who'd been bugging him for years to bring around a girl, didn't make a big deal out of Alice being there. His family welcomed her into the chaos and cacophony of a McManus Sunday dinner, complete with a screaming toddler, a shouting match between his brothers and a platter of dinner rolls dumped all over the living room floor by his fumble-fingered nephew who'd been upended by the dog.

Through it all, Alice beamed. She offered to help his mother with dinner. She listened to Mary's weary complaints about the burdens of child-rearing without rolling her eyes. She fended off Jack's political opinions. By the end of the visit, it was clear to see that his family loved her.

Mick understood how they felt.

"You want to see my baseball trophies?" He was already leading her up the narrow stairs and down the hall, still lined with family pictures including some really embarrassing school portraits.

Alice, her fingers linked with his, gave a low laugh. "Is that sort of like asking me to see your etchings?"

"I don't have any idea what that means," he told her as he opened the door to the tiny room at the end of the hall he'd slept in as a child. "But if you're accusing me of trying to seduce you, I'm offended."

She swatted him lightly as she followed him into the room. "You are not. You're a dirty, bad boy. This was your room?"

"Yeah." Once inside it, he wondered if he ought to be more embarrassed about this room than the pictures in the hall. The single bed still made up with the quilted comforter from his childhood, the same pennants on the walls. What would Alice think of him now when she saw who he'd been?

She turned from the wall where she'd been looking over his collection of classic car posters. "I never thought of you as a Camaro sort of boy. I figured you for a Mustang lover."

He came up behind her to settle his hands on her hips, his chin on her shoulder. "I really always wanted a Charger, like the—"

"*Dukes of Hazzard!*" She turned in his arms with a surprised laugh. "Yeah. Me too!"

It was the perfect time to kiss her, which had been his idea all along. She melted into the embrace the way she always did. How was it that she always fit against him so well, that every kiss was perfect?

"We should go downstairs," Alice said against his mouth. "They'll be wondering where we got to."

"You don't want to make out with me on my twin bed?" He took a few backward steps, easing her along with him.

She followed. She let him pull her onto his lap, straddling him. The bed creaked. Alice took his face in her hands to hold him still so he'd have had to work harder to kiss her.

"Why didn't you ever bring anyone home before?" she asked quietly. Her eyes caught his and wouldn't let them go, even though he wanted to look away.

Mick had lied to plenty of women in his life, but so far, never to Alice. Looking at her now, he wondered if he'd ever want to lie to her. Or if he'd be able to, even if he tried.

"I never felt about anyone the way I feel about you," he told her. "Never wanted anyone to meet my family. It didn't seem fair, you know, to bring someone around and have everyone get to like her if I didn't have any intentions of keeping her around."

Alice's smile twisted in that way she had that always told him she had his number, all right. "So, you intend to keep me around, huh?"

"Oh, yeah. Definitely." He rocked her hips toward him, watching for the telltale flutter of her eyelids that always gave away when she was getting turned on.

He loved that about her. That he could do something so simple and make her react that way. That she responded to him like gas to a match, and she never pretended otherwise.

"Alice," Mick said suddenly. The words rose to his lips, those three words that in his experience led to nothing but the eventual end with someone storming away angry. To hurt and heartbreak. Three dumb words that now tasted like Alice did, sweet and savory and intoxicating, every single time.

"Mick! We're getting ready to leave!" Mary's voice from the hallway pushed Mick and Alice apart as fast as if they'd been in high school, caught doing what they shouldn't. Alice skipped backward to the dresser to look over the collection of rocks and shells in a tray there, while Mick adjusted his jeans on the other side of the room. His sister poked her head around the doorway. "Come say good-bye."

"Good-bye," Mick said, deadpan, knowing it would make her crazy.

Mary narrowed her eyes. "Come say good-bye to your nephews, you giant ass."

Alice laughed. Mary gave her an assessing look, but Alice had already passed inspection and was now safe from his sister's disdain. She did give Mick another frown, though.

"I'm coming," he told her. "We'll be down in a minute."

Mary didn't budge. Mick gave her a fierce look of his own until she capitulated with a toss of her hair. That hadn't changed much since high school, either.

When she'd gone, he went to Alice and took her in his arms. He had to kiss her again. One more time, before he had to share her again with everyone else.

She let him, but only for a few seconds, before she nipped his lower lip and pushed him away. "Later."

"Promise?"

With his hand in hers, leading him to the doorway, she glanced over her shoulder at him. "Oh, yeah. I promise."

Chapter 26

"You met his family? That's kind of a big deal, right? How long have you been seeing this guy?" Alice's sister Wendy coughed into the phone. "Sorry. I feel like crap. I didn't want to miss our lunch."

"Better than giving me whatever you have." Alice twirled in her desk chair, glad she'd packed a yogurt and some fruit that would take the place of the lunch she was now going to be missing. "I met him about three months ago. Going on four. Is it a big deal? I feel like it is."

"Meeting a guy's family is always a big deal. Feels like it, anyway. Which reminds me, when are *we* going to meet him?"

Alice laughed. "I don't know. His family has this big Sunday dinner thing every week, it was kind of convenient and not like we had to plan something special."

"You don't have to plan anything special to meet me."

"I know. It's the time and distance thing. Too hard to get together on 'school' nights. We only get to see each other on the weekends."

Wendy's laugh became another cough. "Yeah, yeah, I

get it. And you want to spend all your time together making kissy face."

"Um, duh." Alice let her chair tip back so she could close her eyes, thinking of it now.

It was only Wednesday. Two more days until she could see him, though they hadn't made any specific plans. In four months, she could count on two hands the times they'd actually decided anything in advance. They spent the weekends together, usually ending up at her place because she was the one who always asked if he wanted to spend the night. She should start packing a bag, just to be ready, she thought, in case he ever asked her to stay over.

"You like him that much, huh?"

"Yeah. He's different, Wendy. We have this spark. It's more than just the sex stuff, though I'm not going to lie, that part is amazing."

"TMI," her sister said.

"Shut up." Alice laughed. "Like I didn't have to listen to you raving on and on about Joe Murphey's—"

"Never speak of it again!" Wendy's hoarse voice turned the command into a bark. "We shall refer to it only as the dream penis. Don't remind me of its loss. My lady garden has never bloomed the same way since."

Alice choked with laughter, shaking her head. "His boner might've been a dream, but the rest of him was a nightmare."

"True."

"Mick is . . . he's just . . ." Alice trailed off into a happy sigh. "He makes me laugh. We talk for hours and hours, and we never run out of things to say."

"Sounds like true love to me."

"Ugh." Alice shook her head, though the protest was automatic and not necessarily heartfelt.

Wendy coughed another laugh. "Don't try to deny it.

You've got it bad for this guy. I can tell. When's the last time you spent more than a month with someone who didn't annoy you? Oh, let me think about that, maybe I guess never!"

"I didn't say he didn't annoy me," Alice said.

"Now we're getting somewhere."

"He's always late," Alice added. "Always because something came up he wasn't expecting. He barely makes plans, and then changes them at the last minute because he's running behind or decides something else would be more fun."

"Well. Is it?"

"Sometimes," Alice admitted reluctantly. "But sometimes I really just want to do whatever it is I was planning on doing with him. I don't care if it's dinner or a movie or bowling or whatever, but if I'm thinking about doing one thing and he switches it up, I get . . . you know how I get."

Wendy coughed. "Yeah. I know how you get. Doesn't he? Do you fight about it?"

"We haven't fought, not exactly. I've tried to tell him that I don't like it when he's constantly changing plans we didn't really make in the first place, but I guess I don't want to sound uptight. Because it is fun being with him. I think he's amazing and wonderful, and . . ." She let her words trail away, trying to think of how to describe her insecurities without sounding like one of those girls who started picking out china patterns after two dates.

"And what?"

"I'm not sure what he thinks about me. I know he likes sleeping with me," Alice said, a little harder than she'd intended. "I figure he likes me well enough, too. You don't spend so much time with a person if you don't actually *like* them aside from the sex parts."

Wendy cleared her throat. "Yeah. I'd agree with you,

there. So what's the problem? I've never really known you to be worried about how a guy felt about you before, Alice."

"He doesn't say it." There it was, out loud, and saying it, even to her sister, felt embarrassing and a little needy. Gross. "I mean, he doesn't say anything about how he feels about me. I say something like, 'I think you're amazing,' and he gives me an uncomfortable punch on the shoulder and calls me 'dude.'"

"Shit," Wendy said. "Ouch."

"Yeah. Unless we're fucking or just finished fucking," Alice said flatly. "He's a lot more vocal about what he likes about me then."

"You can spare me the details on that. But you should tell him how you feel, Alice. No good relationship grows without honesty. And not telling him about what makes you mad isn't honest." Wendy cleared her throat with a sigh. "I'm gonna go take some more meds and a hot shower. Sorry about lunch. Good luck with your new boy toy. Don't keep him a secret too much longer, or I'll think he's got a tail or something."

Alice burst into laughter. "Maybe that's why I like him so much."

"You would," Wendy answered and hung up.

With her lunch plans canceled, Alice grudgingly ate the snacks she'd packed instead of going out for pasta and meatballs, which is what she'd been craving. Her resentment fled, though, when Mick's name popped up on her IM list. If she'd been out of the office, she'd have missed him.

Hey, she typed. *Fancy meeting you here.*

No answer. With a sigh, Alice shook her finger at the computer screen. "Pay attention to your messages, McManus!"

Of course that didn't do any good. He'd probably popped online for a second and then left his office again to do something else. Her job as administrative assistant to the head of human resources for Snazzy Nailz nail polish chained her to her chair for most of the day, but most of Mick's time was spent onsite or in meetings about those onsite visits. Still, seeing the green dot beside his name was like a grain of sand in an oyster . . . only there was no pearl, Alice thought half an hour later when she'd finished her meager lunch and he was still online but hadn't replied.

Ugh.

Busying herself with work, she managed to get through a number of assignments that had been put on the back burner for one reason or another. Stomach growling, she gave in and decided to hit the employee cafeteria. The food there was slightly better than fast-food takeout, which would've been her second option. After a quick sandwich and a salad, she was back at her desk . . . to find a message from Mick.

Hey, hot stuff. Heading out to a job in York.

Hey, you there?

USER MCMANUS HAS GONE OFFLINE

"Dammit," Alice muttered as she slid into her chair. Not only had she missed him, but York was only twenty minutes from her office. He never came this close to where she worked, though Jay sometimes had.

She looked at the clock. The messages had come in fifteen minutes ago, which meant he was probably still driving. A quick glance at her workload showed her where she could rearrange things. She called him, heart already skipping a beat at the thought of getting to talk to him midday on a Wednesday. Thumping harder at the idea that if she could finagle things just right, she might even get to see him.

When the call went to voice mail, Alice said, "Hey, it's me. I got your IM, but I wasn't at my desk. Sorry I missed you. When you get to York, if you have a chance, can you give me a call? I could come meet you for a late lunch or something. You're so close."

She hesitated, then added, "I miss you. Would love to see you today. Bye."

She worked for another hour or so. No call from Mick. She thought about sending him a text, but this close to the end of the month she was in danger of going over her texting allotment, and she'd learned her lesson last month about how expensive that could be. She should bump it up another thousand messages, she thought randomly as she forced herself to focus on work and not her silent cell phone. But she already had a phone plan for five hundred a month, who the hell would ever need to use that many texts?

By the end of the day, any hope she'd had that he was going to call her from the site had fled. When her phone did ring as she was packing up to leave, it was Jay. She tried not to sound disappointed.

"I need a hump day happy hour," he said without preamble. "Come meet me."

"Jay . . . I have to work tomorrow."

He spoke almost before she'd finished her excuse. "You can crash at my place."

"And get up an hour and a half early to make it to work on time? Ugh." Phone cradled to her shoulder, Alice zipped her purse.

"I think Paul is cheating on me."

Alice paused. "Shit. I'm sorry, Jay."

"Yeah. Well. Is it really cheating when the other person won't exactly fully commit?"

"I guess it's cheating if it feels like it," she told him. "To you, anyway."

"Happy hour. C'mon, Alice. We haven't been out together in forever. You've been spending all your time with Mick on the weekends."

"He told you that? Does he talk about me? Were you working with him today?" The thought intrigued and made her nervous. "What did he say?"

Jay huffed. "He didn't say anything. I haven't worked with him in weeks. I just know that's who you've been with, because you've barely called me."

"Sorry." She was chagrined, but not too much.

They arranged a meeting place and time. One more time, Alice checked her instant messages, but Mick hadn't come online again. She shut down her computer and headed out. Traffic was a bitch, as it always was the closer she got to Baltimore. When she passed the exit for Timonium, where Mick lived, her foot unconsciously lifted from the gas, earning her a little road rage from the asshole who'd been tailgating her. She kept going with only a look in the rearview and a sigh, her silent phone mocking her from her purse. By the time she got to the restaurant where she was meeting Jay, she was starving and cranky.

Bless him, though, he'd ordered appetizers and two margaritas, so she didn't have to wait. Alice gave him a squeeze and a kiss on the cheek. Jay pushed her margarita toward her.

"So," she said. "What's going on?"

He told her. The secretive phone calls that ended when Jay walked into the room. The way Paul had stopped returning his calls right away, sometimes going hours or even a day or so. How he seemed distracted, even in bed.

"All the classic signs," Jay said with a vicious stab into the loaded potato skins.

Alice had been cheated on a couple of times, and she wasn't proud to admit it, but she'd cheated once, herself. She'd never condone it, but she couldn't exactly be judgmental. Well, except that Paul was an asshole. "Just ask him about it, Jay. Don't torture yourself."

"What if he won't admit it?"

"You can pretend you don't know and keep going on, or you can break it off anyway," she told him.

"What if he does admit it?"

Alice smiled gently. "Same thing, honey. But if you don't say something, you're going to kill yourself over it. I know it sucks and it hurts, but is he worth it?"

Jay said nothing, which was his answer. Alice sighed and drank some of her margarita while she thought of what to say. No advice came to mind, unfortunately. Love was love, and you couldn't choose it. It just happened to you, no matter how wonderful and terrible it was.

"I don't want to talk about him any more right now," Jay said suddenly. "Let's just eat fried food and get a little drunkish. Okay?"

"Okay, sure. Whatever you want."

A little drunkish turned into Jay downing four margaritas and confessing that he'd snuck through Paul's computer files and e-mails in an attempt to figure out the truth. Alice, who'd limited herself to two drinks over the course of the night, drove him home and forced him to take a shower and a couple of aspirin, drink a glass of water. Then she put him to bed.

"Are you staying?" Jay asked. "You can sleep here."

Alice shook her head. "I'm going to head home."

"It's late," he said without much force.

"I'd rather sleep in my own bed, even if I have to drive tonight, than wake up early."

"You hate early." Jay turned to put his face into the pillow. "G'night."

He'd be fine, she knew that, but still Alice sat with him for a few more minutes until he started to snore. She stroked his hair, hating that Paul was hurting him, wishing she could do more. Not enough to be there in the morning to help him with the hangover, though.

Mick had not called her back. It was just past eleven thirty at night. He could be in bed by now, she told herself. She shouldn't call him, if he'd wanted to talk to her, he'd have returned her call. She was being stupid, Alice thought, but remembered Jay's despondent story of how Paul had stopped replying.

She called him.

"It's me," she said when Mick answered. "I'm twenty minutes away. Can I come see you?"

"Are you okay? What's wrong?"

Nothing was wrong. Not exactly. But she'd been struck with the overwhelming urge to see him. Smell him. Taste him. The fierceness of her desire churned her stomach and dried her throat.

"I want you," Alice said simply. "Please let me come over."

She was there in eighteen minutes. In his arms a minute after that. Mouths open, tongues stroking, hands roaming.

"I want you," Alice said as she pulled his shirt over his head. "Want you, want you, want you."

Her mouth found the smoothness of his chest. Teeth pressed, nibbling. He made a low noise when she flicked his nipples with her tongue, and his hand sunk into her hair at the base of her neck. His fingers dug in, just right, and Alice shuddered with desire.

Her fingernails skidded along his back. She went to the waistband of his pajama bottoms, pulling them down as she followed all his exposed flesh with her lips and tongue. On her knees in front of him, hand circling the base of his cock, Alice looked up at him. His expression—blazing eyes, grim mouth, still somehow looked tender. He stroked a hand over her hair to push it off her face.

She took him in her mouth. All the way, deep, her lips bumping his lower belly. She opened for him, then withdrew, slowly, sucking just enough at the head of his cock to make his hips thrust.

"Shit, Alice . . . shit."

Grinning, she did it again. Closing her eyes, Alice lost herself in his flavor, in the heat and thickness of him. Hand and mouth, she moved on his prick. Teasing him. Her hand went between her legs, under her skirt, along the seam of her pantyhose. She was so turned on that even though the sensations were blunted, she wasn't going to have any trouble getting off.

She'd never been a woman who craved fellatio. She'd enjoyed it, sure, but now, here on her knees in front of Mick, all she could think about was how much she wanted his cock in her mouth. How much she wanted to make him lose all control, to fuck into her mouth. She wanted to make him lose his mind.

Her fingertips circled on her clit. Shuddering, Alice moaned around Mick's cock. Her pussy clenched as she started tipping over into orgasm. So soon, so fast, she might've tried to hold it off except that Mick was saying her name over and over in that rough rasp she knew meant he was going to come.

He tried to pull away from her with a sound of warning, but caught up in the climax rippling through her, Alice refused to let him go. Her hand slid along his slick cock in time with the stroke of her lips and tongue, the teasing, gentle press of her teeth. When she sucked gently on the head of him, Mick at last went over the edge. With a cry, he flooded her mouth. Wracked with shudders of pleasure, Alice carried them both through until the end.

Breathing hard, Mick looked down at her when she at last let him go. He cupped her cheek for a second. Then, to her surprise, he folded onto his knees in front of her. He kissed her, hard.

"Holy shit," Mick said.

Chapter 27

Alice's mouth opened, but before she could answer, Mick kissed her again. He tasted himself on her tongue and a fresh surge of emotion clobbered him over the head. Fuck, what the hell was going on? An unfamiliar burning stabbed the backs of his eyes and closed his throat.

When had they stopped kissing? How had they started hugging? He was nearly naked and she was still fully dressed, and shit, goose bumps had started breaking out all over him, and oh, fuck, was he going to do something insane like . . . what, like tell her he loved her?

He laughed, his momentary insanity fading. The woman in front of him had just given him the best head of his entire life; no wonder he'd lost his shit a little bit. But it was more than that, and he'd known it for a while.

Love.

Shit.

"My knees hurt," she said when he didn't speak. "Umm . . ."

"Shit, yeah. C'mon." He got to his feet and helped her

up, then snagged his pajama bottoms and pulled them up. His T-shirt seemed to have disappeared, flung who knew where. Alice smoothed her skirt and then ran her fingers through her hair, looking completely put together in a few seconds.

Neither of them said anything for a minute.

"So," she said finally, "are you going to ask me to stay?"

Mick coughed, caught off guard. "Yeah, you want to?"

"It's late," she said. "I didn't bring anything with me to stay over in, and I'll have to leave really early to get up for work in the morning. . . ."

Was that a yes? A no? Still fuzzy from the force of coming hard enough to knock a hole in the wall, Mick could only stare. Alice looked expectant.

"Can I borrow a T-shirt and a pair of boxers?"

"Yeah, of course. And a toothbrush. I have an extra, I think." He pulled her close again for a kiss. "Of course you can stay."

Upstairs, he pulled a clean T-shirt and pair of pajama bottoms from the drawer and showed her the shower. The bathroom was a mess, something he only noticed when seeing it through Alice's eyes, but if it bothered her, she didn't say anything. He found a clean towel and washcloth for her. A spare toothbrush. In the bedroom while she showered, he quickly stripped the sheets that had been on the bed for . . . well, he didn't remember the last time he'd changed them, so it was time. He was just shoving an extra pillow into a fresh case when she came out of the bathroom.

"You look good in my clothes," Mick said.

Alice smiled. With her face scrubbed and wet hair slicked back from her forehead, she still looked luminous and beautiful enough to stop his heart. She looked a little shy, though.

"Are you sure this is okay?"

Mick pulled back the blankets. "Get in."

She hopped into bed, scooting over and turning on her side so he could spoon her. He buried his face in her damp hair, breathing her in. His hand fit naturally on her belly, just below the hem of his T-shirt. He was already falling asleep when she spoke.

"Hey."

Mick yawned. "Yeah?"

"I don't like it when you don't call me back," Alice said after a second or so.

Her voice had been matter-of-fact and low, not confrontational or bitchy. Still, it set him back a little. Mick's fingers twitched on her bare skin.

"Okay," was all he said.

Alice was silent.

"I can't always get back to you right away," Mick said after another few seconds had passed. "I mean, sometimes I'm busy."

She shifted to look at him. "Well, yeah. I know that. I'm just saying that in general, I don't like it when you don't answer me. I know sometimes you're busy, we all are. But when you just don't answer me at all, well, that's not cool."

"I always answer you." Defensive, Mick moved away from her a little bit.

"You didn't today. I called and left a message for you, and you didn't answer."

He thought about that, knowing she was right but still not willing to take blame for what he didn't think needed it. "I would have called you tomorrow, Alice. You know that."

"I hope so," was all she said and tucked herself back against him.

Shit. This wasn't an argument, but it had the flavor of one. He thought of a comeback and discarded it. Then another. He listened to the soft sound of her breathing slow and felt her relax against him. She was falling asleep, but now Mick was wide-eyed. Not quite with indignation, that was too strong a word for it. But definitely irritation.

"I always answer you," he said again. "Maybe it takes me awhile, but I do."

Alice's breathing caught, and she twitched. Her voice, thick with sleep, rasped. "You didn't today, and we could've had lunch together or something, because you were in York, but you didn't call me back."

"I was busy working, Alice, I didn't have time for lunch."

She pushed away from him this time to sit up. She rubbed at her face. "Well, I didn't know that. If you'd called to let me know, I wouldn't have gotten my hopes up."

Mick sat, too. "What's the big deal? I don't get it."

"It's just that . . . I was missing you. And when you IM'd me, I got excited, I thought maybe we'd get to see each other in the middle of the week, and I wouldn't have to wait until Friday or Saturday." She paused. "If you'd called me back and told me you were too busy with work, I'd have been disappointed, but I'd have understood. But you didn't."

"We still got to see each other," Mick pointed out. "You're here now."

"Because I called you! Because Jay asked me out for happy hour, and I was close enough to stop here! That's the only reason!"

This was not the kind of conversation he wanted to be having at nearly two in the morning. And he definitely didn't want her to start crying or some shit like that, but there were tears in her voice. With a scowl, Mick ran his hands through his hair to keep himself from saying something he'd regret.

"Never mind," Alice said sullenly. She moved to the edge of the bed, her back to him. "I'll be out of here by five or so."

Mick lay back, staring at the ceiling, jaw clenched. Beside him, too far away to touch but close enough he could still feel every move she made, Alice was as still as a corpse. Maybe she'd been able to fall asleep, but there was no way Mick was going to.

She was right. He had not called her back, nor had he intended to. Well, sure, he would've called her the next day, but he really hadn't returned her call today on purpose. No special reason, other than she'd caught him when he was busy and by the time he got home all he wanted was to eat dinner and watch a few hours of TV and crash. He'd thought about calling her, but in the end, he'd been unable to muster the energy for a conversation.

"I needed a break," Mick said aloud.

From the edge of the bed, Alice made no sound but the subtle, hesitant shift of her breathing.

"I was tired, and I knew if I called you back that you'd want me to meet up because I was so close, and I didn't have time for lunch, so I figured you'd angle for dinner, and I really just wanted to get home."

Quietly, smoothly, Alice sat. In the dark, she was only a silhouette, which meant he didn't have to see her face. Mick wasn't sure he wanted to.

"I see," she said.

"I was tired."

He heard her swallow. "Okay."

"I would've called you tomorrow, Alice. You know I would have."

"I don't know that," she told him, and shit, she was crying, he could hear it. "I hope that you would, but I don't know that you would. Not really. Because I thought you'd call me back today, and you didn't. And I thought you'd call me back last week, but you didn't then, either. So, I get it. You needed a break. Sorry. I shouldn't have come over—"

"Don't," he said as a way to cut her off before this got out of hand.

She shrugged off his touch and got out of bed. "Don't what? Go home? If you need a break so bad, I shouldn't be here, right? Let me give you a break."

"No, Alice, c'mon, that's not—"

She was already taking off her borrowed clothes, searching for her own, but with only the light coming in from the window, she was having a hard time. Mick watched her for half a minute, then got out of bed. He tried to take her by the arm, but she pulled away.

"I guess it's fine when your dick is in my mouth," she snapped. "Then you don't need a break, huh?"

"That's a shitty thing to say!"

She whirled on him, wearing only her panties and clutching the rest of her clothes to her chest. "It's true, though, isn't it? When I try to make plans with you, you can never manage to give me more than a day's notice or so. You don't return my calls or texts sometimes, and now I find out it's because you need a break. A break, Mick? I see you once or twice a week, and I haven't ever asked you for more than that, because we live just far enough apart to make it kind of a pain to get together. But guess what, I would make the effort to see you, even if I have to get up at five A.M. to get to work the next day. Or even just for dinner and then we both went home. I'd make it work to see you, Mick, because to me, it's worth the effort."

She'd stopped fighting to get away from him, but she didn't let him pull her closer. His fingers had dug into her upper arms, and he relaxed his grip. He let his hands slide down her arms, then let her go.

"When you love somebody, you should make them worth the effort," Alice whispered.

She looked at him, waiting. He knew what she wanted to hear, but he couldn't say it. He could tell her he loved her a dozen times, and it probably wouldn't be enough, because that was how love worked. You fell into it like a deep, dark pit, and you couldn't get out.

Mick frowned. "I took you to see my family. Isn't that making an effort?"

"I liked meeting them. Yes, it was." She put her clothes on the chair and slipped on her shirt, buttoning it over bare flesh. "And when we are together, Mick, we have a good time."

"I have a good time with you, too."

She looked at him. He could barely make out her features, but he could see enough to know that she wasn't crying. At least there was that.

"It's not how it feels when we're together, Mick. It's how it feels when we're apart." Here she gave a low and bitter laugh. "When I'm not with you, I'm never quite sure if you're thinking about me. Or how you feel about me. If you like me or love me or just want to fuck me, I have no idea. And I shouldn't have to guess that. Not ever."

"Why does it have to be all or nothing with you?" The words came out angry, and yeah, he was kind of pissed, but more than that, disappointed. Stung. "Why can't we just have fun?"

"Because this isn't just fun for me!" Alice's shout shoved him back a step. "Not anymore. Dammit, Mick, I'm not asking you to tell me you love me if you don't, but don't play with my feelings this way. That's not fair."

"I do love you," Mick said slowly. "On some level."

Chapter 28

Alice had always known she had a temper. Her mother had told her over and over as a kid that nice girls didn't get mad . . . but maybe, Alice had learned, nice girls got even. At Mick's words, "on some level," two things had happened. One, she'd felt a real and physical pain in her heart as though he'd stabbed her. Two, the rising tide of her fury had swept away the rest of her reasonable thought.

She kissed him hard enough to bruise, then bit his lower lip. Her fingers gouged his shoulder blades, holding him close, though at the sting of her violent kiss, Mick jerked. His mouth opened, and she stabbed inside it with her tongue. One hand went between his legs to cup his balls, then to stroke along his cock through his pajama bottoms. She'd never felt him completely flaccid—every time they'd been together, he'd always been at least semi-hard at her first touch.

Only a few hours ago she'd been on her knees, consumed with the thought of pleasing him. Now, she thought, if she put his dick in her mouth it wouldn't end well. And yet when she pushed him back toward the bed and followed him, straddling him, wearing nothing but her panties and the misbuttoned shirt she'd worn to work, every touch fanned the fire that never really went out between them.

"Alice—"

"Shut up," she ordered, half expecting him to protest, but Mick went quiet except for the low groan easing out of him when she ran her nails up his chest.

Alice squeezed her thighs against his hips. His cock bulged in his pajama bottoms, but she didn't touch it, not even to rub herself against it. Instead, she slipped out of her panties. She cupped her pussy, feeling the heat. She dipped a finger deep. She'd taken a shower but was still slick inside from earlier. Now her fingers slid in and out easily, then up to circle her clit. In the next minute, she moved up over him to kneel over his face.

Without a word, Mick put his mouth on her. His tongue fit automatically to her clit as his hands went to her hips. Alice put her hands on his headboard, her hips already rocking. The unshaven stubble above his lip and on his chin scratched but oh so fucking deliciously against her flesh as his lips and tongue worked on her. She rode his mouth, giving him no time to pause. No room to speak.

Only time and space to give her pleasure.

Earlier, her orgasm had rippled like waves, but this, oh, shit, this time she was going to come like a door slamming. Like a fist punching. This climax rose and rose, ripping and tearing, leaving her breathless. She cried out with it. Not his name, she refused to give him that. A low, wordless gasp, rough and harsh and sharp around the edges.

Before it had even passed, Alice moved down his body to kiss him hard. Their tongues and teeth fought. He bit her, maybe by accident, maybe on purpose. She couldn't be sure. Didn't care. She reared back, her hand moving to slap him before his caught her wrist with a thud of flesh on flesh. She was still moving, belly to belly. His cock, rock hard between them even though he'd already come in her mouth earlier. Mick thrust against her, making her shudder, making her hate him even more that he could cause her to react this way even when he made her so fucking angry.

He pushed a hand between them, fingers deep inside and curling, making her hips bump forward. She cried out again, meaning to move away from that magic touch but unable to make herself, not when it felt so good. Oh, so good . . . She lifted to let him fuck deeper into her, his thumb on her clit. Harder, harder, she would regret it in the morning when she was sore, but oh fuck, right now she was hurtling toward another orgasm.

"Fuck me," she gasped out, biting at the words, hating herself for saying them but not enough to take them back.

His cock was already nudging her pussy, and at her words he slipped fully inside her. No friction, nothing but sweet, liquid acceptance, her body to his. He moved and she moved, and they moved together like a rolling ocean, like a train on the tracks, like a key in a lock, like they had always been meant to fit together.

He fucked her fast and hard, both of them shuddering and grunting. When she tried to sit up, he caught her by the wrists and pulled her down to make her kiss him. His tongue fucked her mouth in the same rhythm.

Everything, fire. Everything, pleasure. Everything . . . love.

She came, and this time, Alice said his name. Over and over again, until he answered her. They came together and ended up in a quivering, sweaty heap of tangled limbs. When she could focus and move, Alice still stayed where she was, her face pressed to the curve of his neck, even as he softened and slipped out of her. Only then did she get up and go to the bathroom to clean up.

She would not cry. Would not break. She'd wanted to know how he felt about her. She had no right to complain about the answer, no matter how shitty it had made her feel.

Back in bed, she dove beneath the blankets to breathe herself to calmness. When Mick slid in next to her and spooned her close, Alice didn't mold herself to him the way she always had before.

"I never understood the concept of hate-fucking before," she told him.

Mick kissed her shoulder, bare because she'd taken off her shirt and wore only panties. "I don't want you to hate me, Alice."

She didn't. But this morning she might not even have said she loved him, at least not until he'd said it first. Fortunately, she didn't have to answer him, because the low buzz of his soft snoring told her he'd fallen asleep.

She was still awake when the sun peeked through the window, and she got up and gathered her things. Mick didn't stir when she kissed him. And that was probably for the best, she told herself when she let herself out the front door. That way, she didn't have to say good-bye.

Chapter 29

She didn't call him on Thursday. Or on Friday. And Mick didn't call Alice, either, not sure if she wanted to talk to him. Not sure he wanted to hear what she might say.

On Saturday, he couldn't hold off any longer. Two days without Alice, he'd discovered, was two days longer than he'd ever wanted to go without her. Still, when she answered, the cool tone of her voice made him want to hang up.

"Hey," he said by way of greeting. "What's up?"

"I'm doing laundry. You?"

"Fun Saturday morning. I'm at the grocery store. Want me to get you anything?"

Alice didn't laugh. "Chores, everyone has to do them, right? I guess I'd better hit the store later, too."

He waited for her to ask him what he was doing later. They'd never made plans in advance, something he'd always thought made them spontaneous but now realized had annoyed her. Contrary, he didn't want to say anything about it now. It was stupid, and he knew it, but his mouth still wouldn't make the words.

"Did you have fun . . . did you do anything fun last night?" Lame ass, Mick told himself.

Alice waited a moment before saying, "I went out with my sister and some friends. You?"

"Oh, yeah, got together with some buddies," Mick lied, sure she'd know right away he was making it all up. "Getting together to watch the game later today. Picking up snacks and stuff. Big game. Gotta get moving."

Shit, why had he said that? Now there was no way to ask her to see him later. Idiot.

"Well," Alice said in a clipped voice, "sounds like you're busy. I guess I'll talk to you later. Call me when you have some time for me."

He could've asked her to wait, told her he had all the time in the world for her. He could have asked her out for tonight, but Mick hated it when women acted like they were the only ones who got to be upset about stuff. Or that it was only the guy's responsibility to fix things. His ex Shanna had been like that, always expecting him to read her mind or make things up to her for crimes he hadn't even known he'd committed.

Alice was nothing like Shanna.

And Mick knew it, too, just like he knew she had a right to be upset with him, even if he hadn't meant to upset her. But there seemed to be no good way to say so now without reminding her they'd had a fight . . . sort of . . . and that it hadn't been resolved. She'd snuck out in the morning without so much as a kiss, not even a note, and she hadn't said a goddamn word to him since then, but it was his job to patch things up?

It had taken him about thirty seconds to think of all that, but thirty seconds is a really long time for silence on a telephone call. The soft huff of her breathing sounded pissed off. Well, guess what, he thought. He was still pissed off, too.

"Later," Mick said, and hung up before she could say anything.

He regretted it immediately. He had no plans for tonight, because he'd assumed he'd be with her. And shit, even if they hadn't specifically said anything, why shouldn't she assume the same thing? Why did he have to spell it out for her? If she wanted him to be the guy who showed up for every date with flowers and candy, Mick thought sourly as he passed the chocolate aisle, she had the wrong guy.

"I should never have to guess how you feel," she'd said, and remembering that pissed him off all over again.

How could she even wonder if he thought about her? Fuck, he thought about her all the damn time. She drove him crazy, that's what Alice did. Distracted him, made it hard to do anything else *but* think about her.

How could she not know that?

Mick flipped open his phone and dialed her number. He was going to lay it all out to her, right there in the kosher foods aisle. He did think about her, he did want to see her, and he did love her. Okay, so it wasn't easy for him to say things. Most guys were like that, weren't they? Did she have to expect so much from him?

Angrily, Mick listened to the ringing of his unanswered call, but hung up before it went to voice mail. He wasn't about to leave her a message that she could ignore and not answer just to get back at him. That shit wasn't right, he told himself as he pushed his cart, filling it with stuff he barely paid attention to. Playing games.

Fuck that. He wasn't going to call her again. No matter how much he wanted to talk to her, or see her. Let her come to him, Mick thought bitterly.

Let her wait.

Chapter 30

Alice waited a week before she deleted his name from her instant message list. It had killed her to see him come online every night, same time as always, but never ping her. So had the silence of her phone. But she'd meant what she'd said. No matter how quickly the words had slipped from her lips, they'd been sincere.

Call me when you have time for me.

No call. Therefore, no time. It stung, first like a slap and then every day after that with the slow, dull throb and ache of a muscle-deep bruise that refused to heal.

Another week passed. A third. She gave up believing he'd call her, but not hoping.

She didn't speak of it to Jay, who asked only once or twice before wisely choosing to change the subject. Things with him and Paul had been patched up. Jay was happy about it, and if Alice didn't quite believe Paul wouldn't end up breaking her friend's heart, she knew better than to taint Jay with her own bitterness about her situation.

Wendy hadn't been quite so understanding.

"Men," she said flatly, "are assholes. Why are they such assholes?"

Alice picked at her salad. No appetite. At least she wasn't eating her feelings.

"Hey. Don't let him do this to you." Wendy rapped a fingertip on the table to get Alice to look at her.

Alice shrugged. "He didn't do anything to me that I didn't let him do. Things happen. Sometimes the things that burn the brightest also die the fastest."

"He said he loved you 'on some level,'" her sister said with a sneer. "That's just gross."

Her sister's affront on her behalf made her want to cry. "I don't know. I guess I'd rather he said that than lied to me about how he felt."

"He's scared."

"That's just what we always say about men when they don't give us what we want," Alice said. "It's a nice way of making ourselves feel superior, or something."

"Okay, so he wasn't scared, he was just a dick!" Wendy said.

Alice dragged her fork through the pile of unappetizing lettuce and gave her sister a small smile. "I'm trying to be philosophical here, and the best you can come up with is that he's a dick?"

"A giant one." Wendy nodded. "Riddled with oozing sores. No, not a big one. A tiny, teeny weeny blister-covered prick!"

Alice snorted laughter. After a second or so, the giggles turned to chuckles, and then to guffaws. In another minute, she and Wendy were laughing hard enough to send tears rolling down their cheeks . . . and then she was crying. Sobbing. Alice buried her face in her hands.

She hadn't cried at all this entire time, but now the gasping sobs rose up and choked her. The tears seared her, burning. Everything tasted of salt and sorrow, and Alice pressed the heels of her hands to her eyes to stop herself from crying but could not.

"Thank God you came here for lunch instead of Olive Garden," she heard Wendy say, and lost it all over again.

She cried long enough to soak the tablecloth in front of her, and her sister handed her tissue after tissue until finally, Alice was able to stop. Her eyes had swollen so much her sister was nothing more than a blurry lump. Her nose, a running faucet. Even her tongue felt cracked and sore.

Wendy handed her a wet cloth from the sink and squeezed her shoulder gently. "Feel better?"

"No." Alice shook her head as she wiped her face with the cloth. Another surge of tears threatened, like waves of sickness, but she pressed the cool cloth to her face and managed to keep it under control. "I fucked up, Wendy. So much."

"Shh, hey," her sister said. "He fucked up. Not you. Even if you did, I mean, we all do, he still should call you. You told him to when he had some time, and he hasn't. That's just a dick move."

Alice wiped her face and took the cloth away to look at her sister. "It's playing games, and it's stupid, but I'm doing it, too. So we're both idiots."

"So . . . call him," Wendy said.

Alice gave her sister a long, hard look, until Wendy nodded with a sigh. "It's a thing with him, Wendy. And it will probably always be a thing with him. So, the question is, can I deal with that thing? Or will it keep making me crazy?"

"It will keep making you crazy." Wendy shook her head.

"So . . . I call him, he doesn't call me back. Then I'm

right back where we started. It sucks. It's stupid. We're both stubborn, we're both assholes." Alice shrugged helplessly, feeling the tears welling again. Hating herself for not being able to stop feeling so fucking sad. "But I told him to call me when he had time for me, and he hasn't. Should I chase him?"

"No. But do you want him to chase you?"

Wendy had a point, one Alice had thought about a lot. "He doesn't have to chase me. I'm right here. Right where I've always been. All he has to do is reach out, and here I am."

"I'm sorry." Wendy reached to grab Alice's hand for a squeeze. "It sucks all around."

"Yeah. It does." Alice drew a deep breath and gave her sister a water-logged smile.

"Hey, I know what would make this better. Soft serve from Peggy's." Wendy waggled her brows and grinned.

The last thing in the world Alice wanted was ice cream, really, but her sister was trying to cheer her up.

"By the time we get there," Wendy said, "you'll want some. I promise."

Face washed, positive attitude implemented, in her sister's passenger seat, Alice turned the music up loud and rolled down the window to let the wind blow her hair. It was summer. She was with her sister. And ice cream really could make everything better.

They were both laughing and singing along with the radio when the pickup truck ran the red light and rear-ended them.

Chapter 31

He'd known there would be questions when he showed up to Sunday dinner without Alice, but all Mick said was that she hadn't been able to make it. Jimmy and Jack didn't give a shit, of course. Pop, God bless him, wouldn't have noticed the Pope if he walked in. Mick's mother gave him an extra-long hug and pat on the back and served him two portions of turkey before she'd even let Jack have a second. It was Mary who cornered him in the kitchen after dinner, when Mick was getting something down from the high cupboard for Ma.

"What happened?"

Mick set the platter on the table and gave his sister a shrug he knew damn well wouldn't put her off for long. Mary, who could be a dog with a bone, gave him a sad look. Mick shrugged.

His sister watched him, her arms crossed. She'd started looking so much like their mother it was scary, except that Ma was soft-spoken and never pried. Mary could take a lesson, Mick thought, and felt bad at once.

"She was good for you," Mary repeated. "What did you do?"

Mick cracked open the bottle and took a long pull. He could escape into the living room and the TV with his dad, brothers, and nephews, but he stayed. Not sure why.

"I didn't call her back."

Mary groaned. "Oh. That. What is it with you? With most men, actually. It's not brain surgery. Someone calls you, you call them back, why is it so hard?"

"I didn't feel like talking to her right then, and then it got late and I was going to call her the next day. That's all." Mick shrugged again. The beer tasted sour, and he poured it down the sink.

"Did you fight about it?"

He nodded.

Mary sighed. "So, call her now."

Mick said nothing. Mary's brows rose. She put her hands on her hips.

"Mick!"

"She said she didn't like it when we didn't make plans, that it was always last minute."

Mary looked at him like he was stupid. "Makes sense to me."

"I'm spontaneous!" Mick protested.

"You're not spontaneous," his sister told him. "You're disorganized and you're always looking for the next best thing, so you can't commit to what's in front of you in case something more exciting comes along."

That hit him to the core, but if anyone in the world knew him, it was Mary. "Shit. That's cold."

"It's true," she said, but gently. "I love you, Mickey, but my God, I've watched you do this dance for years. You're going to lose her if you don't step up."

"She told me to call her when I had time for her, like I

never made time for her, when I did. All the time. I gave that girl more time than I've ever given anyone! Why can't women ever just be satisfied?"

"I'm disgusted with you," Mary said flatly. "Satisfied? You want her to be satisfied with what you give her? Don't be arrogant, Mick. She wants to spend time with you because she likes you. And you turn around and knock her down for it?"

"She pissed me off, Mare. I need time to cool down, so I don't lose my temper and totally fuck everything up, say things I'll regret."

Mary rolled her eyes. "Let me get this straight. You had a fight about you not calling her back and about not making plans. She told you to call her when you had time for her. And you're not calling her?"

It sounded stupid because it was stupid, but all Mick could do was give Mary a stubborn glare. His sister shook her head, clearly giving up on him. "I don't want to be an idiot, Mary."

"Well," she said. "You are."

Chapter 32

Alice had been in the ER for hours. Nothing broken, though she'd needed stitches in her arm and hand. They hadn't admitted her, though they'd taken Wendy upstairs an hour ago. Her sister had suffered the brunt of the accident and was being kept overnight for observation, though both of them had been fortunate not to suffer serious injuries. The driver of the truck had walked away without even being admitted. Everything could've been much worse.

Her clothes had started going stiff from the blood. She didn't know if it were hers or Wendy's, but she wanted a hot shower, clean pajamas, some ice packs, and her bed. Everything hurt. She was already purple with bruises.

"I just want to go home." Alice turned her head to look away from the doctor who was poking and prodding her.

"You have a ride?" the doctor asked.

She hesitated. "I called my . . . a friend. To come and get me. But he hasn't answered me yet."

The doctor gave her a sympathetic smile. "Do you have any other friends who you can call?"

She did, but she didn't want any of them. She wanted Mick. She needed him.

"Do you want to give your friend some more time to answer you? Or we can call you a cab." The doctor was already looking harried, not that Alice blamed him. The ER was overflowing with patients in worse condition than hers.

Alice checked her phone, but Mick hadn't returned her call. She took a deep breath that hurt everything inside her and shook her head. "Yeah. A cab would be great."

Chapter 33

"Mick. It's me. I've been in an accident, a car accident. They're keeping my sister, she's banged up pretty bad, but they're letting me go home. I'm okay, but . . . I need you. . . . Can you come get me? Please call me back. I need you."

He'd listened to the message ten times, at least, each time feeling sicker and sicker inside. It had come in around two thirty on Sunday afternoon, while he was driving home from his parents'. He hadn't listened to it until just before he went to bed. Not on purpose. Not to be a dick. Just because he hadn't noticed it until then.

He'd called her back as soon as he'd listened, but had gone straight to voice mail. Three times, though he hadn't left a message after the first. At a loss, he'd called Jay, but he hadn't answered, either.

Monday morning, exhausted from being unable to sleep, he'd missed the alarm. Got to work late. He'd called Jay again, this time at the office, but got an out-of-office voice mail. Useless for anything, Mick canceled his onsite visits. He logged into his computer, but Alice's name didn't appear in his list of contacts.

He called her again. "Alice. Call me, please. I'm sorry I didn't get your message before. I really am. But please, call me back, okay?"

She didn't call him back. Not all day, and by five o'clock, Mick couldn't stand it anymore. With rush hour traffic it took him close to two hours to get to her place, and by the time he did, he was starving. Worried. Anxious and a little angry, too.

When she opened the door, all the breath left him. She looked like . . . shit, she looked like she'd been hit by a truck. He wanted to take her in his arms, but the way she stood so stiffly, as though merely looking at him hurt her, kept him from touching her.

"Can I come in?"

Silently, she stood aside to let him pass, then closed the door after him. Without a word she went into the living room and settled onto the couch, where it was clear she'd been for a long time. Blankets, a bowl of half-eaten soup, ice packs. The TV was playing something in black and white, but on mute.

"Alice . . ."

She looked at him, her expression completely blank. She'd done nothing to cover the bruises on her face, and they stood out starkly in shades of purple, blue, and even black. It broke him to see them, along with the railroad track pattern of stitches on her forearm and the back of her hand.

It broke him worse the way she looked at him. Not cutting her gaze. Flat and disinterested and emotionless.

Mick knelt beside her, tried to take her good hand. She tugged it gently away and put it under the blanket. His insides twisted.

"I'm sorry," Mick said. "Baby, I'm so, so sorry I wasn't there for you."

Something glittered in her gaze. "No. You weren't. I called you, and you didn't answer. And this time, Mick, it wasn't about whether or not we were going to lunch. This time, I really needed you, and you were not there."

"I'm sorry," he said again, helpless to do anything but repeat it until maybe she'd hear him.

Alice only stared, silent. She'd heard him, Mick realized. But she would not listen. He got to his feet.

"You want me to go," he said, not a question.

"If you can't be there for me when I need you," Alice told him, "then I don't want you."

She swallowed, her mouth thinning. She blinked rapidly, and it killed him that she was trying so hard not to cry in front of him. He'd done that to her. Hurt her worse than that truck. Left her with worse than bruises. Worse than scars.

It was over.

Mick to Alice

Don't you believe in second chances?
—Mick to Alice

Chapter 34

Time had passed, but could anyone really ever change? That was the question that came to Alice's mind in the darkness of her room with Mick breathing soft and steady in the bed beside her. His declaration had led to an embrace, which led to a kiss, which had taken them to her bed. Toe bone connected to the shinbone, Alice thought and rolled to face him. Her fingertips drifted down the line of his bare shoulder and arm to rest for a moment on his hip before she rolled onto her back again. Mick hadn't stirred.

He'd always slept hard and deep. She was the one who tossed and turned and woke in the night to go to the bathroom. Now, though she really could've waited until morning, Alice got up and used the toilet. She rinsed her mouth at the sink, then looked at her own reflection, turning her face from side to side as though she'd find some answers in the slope of her cheekbones or the shadows under her eyes.

What in holy hell was she doing?

"I want you," Mick had said. "Let me prove it to you."

If orgasms were proof of desire, he'd done as

promised. Her cheeks heated. Time had passed, indeed, but Mick still knew her body better than any man ever had. Maybe ever would, she had to admit. She'd had a few boyfriends since breaking up with Mick, but none who'd turned her inside out and many who'd never even turned her on.

In bed, she rolled over so he could spoon her. Eventually, she slipped into dreams. Fractured images of crashing waves and fields of flowers. She woke again to the first hint of light in the sky and listened to the steady in-out of Mick's breathing, wondering how on earth she was ever going to give this up all over again.

Now that she'd had him again, how could she go back to living without her Mick?

"Are you awake?" he whispered against the back of her neck.

She almost didn't answer, not wanting to wipe away the brilliance of the night with the mundane morning. She wriggled against him after a moment, her ass pressed to Mick's very impressive waking erection. She hadn't meant anything by it, not really. More a silent acknowledgment of her wakefulness than a come-on . . . but that didn't matter when his hand slid over her belly and between her legs.

His fingers found her clit with unerring precision. Smooth circles, perfect pace. He had her on the edge in a minute or so, then eased off to tease her while his teeth found the back of her neck and the slope of her shoulder. They moved together, shifting until he was inside her. As always, in that first moment when he filled her, Alice made a low noise.

Leisurely, they moved. Dreamlike. Her orgasm rolled through her; she cried out, wordless and breathless and gasping. Mick thrust once, twice more, and shuddered against her.

They slept.

Alice woke to the scent of coffee and frying bacon and toast—did she even have bacon in the house? Bleary-eyed and tousled, she threw on a robe and went to the kitchen to find a feast spread out on the table waiting for her. Cream and sugar had been set out by her mug, which Mick filled for her as soon as she appeared in the doorway. He kissed her when he pressed her mug into her hand. He wore jeans but no shirt. Bare feet, too. Clearly, he was trying to kill her with the sexy.

"Wow," she said. "You are really going all out."

"Got hungry. Took a run to the market. Figured I could treat you to breakfast. And lunch, if you'll let me. Dinner, too." He grinned and kissed her again.

Alice held the mug of hot coffee away from her body so it didn't slop. In the light of mid-morning—God, how late had she slept?—Mick looked even better than he had last night. She, on the other hand . . .

"You're so gorgeous, you know that?"

Alice burst into guffaws. "Oh, shut up! Oh, my God."

"It's true." Mick looked serious. "First thing in the morning like this? Right out of bed? I've never seen a more beautiful woman."

She sipped coffee for a second before putting the mug on the table and her hands on her hips. "Look. Let's just get something straight."

"Anything." He looked expectant before turning to the stove to shut off the burners and slide the bacon onto a plate, which he put on the table before focusing on her again. "What is it?"

She'd watched this domesticity with a raised brow. No denying that a man who cooked for her was sexy. Still, she had some things to say. "Just because I went to bed with you last night does not mean we can just pick up where we left off."

"Where we left off was pretty bad," Mick said. "I was kind of hoping we'd start off in a different place. I meant what I said last night, Alice."

He'd said he wanted her more than he'd ever wanted any woman. What that meant beyond the physical, Alice wasn't sure. She focused on her own bare toes for a moment before looking up at him, her fists clenched until she forced herself to open them. "Why did you go to Bernie and Cookie's party?"

"Because they invited me, and it was a big deal. It didn't seem right to miss it."

That had ostensibly been her reason, too, and she wasn't about to tell him any different.

"And I thought we'd be able to . . . you know. Catch up."

Alice's eyebrows rose. "What, like we were old high school pals who hadn't seen each other in a few years? Like maybe we'd worked together at summer camp? After everything, Mick, you thought we'd just . . . catch up?"

"I wanted to see you again," he told her. "And yeah. Catch up. Find out how you'd been. I know you think I didn't care—"

"I didn't say that." Though she'd thought it, more than once, as the years had passed without a word from him.

Mick gave her a steady look. "Don't you believe in second chances, Alice? Remember once how you told me that you were willing to make the effort? That what we had was worth it?"

Like she could've forgotten it. Some parts of her relationship with Mick had gone fuzzy over the years, blurred around the edges like a vignette. That conversation was not one of them.

"I love you," he'd told her. "On some level."

Oh, the anger had dimmed, after a time. But never the sting of those words. They still burned and bit her in her tender places, remembering.

He took her hand. The one with the scar. It had faded to white over the years. Only someone who knew it was there would even notice it. Mick stroked it now. Then kissed it, sending shivers all through her. He pulled her close, their fingers curled, and put her hand on his heart.

"It's worth trying," Mick said. "Isn't it?"

Their relationship had been over the night of her accident, though they had limped along for a month or so after that before it finally ended. Fighting, mostly. Making up and making love, but the damage had been done, and they'd never really recovered from it. It had been the best and worst month of her life—the sex had been fierce and sometimes brutal. The words they'd thrown at each other, both in person and in letters harsh and ultimately, unforgivable. But the passion? That had been undeniable.

She supposed everything about the two of them together had always been undeniable.

Alice went to the small, built-in desk in the corner of her kitchen and opened the drawer. Inside was a tightly bound packet of letters she'd shoved there some time ago because she'd been unable to convince herself to burn them, but hadn't wanted to be reminded of them all the time. She held them out to Mick.

"I kept these," she said. "I haven't read them in a long time. But I used to read them all the time. I've read them so often I memorized most of them. They all hurt me."

Mick winced, but Alice kept going.

"The angry letters were meant to hurt me, I guess, but the love letters always hurt me, too, because I could remember, so much, how it felt when we were together. I would read them and cry, torturing myself, because . . . because they were all I had left of you. All I thought I would ever have of you, and I could never bring myself to let them go. Ten years is a long time to hold on to something, Mick. It's a really long time not to let go."

He crossed to her. Pulled her close. She buried her face against his chest, breathing in the clean, warm scent of Mick's skin. It hadn't changed, not in all these years.

He kissed the top of her head. "I kept yours, too."

Alice to Mick

Last night I dreamed of a long hallway lined with doors of black and white, all but the one at the end. That one was red. I walked toward it, not bothering even to knock at any of the others. I didn't care what was behind them. I only wanted to get to the red door, because somehow I knew already what was behind it. The more I tried to get there, the longer the hallway got. Total cliché. Even in the dream, I knew it, and suddenly I knew it was a dream, and that I could control it, so I yelled out, "I want to get to the red door!"

Everything stopped.

I stood in front of the red door.

And there you were.

—Alice to Mick, unsent

Chapter 35

It had been a long time since Mick had put pen to paper this way. Not merely a scribbled to-do list or a signed birthday card, but an actual letter. The last time that he could remember writing something like this, in fact, had been to Alice. A long time ago.

It felt right, though. The scratch of the nib against the creamy thickness of the paper. The way the lines flowed, one into the other, making words. Handwriting was so different than typing on a computer or on a phone screen. He had to be very certain of what he wanted to say before he wrote it down. No backspace. No erasing.

It felt very fitting.

It had only been two weeks since he'd shown up at Alice's door. They'd agreed to take things slow. It was easier, in a way, than it had been back then. Now they both had smartphones, social media, unlimited texting. Maturity, he thought with a snort as he twirled the heavy fountain pen in his fingers and thought about what to write next.

The letters had been his suggestion. They'd written to

each other a lot the first time around. Funny cards or little notes. During the breakup, they'd sent even more letters. It had been easier to write what they felt instead of saying it aloud, at least for him. During that last horrific month when they'd both been clinging to each other and trying to tear each other apart, writing those letters had been like lancing a boil. The sight of an envelope in his mailbox, addressed in Alice's familiar hand, had always simultaneously lifted him and cast him down. And after it had ended for good, that last final letter from her that had told him never to contact her again, Mick had still kept writing letters he never sent.

There'd been girls before Alice and a few after, but he'd never done that for any of them. Held on that way. He didn't pull those unsent letters out to read them now, but he remembered all too well the words in them. He'd been angry. Pleading. Contrite. Sarcastic. Despondent. Vengeful, too.

This time around was going to be different.

In high school, his teacher had been adamant about making a rough draft before the final copy. There was something to be said for that, but in letter writing, Mick had found the first words were the best words. Okay, so maybe he spelled some things wrongs, or scratched them out, or repeated things. He wasn't an author, just a guy trying to get his girl back.

First words, he thought. Best ones.

Dear Alice, he wrote. *I wish you were here.*

Mick to Alice

Today I was onsite and stopped at a little deli for lunch. I got an egg salad sandwich because the last time I was at your place, you were boiling eggs to make some. I didn't get to try any of your extra-special egg salad, and I'm pretty sure this deli's didn't even come close, but it was a pretty good sandwich, anyway. By the time you get this letter the weekend will probably have come and gone, and I'll already have been able to say this to your face, but in case something weird has happened and the zombie apocalypse came or something like that (which is the only thing that would prevent me from seeing you) I wanted to send you this letter and tell you this . . .

I ate egg salad today because it made me think of you.

—Mick to Alice

Chapter 36

There were good days, and there were bad days. This was one of the bad ones. Wendy had called Alice at work, asking her to come over to help out with the kids for a few hours until her husband Raj could make it back from an unexpected business meeting.

Alice didn't usually mind helping out with her niece and nephew. They were the light of her life, those two punkins, but Alice didn't envy her sister's domestic bliss. Alice had known for a long time she probably never wanted children of her own. She loved Benjamin and Mallory, but pregnancy, childbirth, diapers, toddlers . .. all of that was much better experienced vicariously and from afar. And the husband thing seemed great, except of course when it didn't.

"Go take a shower," she told Benjamin, and gave Mallory a significant look. "You're next."

The twins, age six, were pretty good about the bedtime ritual, even on the exciting days when Auntie came over. Tonight they'd already finished up their dinner and watched a movie. Alice was willing to let them stay up an hour later to read in their rooms, a treat they giggled over like it was a conspiracy. They didn't know their mom was on board with it.

When both kids had bathed and been tucked into their beds, and Raj not yet home, Alice went into her sister's bedroom. Wendy was in bed, a damp cloth over her eyes preventing her from watching the TV, which was muttering in the corner. She shifted when Alice came in, but Alice shushed her.

"Don't get up. How's the head?"

Wendy waved a languid hand. "Hurts. Meds help."

Alice sat on the edge of her sister's bed. "No kidding. How about you share some of that good stuff with your favorite sister?"

The comment earned a laugh, weak but genuine. Getting hit by a truck had left Wendy prone to migraines, what the doctors often called cluster headaches. They hit her without warning, not set off by normal triggers, and left her basically unable to function normally until they faded. Alice had been left with scars, but her sister had suffered worse long-term effects.

"The kids in bed?"

"Yeah. Reading. Can I get you anything?" Alice yawned, thinking about heading home. Thinking about staying. The distance from here to work was the same as from home, and she'd brought an overnight bag as always, just in case she didn't feel like making the drive.

Wendy tugged the cloth up a little bit to peek out. "A new brain?"

"Girl, you've needed one of those since you were born."

"Don't make me laugh," Wendy protested weakly but laughed anyway. Some color came back into her cheeks. That was good.

"What time's Raj supposed to get home?"

Wendy sighed. "I don't know. They have him on this huge project, and he wasn't supposed to need to be at any of these meetings, but . . . you see how that worked out."

"No worries. I can stay, if you want. I don't have anything going on at home." Alice paused, thinking of Mick.

They'd talked last night, as they'd done every night for the past two weeks. They'd returned to at least one old habit, their daily "good nights," though these days they were often made via video chat or text instead of instant message. They'd spent the past weekend together, too, some of it in bed, but most of it actually doing things that were not clothing-optional.

She wasn't sure what she thought about all of it. Not yet. Too early.

She had a letter from him in her bag. It had been waiting for her when she got home from seeing him, and she hadn't read it yet. In the times of almost instant digital communication, the old-fashioned letters were special. A treat. The anticipation of it was like knowing she had a piece of gourmet chocolate waiting for her. She wanted to savor it.

She hadn't yet told Wendy she and Mick were making another go of things.

"You don't have to. You can if you want to." Wendy yawned. "I'm going to sleep, soon. I hope."

Alice stood. "Want me to turn off the TV?"

"No. Hey. Sit a minute." Wendy patted the bed next to her. "What's going on with you?"

"Huh? Nothing." Alice sat.

Wendy smiled. "Don't lie to me. I can hear it in your voice. You're bursting to tell me something. What is it? Spill!"

"God, it's like you got Spidey senses or something going on in there," Alice said. "Maybe your head hurts so often because you're having, like, psychic waves."

Wendy laughed again, harder this time. "I wish."

Alice thought for a moment about what to say. Wendy had been with her through the breakup, but then her sister had been with her through all her breakups. Alice shouldn't be embarrassed to tell her she'd been hooking up with Mick again.

"Mick," she said suddenly, and couldn't bring herself to say anything else.

Wendy waited, but when Alice didn't say anything, she took the cloth off her eyes. "What about him?"

"He was at Bernie and Cookie's the last time I went."

Wendy's brows rose. "Did you know he was going to be there?"

"Yeah. They told me he'd been invited."

Wendy's mouth twisted. "And you went anyway?"

"It was their anniversary party. It's been years. I figured it would be okay."

"And? Was it?"

"We . . . um . . ." Alice coughed. "We're . . . um . . ."

"Oh, my God," Wendy said, sitting up in bed fast enough to wince and fall back on the pillows with a groan. "You and Mick? *Mick the Dick*?"

"Hey, take it easy. You don't want to set it off again. You need another pill?" Alice opened the bedside drawer to look for the medicine bottle, but Wendy waved her away.

"I'll be fine. It's fading, thank God. But you and Mick. I, wow. Can't believe it. That guy broke you, Alice. I mean, really broke you." Wendy paused. "Sorry, but it's the truth."

"I know. Believe me, I remember."

Wendy's eyes widened a little. "How did this even happen? I mean at the party, sure, but then . . . ?"

"He showed up at my house."

"Oh." Wendy paused. "He likes to do that, huh? That's only a little creepy."

Alice burst into laughter. "Stop!"

"I'm just saying." Wendy grinned.

"He said he wanted me more than he's ever wanted any woman. Ever."

Wendy didn't say anything for a few seconds. "Wow. That's something, huh?"

"It's dick feelings," Alice said flatly. "Dick feelings don't count."

"How do *you* feel about it?"

"I don't know how I'm supposed to feel. I went there for the weekend. He was there. The second I saw him, it was like I'd been in a dark room and someone came in and turned on all the lights." Alice blinked rapidly, remembering. "Only it didn't hurt my eyes. It just made me able to see everything that had been in shadows before."

"Oh, shit," Wendy said softly.

"Yeah. So. For now I'm just seeing what happens. I mean, people don't change, do they?"

"Sure they do. All the time." Wendy patted Alice's hand.

"I don't feel like I have."

Wendy made a face, gingerly, as though it hurt. "Has he? That might be the important question."

"He's trying hard to act like he has."

"Well," Wendy said. "There's that."

Alice's phone chirped from her pocket and she slid it out, anticipating a text from Mick. It was Bill. She swiped the screen to see the message, laughed a little, and typed out a quick reply. When she looked up, Wendy was staring.

"Was that him?"

"No, that was some other guy. Bill. I met him a few weeks ago. He keeps texting me," Alice said.

"Are you seeing him?"

"I've seen him," Alice said. "A couple of times. Not recently. Not since Mick. But I don't have to stop talking to Bill just because Mick suddenly decided he made a huge mistake and wants me back," Alice said.

"You don't have to explain that to me." Wendy reached for the glass of water on the nightstand and sipped it. "Nothing wrong with keeping your options open."

"It's not . . . I'm not . . ." Alice shut up. There was no point in lying to her sister, even if she'd been lying to herself. "I like Bill."

"That's okay."

Alice shook her head. "No. I mean, yes, it's okay to like him. He's nice. He makes me laugh."

"But he's no Mick."

"He also didn't roll over my heart in an eighteen wheeler, then put it in reverse so he could back up and roll over it again," Alice said darkly.

Wendy smiled. "He could, though. Right?"

"Anyone could. But Mick already did." Alice frowned.

"So . . . tell me again why you're seeing Mick?"

Alice sighed and fell back on the bed with a groan. "You know why."

Wendy started to giggle. "Mick has the magic peen!"

Alice frowned, but there was no denying it. Mick McManus had a cock made of magic, and she couldn't get enough of it. The question was, would that be enough?

Alice to Mick

Knock, knock.

Who's there?

Ewan.

Ewan who?

Nobody. It's just me.

—Alice to Mick

Chapter 37

"So, did it work?"

Mick turned away from the coffeepot, then grinned when he saw Jay. Mick clapped him on the shoulder. "Hey, man. I didn't know you were coming to the office first. It worked. I went to her house, did the whole grand gesture thing. It absolutely worked. Thanks."

Jay looked thoughtful, but shrugged. "Good."

"What?"

"I'm just surprised, that's all. I mean, it's great, don't get me wrong. I'm glad." Jay grabbed a mug and held it out. "Can I get one of those?"

Mick filled both mugs. "Why are you surprised? You're the one who told me what to do."

"I did. I just didn't think it would actually work." Jay sipped and grimaced. "The coffee here is shit, you know that? You want to grab something on the way to the site?"

Mick wasn't going to argue with that. He dumped his mug and headed for his office, Jay following. "Yeah. Let me grab my stuff. You want to drive together?"

"Sure. I've got some plans later back this direction.

That's why I stopped in here first. You want to go in my car?"

"Nah, I got it." Mick stopped to grab his keys, then took another minute to hop on his computer and check to see if Alice had answered his instant message. The method was old-school, but was also nostalgic. How it had been with them, before. She'd been sending him goofy knock-knock jokes all morning. The punchline to this one made him laugh under his breath. He typed out a quick response, then waited for the little pencil icon to show up in the box to alert him that Alice was typing a reply. She wasn't, so he shut down his computer and looked at Jay. "Ready?"

Some onsites were simple fixes. Swoop in like a superhero, take care of the issues, clean up the mess. Some, like this one, were an insane pain in the ass. Because Mick worked on the tech side and Jay on the management side, it took both of them almost the entire day to get the situation in this branch back on track, and only then because Mick was able to call in a last-minute order for some new conference room equipment the branch manager insisted he'd requested a month before and needed for the client meeting next week.

"You earned your bonus," Jay told him when they'd finally put everything back on track for this branch's reopening and were heading back to Mick's office. "Hey, you want to grab a drink? I've got some time to kill before my date."

Mick, feeling accomplished about the day's work, had been tapping the steering wheel to the beat of the song on the radio. Now he gave Jay a sideways look. "Date, huh?"

"Yeah. New guy."

Mick wasn't one to get in anyone's business, but this

startled him. "What happened with Paul? I thought you two were back together."

Jay was silent for a minute. Mick concentrated on driving. Jay would talk when he was ready.

"Ten years is a long time to let someone treat you like shit, over and over," Jay said finally. Stiffly. Like the words hurt coming out. "I got tired of being treated like shit."

"I don't blame you, man."

Jay made a disgusted sound. "Anyway, let him do what he wants, with whoever he wants. I'm done."

They went to a sports bar near Mick's office. Jay's date was meeting him there and would give him a ride back to his car later. They settled into a booth, ordered some drinks and food. While Jay answered a message from his date, Mick checked his phone.

Nothing from Alice.

He sent her a message anyway, just a quick forward of a funny picture he'd gleaned from his newsfeed. It was in the spirit of the knock-knock jokes from earlier that day. She replied with a laughing emoticon, and before he had time to say more, Jay had put away his phone, and the drinks had arrived.

They talked about work for a few minutes before the conversation turned to the next weekend at Bernie and Cookie's house. They'd planned their traditional big Fourth of July party. Mick hadn't talked to Alice yet about going, but Jay wasn't sure he was going to make it.

"Paul got invited too, of course," he explained. "And it's too late to tell Bernie not to invite him, which I wouldn't do anyway, because that would make me the asshole. It would never occur to Paul that Bernie was my friend first, or that he should stay the hell home because we broke up, which is just going to make everything super awkward and not only because of the rooming arrangements." Jay stabbed a fork into the small plastic cup of guacamole that had come on the side of his quesadilla.

Mick knew how that had felt, but he'd also declined years of invitations from Bernie upon the assumption Alice would be there and had only too late learned she'd been doing the same. "You guys were broken up the last time you were there."

"So were you and Alice. Something must've been in the water that weekend," Jay said sourly, then gave Mick an apologetic look. "Sorry. I'm sure it's all cool with you and Alice."

Mick dunked a celery stick into the bleu cheese and crunched loudly. "Let's just say yeah, it's all really cool. Kind of hard to believe. But cool. Hey, want me to tell him to fuck off, make sure he doesn't go to Bernie's?"

"Who, Paul?" Jay looked surprised.

"Yeah." Mick grabbed another hot wing. "I don't care. I'll tell him to keep his punk ass home."

Jay laughed and shook his head. "Wow. Thanks. But nah, it's fine. I might have plans for the Fourth anyway with this new guy, and as much as I love the lake house parties, I'm not about to bring around another person there until I'm sure. You know. That it's going to work out."

"I haven't talked to Alice about going." Mick thought a moment. "Maybe she wants to go someplace else, too."

Jay looked thoughtful. "You haven't said anything at all?"

"Nope. But maybe we'll go someplace romantic. Or something." Mick grinned.

"Yeah . . . but . . ." Jay's phone rang, interrupting him. He held up a finger to Mick while he took the call.

Mick pulled out his own phone, typing a message to Alice. *What are you up to?*

Her reply didn't come right away, but Jay was trying to give directions over the phone, so Mick had nothing to do but wait. After a few minutes, Alice's answer came in the form of a picture message—a platter of spaghetti and a glass of wine. No text or explanation. Just a picture. Mick took a shot of his beer and sent that off just as Jay disconnected.

"Sorry about that. He's lost. He'll be here in about ten minutes."

"I'll get out of here, then. Leave you some privacy." Mick waggled his eyebrows until Jay laughed.

Jay held up his bottle. "Hey, thanks for coming out with me. And about Alice . . ."

"I know, I know, man. You'll kick my ass."

Jay looked solemn. "I was going to say I hope it works out for you."

"It's going to this time." Mick clinked the bottle against Jay's. "I know it."

By the time Mick was ready to leave, Alice had replied to his text, so he called her on the way home. "Hey, gorgeous."

She sounded sleepy. "Hi. What's up?"

"Heading home. Had a drink with Jay after work. He was waiting for a date. Are you in bed already?"

"Oh, really?" There was a soft shuffling. He imagined her turning in the sheets. "Yeah. I was reading in bed, guess I fell asleep. What time is it?"

"A little after nine. I'll let you go."

Alice laughed gently. "No, no, don't do that. Talk to me."

He had another twenty minutes' drive. So he talked. He had her giggling over some silly story when he pulled into his driveway. He cut the ignition but left the radio on so he could keep talking using his phone's Bluetooth connection.

"So, what are you wearing?" He pitched his voice low and sexy. Or at least tried to.

Alice sounded amused. "Pajamas."

"What kind?"

"Silky bottoms with a cotton top." She paused. "Too bad you can't come over and see them on my bedroom floor."

His pulse quickened at the thought. "Damn."

"Yep." She laughed again, low and sweet.

He looked at the clock. It was nearly ten. Even if he backed out of the driveway without packing a bag and headed for her place, he wouldn't get there until nearly midnight. They'd both agreed to keep weekly dates short, for both their sakes, but damn if he wasn't tempted to get to her anyway.

"You're still coming here right after work on Friday, right?" he asked.

"Yep. I thought on Saturday we could go to the farmers' market in Lancaster. It's a bit of a drive, but worth it. We could spend the day? They have the most amazing pie place there. And a flea market. I'll buy you a whoopie pie."

"Sure, we'll see how we feel. Hey, listen, my radio's about to shut off so I'm going to lose you. I'll let you get back to sleep."

"Okay, but—" Alice said.

Too late, his radio clicked off, cutting the call. Mick gathered his phone and bag, the mail, a bunch of garbage from the past few days, and juggling all of it, went inside. A text came through while he was tossing some laundry in the washer. Then he forgot his phone on the kitchen counter while he took a bunch of towels out of the drier and carried them upstairs to fold. By the time he checked it, another forty minutes had passed.

It was from Alice, and made him smile. *GNM.*

GNA, he typed, but she must've gone to sleep because she didn't reply.

Mick to Alice

Open the envelope, it's a surprise!
—Mick to Alice

Chapter 38

They never made it to the farmers' market. Alice's plans for Amish quilts and fattening pastries had been circumvented by Mick surprising her with tickets to a concert. He'd looked so pleased with himself when he handed her the envelope containing the tickets he'd printed that she couldn't even be mad. Okay, so it wasn't a trip to horse-and-buggy country, but it was still going to be a good time. Did it matter what they did, she told herself, so long as they were doing it together?

Besides, the Lion's Head had always been one of Alice's favorite places to see live music. The venue was touted as "intimate," which translated into small. A stage, front and center. Bars on either side. A balcony above. She'd been to barely attended acoustic performances and also shows so crowded it had been almost impossible to move. Tonight's show, a hard rock Irish band called the Dirty Dubliners, promised to be one of the latter, but that kind of added to the fun.

"I've never seen them live," she confessed to Mick as

they waited in line to get in. "But their last album was amazing."

"I knew you'd love it. Glad I got that announcement about the show last night."

Inside, she directed him to the side farthest from the stage. The bar back there generally had much shorter lines and less of a crowd, with a decent view of the stage. It was closer to the bathroom, too, always a plus when in a crowd.

"You don't want to be front row?" Mick asked as they wove their way through the audience, her hand in his, leading him.

"I'm too old to be in the front row of a crowd like this." Alice laughed. Her fingers curled in his. It was a good excuse to hold his hand, and she didn't let it drop even when they got to a clear spot on the floor.

Mick pulled her close for a second. "You don't want to be in the mosh pit, huh?"

"No." She let him nuzzle her. "Hell, no."

Mick laughed. "You want a drink?"

"Absolutely. Jameson and ginger ale." Grinning, she watched his brows raise. "Hey, we're here to see the Dirty Dubliners, gotta go Irish."

Under cover of the shadows and the massive number of other people, Mick took her hand and pressed it briefly to his crotch. "You need some Irish? I got some for you, right here."

It was funny and dirty and kind of trashy, but oh so sexy just the same. It made her forget all about how she'd wanted to look at quilts and cornfields this weekend, how irritated she'd been that he'd once again switched up the plans without asking her first. His hand covered hers, moving it over the bulge of his denim-covered cock. The heat in his gaze sparked her own; Alice pressed her body to his and lifted her mouth for a kiss.

"Let me get that drink," Mick said a few breaths later, when the jostling crowd made it awkward for them to make out.

They'd need to find a quieter place for that.

Alice staked out their spot while Mick got the drinks. Her Jameson and ginger was tingly and warm and tasty, though not as delicious as Mick's kiss. She'd found a place near a pillar so he could lean against it. He pulled her back against him, one hand hooked into her belt loop to rock her ass against his crotch.

Bill would never have come to see this band with her, Alice thought as the crowd roared and cheered at the opening band's first notes. He would never even have known how much she loved the Dirty Dubliners. Mick, on the other hand, had been the one to first introduce her to the band way back when the band was selling CDs out of the back of their van. She had one of those CDs, signed by the original members. Years had passed and she still listened to it.

Alice let her body mold to Mick's as they moved to the beat. There was nobody else she wanted to be with, and that thought sent competing shivers of heat and cold all through her, peaking her nipples and sending a flush up her throat to her cheeks and making her grateful for the darkness that hid them. Mick rolled his hips, and Alice lost herself in feeling him against her. It didn't matter the beat of the song, fast or slow, they moved together in perfect sync the way they always did.

When he slid a hand along the back of her skull to twist his fingers in her hair, pulling her head back, Alice closed her eyes. This, this, oh this, she thought as Mick's breath caressed her cheek. His lips found her ear. His tongue flicked. She pushed herself back against him.

"You know my fantasy," he said into her ear. "About a dark hallway in a club . . ."

She knew, all right. It was so unfair, how much she remembered about him. How he'd told her once, long ago, that he wanted to take her into the shadows while a rock band played and get his hands all over her. His mouth.

There was a dark hallway here, beyond the bathrooms. It led to an outside exit where people went to smoke. It also had a small alcove hung with a coatrack nobody ever used, because who left their coat unattended in a bar?

Maybe it was the drink. Maybe it was Mick. Whatever it was, Alice couldn't fight it. Hell. She didn't *want* to. When he tugged her hair again, everything inside her went molten.

Mick made her lose her fucking mind.

She tossed her empty plastic cup into the nearby trash can and took his from his hand to toss that, too. At his confused look, Alice smiled. She took his hand.

"C'mon."

Again, she led him through the crowd with their fingers linked. Inside the alcove, she found his mouth, already open for her. In seconds, Mick turned her. Put her up against the wall. He raked her throat with his teeth until she gasped. Her knees went weak, and if he hadn't put his thigh between hers, she might have stumbled.

"You," he breathed into her ear, but said no more than that.

"Me?"

His thigh nudged upward, pressing her in just the right spot, and all other speech fled her. She should've worn a dress, Alice thought incoherently. Then he could've put his hand up it, in her panties, inside her. . . .

Oh, God, she was going to come. Unbelievably, unavoidably, and undeniably. Pleasure spiked as Mick rocked her against his thigh. His mouth plundered hers, tongue fucking deep inside. Her hands went to the back of his, seeking purchase in his hair, but it was too short now to lose her fingers inside. His hand, though, went back to where it had been before. Her fingers twisted, tugged, pulled. Then, without warning, yanked.

Alice came with a low moan into Mick's mouth. She shuddered. Her pussy clenched, spasming, and her back arched. Blinking, she eased down from the high of climax. They'd only been in the alcove for about three minutes, tops. A couple stumbled down the hall, veering toward the alcove before seeing them and bursting into laughter.

Mick moved to shield her automatically, keeping her from view. That, Alice thought in a daze, was why she loved him. Because of things like that. Simple, but important, showing that he cared enough to protect her.

And oh, she thought. Oh, *love*. Oh, no.

"I want to fuck you right now," Mick said into her ear.

Alice shuddered. They couldn't. They'd already gone further than they should've. But she couldn't deny that she wanted him inside her, right there, fucking to the steady thumping beat of the opening band's last song. He was hard against her, his breath hot on her neck. His hands gripped her hips. They stayed that way for another minute before another passing couple interrupted, and then, no matter how much she wanted to stay, Alice knew it was time for them to get out of there.

"Later," she promised him. "Later, you can do anything and everything you want."

Alice to Mick

Listen to this song. It always makes me think of you.
—Alice to Mick

Chapter 39

She was amazing, and Mick couldn't get enough. Not only had she remembered his old fantasy, but she'd made it come true. Making out with her in that alcove, getting her off . . . He could've moved a stone block with his dick right now.

The Dirty Dubliners had taken the stage and hadn't stopped rocking for the past hour. Mick had been watching Alice more than he'd been looking at the band. She bounced along to the music, throwing him a grin every now and then, and Mick found her more intoxicating than the Jameson and ginger. Everything about her was light and joy, and every time she looked at him, all he could think about was how much he wanted to be the man to always make her look that way.

He was aching to taste her. Get inside her. But it would've been kind of a dick move to ask her to leave early so he could get her home just for that, so Mick forced himself to stop thinking about his half-hard cock and the heat of her against his thigh, and how she'd moaned and shook. . . .

"That's my favorite song," Alice said as the band finished one of their recent hits and started immediately into a rare ballad. Her gaze glittered for a moment at the opening notes. Some of the joy faded from her face.

Mick knew this song. It was from the Dubliners' first album, before they got signed to a major label. It had been written while the band was trying to find its voice and wasn't typical of the band's style. It was about love and loss and heartbreak, and once, Mick remembered, Alice had burned a copy of it onto a CD and sent it to him along with a short, viciously sad letter telling him she never wanted to see him again.

It had been the last thing she sent him.

Facing him, Alice met his gaze in that steady way she always had, not looking away. Her eyes glittered with blue and green reflections from the lighting. She wasn't crying, but he pulled her close to him anyway. He couldn't take away what had happened in the past, so he did the only thing he could; he held her close and tight and breathed her in and hoped it would be enough to stop her thinking about what had been and start her thinking about what could be.

When the song ended, she squeezed him hard and stepped away. "Gonna run to the bathroom."

By the time she got back, the band was heading into an encore. When she asked him if he wanted to get out of there before the rest of the crowd, Mick agreed. They made it through the doors and to the parking garage before the rest of the traffic hit.

"Are you hungry or anything?" he asked as he navigated out of the city and onto the highway.

Alice, who'd been quiet since leaving the club, shook her head. "No. Let's just go back to your place, okay?"

That had been the idea on his mind all night, but

again, he didn't want to seem like he was making it all about getting her into bed. "Sure. If that's what you want."

"If it's what *you* want," Alice said. "I guess I could just go back to my place. If *that's* what you want."

Mick bit back his irritation. "You can go home if you want. Or we can go back to my place. Whatever you want."

"I don't want to make you do something you don't want to do," Alice said sharply.

"I want you to come back to my place!"

She looked at him then. "Good! Because that's what I want to do!"

It felt like half a fight, and he didn't know why they were heading that direction, but he did know enough to shut up about it after that. Alice turned on the radio, so at least the drive to his house wasn't too awkward, though it was quiet. By the time they got there, she was even singing along under her breath.

Inside, he offered her a drink, but she declined. Same to food. It wasn't early, but it wasn't late, either, not by Friday night standards.

"Want to watch a movie or something?" Mick asked, trying to figure out what he could do to make her happy.

Alice shook her head and gave him a look from the corner of her eye. "Do *you* want to watch a movie?"

"No," he said, deciding to be bold. "I want to take you upstairs and get my mouth between your legs until you scream my name."

A low, raw noise slipped out of her. Just like that, heat blazed between them. He had her in his arms half a minute after that. Somehow, she jumped. He lifted. Her legs went around his waist, his hands beneath her ass. If they'd been close to a table or a counter he'd have seated her on it, but all he could do was take a few unsteady steps toward the stairs.

"Shit, Alice, I'm going to drop you," he muttered into her mouth as he put one foot on the bottom step.

They both moved, ending up with her sitting and him between her legs. Arms tangled. Mouths sliding every place they could get to. She broke the kiss with a gasp, a hand on his chest to push him back.

"Upstairs," she said. "Bed."

She got to her feet and moved, Mick on her heels. She took her shirt off as she walked, tossing it at him along with a sultry glance over one shoulder that had his tongue lolling out like a cartoon dog. Her bra came next, showing off those perfect tits, though she covered them with her hands and gave him a coy raise of her brows.

In his bedroom, more kissing. More hands. More tongue. She urged him to tear off his long-sleeved shirt, then let out a laugh at the sight of the T-shirt he wore beneath.

"You and layers." She shook her head. "Get naked faster!"

Mick was happy to oblige. Alice fell back onto the bed, lifting her hips so he could tug off her jeans, though neither of them had remembered to take off her boots first. Laughing, they struggled, and he paused to soak in, once more, how truly fucking beautiful Alice was.

"What?" she asked self-consciously.

Mick shook his head and finished shucking out of his jeans and briefs. Her gaze dropped to his cock, hard as iron now. Fuck, he loved the way her eyes went all dreamy when she looked at him.

"I love watching you get turned on," Mick said.

She looked at his face, mouth open as though to say

something, but all she did was lick her lips. Then slowly, deliberately, she moved back on the bed and let her thighs fall open. One hand drifted along her inner thigh to stroke a fingertip along her pussy. Then, oh fuck, she stuck out her tongue to lick the same fingertip. Her eyes never left his.

Mick knew an invitation when he got one. In a heartbeat, he was between her legs. Hands slipping beneath her ass to lift her close so he could feast on her. At that first long lick, she gave a low cry. When he found her clit and let the flat of his tongue stroke over it, her hand went to the top of his head.

He loved it when he made her react this way. He loved turning her on. And hell yeah, Mick loved making Alice come.

He flicked his tongue over her slick flesh until she cried out again. Then he moved up the bed, rolling onto this back and pulling her along with him until she ended up straddling his face. Much better, now she could ride his mouth and tongue, really getting herself off, and all he had to do was lay back and enjoy every second of it.

Mick closed his eyes, letting himself get lost in every smell, every taste of her. Alice moved on his mouth. Slowly at first, then faster. Her hand reached behind her to stroke his cock, and the arch of her back pressed her pussy harder against his mouth. He was drowning in her and didn't care; all that mattered was how good this felt.

When she started to shake, he knew she was close. Her stroking hand faltered, edging him. Mick gripped her hips to keep her from moving off him. He wanted her to finish right there, right on his mouth, he needed to feel her come on his tongue. Just. Like. That.

She shouted his name, hoarse. Her pussy throbbed and pulsed under his tongue. He drank her in, savoring every second of her climax, his balls aching for release. He protested with a groan when she moved off his face.

Alice laughed, low and throaty, but her giggle turned to a groan when she seated herself on him. For a moment, neither of them moved. Breathing hard, she looked down at him. Mick ran his hands up her body to cover her breasts, and when she reacted with a sigh and another of those dreamy looks, he pinched her nipples lightly.

"Oh," Alice said. "Yeah. That. Again."

So he did it again. And again, when she asked. When she started to move on him, Mick gave himself up to everything. The slow, building pressure in his balls. The sharp sting of her nails digging into him.

He wanted to fuck her forever, but he wasn't going to last more than another minute. Alice moved faster, focusing on his face now. She looked determined. Riding him. Responding to his reactions.

"Come for me, baby," Alice said like he'd be giving her a gift.

Mick gave her what she wanted. Pleasure exploded through him, so fierce he was sure he knew what dying felt like. There was nothing else but this ecstasy. Nothing more than the feeling of her body gripping his, urging him to the edge and hurtling him over it. In that moment, there was nothing else for him but Alice.

She collapsed on top of him, her mouth on his throat and her hair a delicious tangle all over his face. His arms went around her, holding her close. When she finally rolled off him to flop, spread eagled on the bed, he could barely muster the strength to move. But he had to. He needed to look at her face. It was the last sight he wanted in his vision before he fell asleep.

"What?" Alice said when she noticed him staring. She rolled to face him. "What?"

"That was fun."

She smiled, but only after a second or so, as though she hadn't quite been certain of how she wanted to react to what he said. Then she moved in close and kissed his mouth. She took a fingertip and pressed it to each eye, closing them.

"Sleep," she whispered, and he gave her that, too.

Mick to Alice

Hello, gorgeous. I had to leave before you got up. I started the coffee for you and fixed that squeaking drawer in your bathroom. See you later.
—Mick to Alice

Chapter 40

Dayna had pinged Alice online that morning, and with the barest amount of prompting had admitted that she'd been with Paul the night before. Alice had immediately invited her to lunch. There were conversations you simply couldn't have in a text window.

"The sex was amazing," Dayna said. "It's always amazing, even when I'm wracked with guilt about it."

"What do you feel guilty about?"

"Jay." Dayna looked sad. "I know he's in love with Paul as much as I am. I think sometimes that if I weren't around, Paul would maybe make a real effort with him. Make it work."

Alice thought about that. Jay had told her he'd finally broken it off with Paul. He was dating a new guy, a few of them, in fact. He wasn't happy about the breakup, but really, who ever was, even when it was the best choice?

"If Jay weren't around, do you think Paul would make a real effort to make it work with you?"

Dayna looked faintly surprised, then frowned. "He got a phone call while we were watching TV, and he got up to take it in the other room. It might've been Jay, though I've heard him talking to Jay before, and I don't think it was. I think he was talking to another woman. So, do I think if Jay weren't around that Paul would make the effort? I don't know. I guess not. But then he calls me up and he knows all the right things to say, and he knows just where to touch me, and the next thing I know, we're in bed."

"I'm the last person to tell you not to give in to a magic cock," Alice said. "Believe me, I get it. Especially after a long, long dry spell, finding that person who makes everything work just right is super hard to give up. Even when you know you should."

"*Oh,* really? Are you talking about that guy you met the last time we went out? Bill?" Dayna stirred sugar and cream into her coffee and set the spoon on her plate before giving Alice a significant look.

Alice laughed and shook her head.

"No way. Mick?"

Alice smiled.

Dayna laughed. "Wow. You guys. Again. Kind of gives a girl hope."

"It's either going to be the greatest love story ever told, or the greatest tragedy." Alice sipped her own coffee and contemplated ordering cheesecake. Not that she needed it or was even that hungry after the giant salad she'd had for lunch, but because . . . cheesecake.

"Thanks for meeting me."

Alice looked up at Dayna's off tone. "Sure."

"I just needed to talk to someone about stuff. And nobody knows like you do, about everything." Dayna took a deep breath. "And look, I know Jay's your friend . . ."

"I love Jay, and we've been friends for a million years," Alice said, "but you're my friend, too."

"And you don't like Paul."

Alice couldn't deny that, not exactly. "I like Paul just fine. I don't like the way he treats the people who love him so much."

"And you don't understand why we do." Dayna turned her cup in her hands and looked sad.

"Honestly, I don't understand why anyone falls in love with anyone," Alice said somewhat sourly.

Dayna looked surprised. "Uh-oh. Sounds like that's heading more toward tragedy than love story."

Alice was silent for a moment while she tried to put her feelings into words. She thought about seeing Mick at Bernie and Cookie's house for the first time after so long. That first weekend, the kissing, the touching. The passion. Then his phone call, opening the door to him, his declaration. All the months that had passed since then.

"It's like you're elated, right? You get this high from being around the other person. Whatever it is, chemistry or whatever, you get a zing."

"Yeah," Dayna said with a sort of dreamy sigh. "The zing."

"But you can't be high forever. You have to come down, sometime. And the higher you were, the harder it is to hit the ground."

Dayna waved to the server. "Deep philosophical questions need dessert. Two chocolate cheesecakes with strawberries, please." To Alice, she said, "But that's why people keep falling in love. Because it feels so good when you're up."

"I was totally and completely in love with him. That first time. God." Alice shivered at the memory of it. "So caught up. Everything he did or said. I couldn't get enough of him. The sex was great. And he could make me laugh the way no man ever has. I was so gone for him."

"And now?"

Alice chewed the inside of her cheek for a second, thinking. "The sex is still great. Better, even, though I would never have imagined that could be. We still talk for hours, and that's great. So long as we're not talking about us. Then all of a sudden it's 'can you hear me now?'"

Dayna laughed. "I've had that conversation myself."

"So why can't I just go along with it? Have fun, like he says? I do have fun with him," Alice said in a low voice. "He still makes me laugh harder than anyone else."

"But . . . ?" Dayna prompted.

"But I haven't forgotten how much he made me cry, too. And I *am* older. I know myself better now. A lot of what I put up with when I was twenty-three, I wouldn't put up with now. I deserve better than to settle for half measures or someone who doesn't listen to me or make me important. I'm trying hard to put it all in perspective. That's all. Keep my expectations reasonable." Alice laughed ruefully. "Look, I know that you can't depend on any one person to make you happy, but damn, it's not good to be with someone who makes you sad."

Dayna looked stunned. "Oh, my God. Oh, wow. Yes. That, all over. That, ten times. Paul never makes me feel important, and he sure as hell makes me feel sad."

The cheesecake arrived, and Alice dug in. The sugar sweetness did its best to chase away the sour taste on her tongue. But it didn't help her to stop thinking about it.

"Does Mick make you sad?"

"He hasn't yet," Alice replied. "But I guess I keep waiting for him to."

"I'm not going to see him again," Dayna said when a minute or so of silence had passed between them while they ate their cheesecake.

Alice looked up. "What? Paul? Really?"

"Yes. I'm done." Dayna drew in a long, shaky breath,

looking pleased. "Oh, my God, I never thought I would say that. All these years, the back and forth, on and off again. I mean, I didn't see him for months or even years at a time, but I always knew we weren't finished. He'd knock, I'd open the door. But now, what you said . . . I'm done."

Surprised and pleased, Alice sat back in her chair. "Wow."

"Shit." Dayna looked surprised, too. "I really mean it. I feel it. It's no good to love someone who doesn't love you back. What good is it to open the door for someone who won't bother to be there when you do?"

Alice held up a hand for Dayna to high five. "No kidding."

"I feel like we need champagne or something for this revelation." Dayna gave a shaky laugh, her gaze bright. She lifted her fork of cheesecake. "I guess we can settle for toasting with chocolate. To not putting up with shit."

"Yes." Alice lifted her fork, too. "To all that."

Alice to Mick

You know when you do something, even though you know you shouldn't, but you do it anyway because it seems as though the benefits outweigh the potential for damage? Sometimes, it's worth it and sometimes you end up wishing you'd been smarter. I think I've started wishing I was smarter.

—Alice to Mick, unsent

Chapter 41

"Hey, babe. It's me. We're starting Sunday dinner, just wanted to know if we should hold it for you." Mick took the beer Jimmy offered him and made an apologetic face at his mother, who was pushing past him with a pan of roast beef.

Alice sounded surprised. "What?"

"I'm at Mom and Dad's. Dinner?"

"Mick, I'm just getting in the car to take Wendy's kids to see a movie. I didn't know I was supposed to come over to your parents' house. I'm sorry." Alice said something in a muffled tone to the kids, and then her voice came back more clearly. "You didn't mention it last night."

"This morning I did," he said. "I said see you later when I kissed you good-bye."

Alice made some more muffled noises and sounded disgruntled when she came back on. "You always say see you later. You didn't say 'see you later at my parents' house for Sunday dinner.' I didn't know I was invited, and besides, I've had plans to take the kids to see this movie for a week."

"Oh." Mick frowned, kind of pissed off that she hadn't mentioned it before now. "My mom was expecting you."

"Tell your mother I'm sorry. I would've loved to come to dinner." Alice paused. "Clearly we miscommunicated. Can I come next week?"

"Yeah. I guess so. See you later . . . will I?"

"I'll be busy with the movie and dinner after until the evening, and then I have to run the kids back home. I'll be home around eight, I think. But I'll call you when I'm finished, okay?"

His mom was giving him the "sit down, it's getting cold" look now.

"Yeah, fine. Okay. Gotta go."

Alice sighed and muttered something he didn't think was to the kids. Louder, she added, "Talk to you later."

"She's not coming," he told his family. "Wires got crossed, she's got plans with her niece and nephew."

"That's nice, that she does things with her niece and nephew." Mary gave him a pointed look, then at her own boys, who'd barely ever given Mick the time of day as little kids and sure didn't now that they'd become teenagers. "What a nice break for her sister, to have a whole Sunday afternoon to herself."

"Her sister gets killer migraines, maybe you'd like one of those?"

Mary rolled her eyes, but didn't keep poking him. Dinner was good. It always was. And nobody pestered him about why Alice had made other plans instead of being here with the family, though her absence was keenly felt by Mick because of the empty chair next to him. He'd been looking forward to some of Mom's amazing home cooking, then maybe hitting the hardware store later to pick up a new faucet for Alice's leaking kitchen faucet. She hadn't mentioned it, but he'd noticed yesterday that it dripped.

He could fix that, no sweat, the way he'd taken care of her squeaking drawer and the oil change for her car. That's what a man did, he took care of his girl.

He could still do those things for her, he guessed, even if it wasn't today. But that still meant he wasn't going to get to see her, and that flat-out sucked. He checked his phone at the table, though his mom always scolded about that, but Alice hadn't texted him.

Jimmy and Jack argued about professional wrestling. Mary ignored her husband, who honestly probably didn't give a damn that he was being given the cold shoulder. Dad shoveled food into his mouth as fast as Mom could put it on the plate for him, and Mom spent so much time getting up and down to bring stuff in from the kitchen that finally, Mick lost all patience.

"Mom, sit, I'll get it," he told her when she'd hopped up for another set of serving spoons. "You sit."

In the kitchen, he got more spoons and another beer, then checked his phone again for a text. Still nothing from Alice. She was busy with the kids, he reminded himself.

He wanted her there.

"I wrapped this up so you could take it home," his mother said in the kitchen as he was getting ready to leave. She pushed a plate of chicken and potatoes at him. "There's plenty for you and Alice, too, if she's hungry later."

"I'm not seeing her tonight, Mom." Mick took the food, knowing it was too much. He'd eat some of it and end up tossing the rest.

His mother didn't look surprised. "Your dad likes her, you know. Alice. Says she's a keeper."

"What? Dad told you that?" Mick couldn't recall his father espousing an opinion on much of anything, much less Mick's romantic partners. There'd been that awkward condom talk in high school, but beyond that, Dad had never even seemed to acknowledge Mick having any sort of love life.

Mom, on the other hand, had always had an opinion about the girls Mick dated, especially, it seemed, the ones he did not bring home. Now she bustled around the kitchen, wiping at the counters. "Yep. Dad says she's a smart one. I like her, too. It's too bad she had plans today."

Mick frowned. "I didn't know. I figured she'd come to dinner, Mom. I'm sorry."

"Oh, honey, I'm not mad." His mom gave him a fond look and a shake of her head. "Next time, I'm sure you'll give her plenty of notice."

From Mary the remark might've sounded snide, but Mick had never known his mom to be that way. Sometimes subtly passive aggressive, but never harsh. "She'll come next week."

"That'll be fine." From the next room came raised voices, Jimmy and Jack shouting at the television, Mary shouting something at one of her sons. Mom gave Mick a long look. "You're a lot like your dad, Mickey. You know that?"

"I've heard it a few times, yeah." Mick had his dad's blue eyes and dark hair, but then, all the McManus kids did.

His mom laughed and folded the dishcloth neatly before putting her hands on her hips. "Do you know that I almost married Gino Batistelli?"

"Gino from Gino's Dairy Dell? Get out of here." Gino's was the best hoagie shop back in his mom's hometown. Mick hadn't been there in years, not since Gam and Pap died.

"Yes. Just think, I could've been the hoagie queen of Elk County." Mom leaned against the counter. "Gino was great, and we had a lot of fun together. But I really liked your dad a lot more. There was this little problem he had, though."

Mick got a plastic shopping bag from the drawer where his mom kept them and settled his foil-wrapped packages inside. "What was it?"

"Your father," Mom said, "never really figured out how to open his mouth and tell me how he felt about me."

Mick laughed. "Yeah? No kidding. Dad's never been a talker."

His mother shook her head, but as fondly as she had earlier. "No. He never has been. And you're like he is, Mickey, except that you got my dad's, your Pap's, golden tongue. So you talk a lot but you don't say the right things, do you?"

This stopped him. "Huh?"

"Do you like Alice?"

"Yeah. Of course I do. I like her a lot."

"Does she know that?"

"She ought to," Mick said.

"Do you tell her?"

Mick frowned. "Sure. I mean . . . well, I do stuff for her."

"Your dad was always doing stuff for me, too. Still does. The difference," Mom said, "is that now I know what it means when he rotates my tires."

"Are you saying I need to rotate Alice's tires? I just changed her oil."

Mom sighed and shook her head again with an expression Mick had long grown used to. "No. I'm saying that if you like her, you'd better tell her so, or else she might end up marrying a Gino."

"Mom, we're not even talking about getting married," Mick said uncomfortably.

His mother shook her head again, looking pained. "Of course you're not. You tell Alice I asked after her, though. You'll do that?"

"Sure, Mom." He had no idea why it mattered but if his mother wanted to send her regards, he'd be sure to pass them along.

At home, he busied himself catching up on all the stuff that went ignored while he was at Alice's. Laundry, bill paying, a few DVR'd shows he wanted to see before the next episodes came out. He fell asleep on the couch and by the time he woke up, it was close to 9:00 P.M. He'd missed a phone call and a video chat request from Alice.

She was probably in bed already. They'd been up until four this morning, doing things that twitched his dick at the memory, but it was a hollow arousal now. Dammit, Mick thought as he loaded the dishwasher and started it running and set the coffeemaker for the morning, he wanted her *here.*

Settling at his kitchen table with his laptop, he pinged her. The video chat program rang for so long he was sure she wasn't going to answer, but right before he was about to give up, the screen shifted from showing his whole face to putting him in a tiny box in the lower corner, with Alice full screen.

"Hey, gorgeous."

"Hi." She yawned. Her hair was wet, and she wore a thin tank top that clung to every curve.

Damn, he liked it when she wore that shirt. "You're in bed, huh?"

"Well," she said, wryly amused, "when you keep me up until it's almost sunrise . . ."

"I like it when you keep me up."

She made a face, but looked pleased. She settled back against her pillows. She must've been using her tablet, because the view shifted for a woozy, unsettling minute before she adjusted. At least, until everything went dark.

"Oops," she said as she came back into view. "Gotta prop you up."

Mick made a little *whoop-whoop* and pushed upward with his hands. "Prop me up, prop prop me up."

Alice burst into laughter, then gave him a lingering look with an expression he couldn't quite interpret. "You make me laugh so much, Mick. I love that about you."

He feigned peeking down her shirt. "Lean forward a little bit."

She did, giving him a full view of her cleavage. When she sat back, her nipples erect and clearly visible through the thin fabric, heat twisted in his belly. It blazed in her eyes, too.

All at once, his longing was enormous and indescribable. He'd almost left her sleeping this morning without a kiss good-bye because he hadn't wanted to wake her, but now he wished he'd kissed her ten times. He hadn't known how much he would miss her tonight until he hadn't seen her all day.

"I want you so much right now," Mick said suddenly.

Alice shifted again to let the thin strap of her tank top fall over her shoulder, exposing her even more. She made a little noise. "Mmmm hmmm."

He'd meant he wanted her to be there with him. In his kitchen, making a bedtime cup of tea. In his bed, leaving her scent all over his pillows. In his bathroom in the morning, with her stuff taking up all the room on the countertop.

But he'd never turn down that view, either.

"So fucking gorgeous," he breathed as she cupped her breasts and thumbed her nipples even harder. "Take it off."

The soft, shivery sigh sent an answering shudder

through him. His jeans were getting tight, and he rubbed at the bulge as she gave him what he asked for. Last night, he'd tongued her nipples while she writhed and gasped, until she'd begged him to use his mouth between her legs.

"I love your tits," Mick said.

Alice's laugh skipped and cracked. "I love it when you talk dirty."

He loved that about her, and always had. Other women might balk at the use of "bad" language, but not his Alice. She might look like an ice princess, but she was all flames and fire.

"I want to watch you touch yourself for me," Mick said.

Alice grinned. "Are you going to give me the same thing?"

He was already taking the laptop into the living room, where he could sprawl on the couch and unbutton his jeans. Mere hours ago they'd been fucking like rabbits on Viagra, but it didn't matter. He wanted her as soon as he saw her. He would never get enough.

It didn't take long—they'd spent so much time on video chat they had their virtual lovemaking down to a science. He was coming all over his fist in a few minutes to the sight of her getting off, too. She'd cried out his name at the end, the surefire way to tip him over.

Breathing hard, Alice brought the table close to her lips so all he could see was her smiling mouth. "You make me so fucking crazy. You know that? Crazy insane."

"That's a good thing, right?" Mick leaned to grab some tissues from the box on the coffee table.

"I guess so. If you like being crazy," Alice said slowly.

He looked at her. "You look tired."

"I am."

"Go to sleep," he told her.

"Mick," she said. "I like you so much."

He winked at her. "That's because you're crazy."

Her smile faded, her expression going a little blank. "Yeah. I guess I am. Okay, I'm exhausted. I'm going to sleep. Night."

"Hey, Alice," Mick said before she could disconnect.

Alice sat back. "Hmmm?"

"I bought you a new faucet."

She looked confused. "For what?"

"The one in the kitchen is leaking. I can replace it for you." Mick leaned a little closer to the computer screen.

Alice blinked. "Sure. Okay. That would be great."

"And I was thinking, next weekend, I could take your car to get the tires rotated." Surely that, he thought, would let her know what he felt.

"Sure . . . if you want to." She gave him a curious look. "Anything else?"

"Do you need anything else?"

She shook her head. "No. I guess I don't."

"'Night, Alice," he told her, and then the screen went dark.

Mick to Alice

I fixed your faucet.
—Mick to Alice

Chapter 42

Long summer days led to dark summer nights. If she had to pick a favorite season, Alice would've chosen autumn, after the summer's heat had faded and before winter's frigid snows. Sweater weather, that's what Alice liked, but today was more like "strip yourself down to skin and then to bone, if you can" kind of weather.

It reminded her of the summer she and Mick had met. Scorching in more ways than one. The blazing temperatures that had peaked at noon dropped so slowly after that it had made little difference. It was like being baked in a pizza oven, waves of rolling, shimmering heat making the cars in the parking lot shimmer. In the five minutes it took to get her from her car to the door of the restaurant, Alice thought she might pass out.

Inside the restaurant she went to the hostess stand to see if Mick had already arrived. He hadn't, of course, which gave her mouth a sour twist. Irrational to be annoyed and she knew it, because he'd likely been stuck in traffic, which was always worse coming from his direction this time of day. Still, when fifteen minutes passed while she waited on a sticky vinyl seat with sweat dripping down her spine, it got harder and harder not to let it get to her. She fanned her face with a takeout menu, which did little good, and considered going to sit at the bar so she could at least get a glass of ice water before she melted.

He was always late.

Always.

"Last-minute Mick," she wanted to call him. Typically, she hadn't been able to pin him down to any specific plans for the weekend, though she'd asked him three times what he might want to do. This morning he'd called her unexpectedly after she'd already arrived at work. He'd asked her to meet him tonight for dinner, on a Tuesday, and it was such a rare occasion that she'd jumped at the chance even though it meant rearranging the plans she'd made to run some errands.

One of these days she was going to tell him no. Let him suffer. Except she knew she probably never would, because even though it made her crazy not to know what was going on, she'd never yet been able to pass up the opportunity to be with him, no matter how inconvenient or last minute.

Finally, he was there, pulling off his sunglasses as he came through the front doors and finding her at once. Grinning, he came to kiss her. "You're early."

Alice bit her tongue and kissed him instead of snapping at him. Too hot, too hungry. She was on her way to Crankytown on the Raging Bitch Express, and she knew it. "I'm not."

"You look great. Nice dress," Mick said as though he knew he needed to mollify her.

Or maybe, Alice told herself once they'd been seated at last, he really liked her dress. With a drink and a breadstick in her belly and more food on the way, her annoyance was rapidly fading, thank God. She didn't want to ruin the night by fighting. Not even if it meant being able to make up.

"What's that smile for?" Mick asked.

Alice touched her mouth for a second, unaware she'd been smiling. "Nothing. Just glad to be here with you."

"I was thinking, you want to go to the batting cages after this? Go-karts?" Mick dipped his breadstick into the small pool of olive oil he'd poured onto his bread plate and swirled it around before biting off the end of it.

Alice laughed. "Seriously?"

"Well . . . yeah." Mick paused, brow furrowed. He licked the oil from his lips, a gesture that normally would have snagged her gaze, but only made her wish he'd used a napkin now. "You don't like that?"

"I do like it. I love go-karts and I suck at batting, but I like it, sure. It's just that I'm totally not dressed for it tonight. And it's like, a million degrees outside."

"What's wrong with what you have on?" Mick looked perplexed, though he'd eyed her outfit up and down earlier and even said he'd liked it, so Alice couldn't begin to think why on earth he'd be confused. She drank to keep herself from making a snarky comment. Mick sat back in his seat. "Don't you have anything to change into?"

It was Alice's turn to look perplexed. "Not for go-karts. I have my gym bag, but I'm not wearing dirty shorts and a T-shirt out in public."

"Oh. Well. That sucks." Mick frowned. "Too bad. I thought it would be fun."

"It would have been fun. I wish I'd known sooner. Say, maybe this morning before I left for work, or last night, even better. Then I could've been prepared." Alice frowned, too.

Mick's mouth thinned further. "How was I supposed to know?"

"I don't know, Mick," she said snidely, "maybe you could've planned it?"

Fortunately, the server arrived with their food, preventing Alice from going into full-bore bitch mode. She cut into her steak with vehemence, though, stabbing a little too hard. She looked up to see Mick glaring.

"If you have something to say to me," he told her, "I wish you'd just say it instead of simmering about it."

Alice took a long, deep breath, ready to let fly . . . and then took another breath, instead. This was not worth an argument that would ruin their night. Let it go, she told herself. Let it go.

"I'm fine. Just starving." To prove her point she forked a bite of steak into her mouth and chewed.

It was good steak, too, and she didn't have to feign her appreciation. With more food in her stomach and another drink, too, it was much easier to relax. Mick had her laughing in minutes the way he almost always did, even when she didn't want to.

He watched her with shining eyes. "You have such a great laugh."

"Hee hee, ha ha, ho ho ho." Alice waved a hand.

"You do," Mick insisted. "I like it when I make you laugh."

"It's better than making me cry," Alice said.

She hadn't meant it to sound serious, but Mick took her hand. His thumb caressed the back of it. Then he pulled it closer and kissed her knuckles.

"I never want to make you cry, Alice."

Unexpected tears sparked behind her eyes. Damn emotions. Too many feels. He was so good at poking them out of her, even when he wasn't trying.

She squeezed his hand. "That's good to know."

She wanted to kiss him all over his face right then, her desire so strong it was as fierce and physical a hunger as any she'd ever had for food. He must've seen it on her face, because his expression shifted into something hungry, too. His thumb moved against her skin in steady, relentless circles.

"I have a better idea of what we can do after dinner," Alice said. "And the best part is, I don't need to change my clothes first."

She did need a shower, though, which she insisted on as soon as they got to her place. Not alone, though, she told him with a grin over her shoulder, as she kicked off her shoes and headed for the bathroom. Mick didn't waste a second.

"Cold!" he shouted when he stepped in.

"Crybaby." Alice adjusted the temperature from chilly to lukewarm and sighed with pleasure as she tipped her face into the spray. "It's too hot out for a hot shower."

"You're crazy," Mick muttered, stepped back out of the spray. "It's freezing!"

Alice laughed and turned to splash him a little, laughing again when he yelped. "C'mere. I'll warm you up."

"Now that's what I'm talking about." Mick let her pull him closer.

Belly to belly, thighs to thighs. Water sluiced over them both as she pushed on her toes to kiss his mouth. His hands smoothed over her slick skin. She moved against him, delighted at the rise of his cock between them.

"I love touching you," she told him.

Her hands moved down his back to the curve of his ass to cup it. She pressed him closer to her. His tongue slid inside her mouth as his hands buried in her hair, and when he moved to nibble at her jaw and throat, Alice broke out in gooseflesh that had nothing to do with the water temperature.

Mick gave an appreciative sigh and bent to take her erect nipple in his lips. He suckled gently, making her shiver again. His hands roamed her back and hips before grabbing her ass to grind her against him.

With a look over her shoulder, Mick found her washcloth and added some shower gel, making sure to suds the cloth before smoothing it over her body. Breasts, belly, legs, back. His fingers delved between her legs, and Alice gave a small, choking cry. He looked at her, his gaze steady and unrelenting as he slipped a finger inside her. Then another. His thumb pressed her clit.

Alice dug her fingernails into Mick's shoulders. "Oh . . ."

When he went to his knees in front of her, she let out another low cry. Mick pushed her gently to sit on the shower's molded seat. He spread her thighs and bent his head between them. His mouth found her clit with the same determination and ease his thumb had a few minutes before.

His hands kept her from sliding off the seat. His mouth worked on her flesh. Nibbling, teasing strokes of his lips and tongue. Every so often he'd shift to the side to let the water from the shower spatter onto her pussy—never hard or direct enough to send her over the edge. All she could do was shake, her muscles tensing and releasing. Pleasure building.

Mick went down on her like it was Judgment Day and the only way to get into heaven was by making her come.

With a moan, Alice gave herself over to the ecstasy. It lasted and lasted, and because she hadn't turned the water very hot, it was a long time before it started to run cold. By that time she was wrung out from mini-climaxes, until finally Mick stopped teasing her. The flat of his tongue worked on her clit, and he slipped two fingers inside her to curl upward.

Alice came so hard she wouldn't have been surprised if the world really had ended. The final orgasm left her spent and shuddering. Mick eased his fingers free of her clutching pussy and kissed her clit. Then her belly. Finally, her mouth.

"It's freaking cold in here," he said. "Can we please get out now?"

Alice to Mick

I was always that kid who touched the hot stove just to make sure it would still burn me, even if I'd already blistered my fingers on it a bunch of times before. A lesson learned easily isn't learned well, that's what my dad always said, and I guess I took him to heart. Somewhere along the way, though, I figured out what my dad really meant by that. It wasn't that you should keep touching that hot stove to prove that it's still going to burn you. What he meant was that it's easy to keep on touching that stove because it's always going to remind you that it burns; what's much harder is reminding yourself that you don't need proof if you've already learned your lesson.

—Alice to Mick, unsent

Chapter 43

"Here, honey, get warmed up," Alice said sympathetically as she handed him a thick terrycloth robe and used a towel to wrap around her hair.

He hadn't minded the cool water so much when he was on his knees in front of her, his mouth on her heated flesh, but toward the end the spray had become frigid. Like needles. His back still stung from it, but drying off now, all he could do was grin.

"That's a self-satisfied smile," Alice noted.

Mick took the towel she handed him to scrub dry his hair. "I love making you come."

"Mmmm." She came up behind him, still naked, and slipped a hand into the folds of the robe. "I like it when you make me come."

Her fingers found his half-hard cock, and she murmured in delight as she moved around to his front. It took only a stroke or two to get him erect again—eating her pussy in the shower had been sweetly torturous because he'd needed to keep both hands on her to make sure she didn't slip off the seat. He'd been unable to stroke himself at the same time.

Now Alice's fingertips found the slick, clear bead of pre-come and spread it around the head of his cock. Muscles in his belly and thighs tensed. His dick throbbed, then jerked in her hand when she let her fingertip smooth down the divot below the head.

Eyes never leaving his, Alice brought her finger to her lips and sucked it gently. The sight of her cleaning that slick fluid off her own skin made him almost finish right there—but Alice wasn't finished with him. Taking his cock in her hand and walking backward, she led him to her bedroom, smiling wickedly the entire time.

There she pushed him back onto the bed. The robe fell open. She climbed up next to him and, without warning, engulfed his cock in her mouth. All the way down to his belly, her lips brushing his skin. Her hand cupped his balls, stroking, before moving up to circle the shaft as she slid her mouth off him.

Perfect. Almost too good; he wasn't going to be able to hold out for long. When she shifted to put her pussy back on his mouth, her lips and tongue still working their magic on his cock, Mick groaned. The muffled noise of his pleasure against her pussy made her laugh, and though he was too far gone to do anything but moan, the sound of her glee pushed him harder to the edge.

He loved making her laugh, he loved making her come. He loved everything about this woman, he thought in that last incoherent moment before the only thing he could think about was exploding. He'd teased her forever before letting her finally orgasm, but Alice was kinder to him than that. She was going to finish him within minutes.

He wanted to make love to her, be inside her, but he couldn't make himself move. His tongue slid along her slick folds and found the hardness of her clit. She cried out when he flicked it—shit, he wanted to make her come again. He wanted her bucking and writhing and covering his face with her desire, but he didn't think he could last long enough to get her off again.

It was all over when she pressed a fingertip to his asshole, pressing just hard enough and surprising him into bucking upward inside her mouth. Every single thought left his brain except the single, repetitive beat of "yes, yes, yes." He cried out, incapable of words.

Alice moved off him a moment after that. At the loss of her he managed to feel a pang of regret that he'd been unable to make her come again. She turned, kissed his mouth and snuggled up next to him with a leg flung over his and her head nestled into the curve of his shoulder. He didn't feel so bad, then, when she gave a happy sigh and said, "Wow."

He dozed, vaguely aware of her getting out of bed and going into the bathroom. When she came back she turned off the light and turned on the ceiling fan, then pulled the sheet up over them. Her breathing slowed and softened.

When her phone rang, she was swift to answer it, cutting off the noise at the second ring. Mick checked the clock—barely eleven. He guessed the days of them partying until two in the morning before stumbling home to fuck had passed . . . and that didn't bother him at all. This was much better.

"No, it's okay," Alice said into the phone. "Are you okay? Is it your head?"

Her sister. She'd told him about how the car accident had left Wendy with intense and frequent migraines, but not much more than that. The accident was a sore subject, seeing as how it had partially led to the fighting that had ended them the first time around.

Alice laughed, so it didn't seem like there could've been an emergency. "No, I'm actually in bed, believe it or not. That's what happens when you get old, I guess. Yeah, that's what I was thinking, too, because Mom asked me about it. For the kids, right? Yeah. Yep. No, that's okay, I told her that one was fine. Yes. One block to the beach. Yeah, it'll be fun! Okay, talk to you later."

She disconnected and put her phone back on the nightstand, then snuggled back next to him with a yawn. She kissed his shoulder. He pressed his lips to her still-damp hair.

"Everything okay?"

"Yeah. My mom was sending my sister links for this house they're renting for the beach, and she wanted to make sure I was cool with sharing a bathroom with the kids. Usually Mom and Dad rent the same house, but this year we decided to get a little closer to the ocean. I guess she hadn't really paid attention a few months ago about the bathroom situation when they rented it. But it's no problem for me." Alice yawned again.

Mick shifted to relieve some of the pressure on his arm. "You're going to the beach?"

"Yeah, they get a place down in Rehoboth Beach every year over the Fourth." She sounded sleepy, but Mick was suddenly wide awake.

"The Fourth? Of July?"

Alice chuckled softly. "Um, yeah."

"As in, next week?"

She paused before answering, her tone cautious. "Yes."

"Well . . . shit, Alice." Mick sat up.

Alice sat, too. "What?"

"I thought you were going to go to Bernie and Cookie's house. I mean, we're all going. Jay's not going, I guess, because of Paul, but . . ."

"Yeah, I know." She didn't reach to turn the light on, and in the shadows all he could see were curves and silhouettes. "I told Bernie months ago I'd be going to my parents' for the Fourth. I've been going there with my family for the past five years."

Shit. Dammit. Mick turned on the lamp on his side of the bed. "Why didn't you tell me?"

"I guess it didn't occur to me. It's my family thing. I planned it long before you and I . . ." She hesitated. "Look, you've known for weeks, at least a month, about this Fourth of July thing. I know you have, because I got the invitation, too. You didn't say a word about it. If you had, I'd have told you that I already had plans, but you didn't say anything. I figured maybe you had plans, too."

"I did. Plans with you."

"Then maybe," Alice said icily, "you should have told me about them instead of assuming I could read your mind."

All his euphoria faded. "When were you going to tell me about this thing with your family?"

"I don't know, Mick. When were you going to ask me about going to Bernie's?" Alice said. Just that. Nothing else, though clearly by the way her mouth thinned, she had other words that wanted to come out.

Mick frowned. "I didn't know I had to ask. You never said anything about it."

She was pissed off. He knew it by the way she turned on her side, facing away from him, even though it wasn't her normal side of the bed. By the way she punched her pillow and shifted away when he dared to come an inch closer.

He hated it when she stewed.

He clicked off the light. On his back, he made sure not to touch her. He listened for the sound of her breathing to slow, meaning she'd fallen asleep, but all he heard was the soft huff of her breath, in and out. Ragged.

Alice sat up. Mick tensed. Bring it, he thought. Come on, then.

"Things really haven't changed. Have they?"

Mick sat, but didn't turn on the light. Somehow this seemed like a conversation better held in darkness. He wished he could get up and find his briefs, but something told him it was wiser to stay put.

"Of course they've changed, Alice."

"No." She shook her head. "Not really. You still want to slide through this thing like it's some kind of game. What, do you get bonus points for fitting the pieces together all last second, like Tetris or something?"

"What the hell does that mean?"

Alice cleared her throat. "It means that unless I specifically lay out what we're going to do, we never make plans. I never know what, exactly, is going on. Sometimes I swear you have conversations in your head where you tell me things and then you act like I should just know them, but I have no clue what you're talking about!"

"Like what?" he demanded.

"Like last week, when you said, out of the blue, Mary had finally decided to go back to school and she was going to quit working to do it, and her husband was being an ass about it."

Mick paused. ". . . Yeah?"

"You said it to me like I had any idea that your sister had ever been considering going back to school. But here's the thing, Mick, it was the first time you'd mentioned it. I've met your sister like, three times. I don't know what's going on in her life."

"But I told you about it. So then you knew."

Alice sighed. "Yeah, but then there was the time you

called me to find out why I was late, and I had no idea you'd meant the CinemaEight instead of the Cinema-Center we usually go to."

"Why would you have assumed it wasn't? It's the one closest to you." He remembered that conversation. She'd been mad then, too. "What difference does it make, you got to the movie on time."

"It's not the one closest to where I work. And yes, I made it on time, but that's not the point."

"What is the point, Alice?" Mick cried, frustrated.

She sighed again and was silent for a few seconds. "For you, this is fun. That's all. Right? So it doesn't much matter where we go or do, it's all just . . . fun."

"It should be fun. Shouldn't it?" He took a chance and moved closer to her. He didn't touch her, but he was close enough to see her in the dark. "I'm not sure what the problem is. What's wrong with fun?"

"There's nothing wrong with fun," she said in a defeated, helpless tone he didn't understand at all. "Fun is great. Fun is fun."

He tried again to hug her, and this time, she let him. Her body didn't mold itself to his the way it usually did, but after a second or so she did put her arms around him. Mick buried his face in her hair, breathing deep. When her shoulders heaved, his heart sank.

"I don't want to make you cry, Alice. I'm sorry."

She didn't answer him with words, but the shaking of her body told him more than he wanted to know. Mick held her closer, and again, she let him but it wasn't the way it had been before. He pushed her gently away, gripping her upper arms, and tried to see her face through the shadows.

"Don't cry. Please."

She drew in a snuffling breath. "I'm okay."

"You're not. C'mon, I don't want to fight," he said.

"No. Me neither."

"That's no fun," he continued, trying to make a joke, to make light. Anything to keep this from going south.

Her chuckle was halfhearted and waterlogged and a little strangled. "Right. Fun. This all should just be fun. Only fun."

It didn't sound like she was agreeing with him, but he took it. "Yep. All fun, all the time. Okay?"

"Sure," Alice said. "All of this is just fun."

And then she hugged him hard enough to make him believe things were going to be all right.

Mick to Alice

Have fun at the beach without me. I'm going to miss you. You should have told me you had other plans, I would have changed mine.

—Mick to Alice, unsent

Chapter 44

Perfect beach weather. Sunny, bright, warm enough to make running into the still-chilly Atlantic waters worth-while, but not hot enough to make you wish you were in hell, where it would be cooler. With a book and a beach towel and a new bikini, Alice was all set.

The only thing missing, of course, was Mick.

She'd met his family a few times, but he'd never met hers, so inviting him along on this vacation, no matter how sexy the prospect, had not been an option. The last place she wanted to introduce him to her parents was in the house where they'd have to be sharing a bed. And it was nice, too, to have time to herself to sit and relax and read and read and read. With Mick along, she'd have been go-karting and paddle boarding and body surfing, she was sure of it.

There were advantages to time apart in a relationship. Ten years ago, Alice hadn't known that and probably wouldn't have believed anyone who'd tried to tell her so. She'd been convinced that being with the person you loved was necessary, like breathing, and being away from each other meant you ached and bled and gnashed your teeth. Well, she was older now, and if she wasn't wiser, at least she was a little more self-aware.

Her time at the beach was something she looked forward to every year and built her vacation time around. She'd never taken a boyfriend along. Either she hadn't had one or whatever relationship she'd been in at the time hadn't been the sort you brought around your family.

Which sort, she wondered, was Mick?

They hadn't tossed around the words boyfriend and girlfriend. Maybe at thirty-three it was silly to label whatever they were doing that way. Or maybe they weren't serious enough to be giving each other titles, she reminded herself. Maybe, she thought, they were just having *fun*.

She should let it go, Alice told herself and took a long drink of lemonade to wash out the bitterness. She turned her face to the sun to soak in the golden glory. She was on vacation, dammit, and she wasn't going to spoil it with any kind of angst and woe. Beside, didn't she know better now than to expect more from Mick than whatever he had to offer. Hadn't she learned her lesson about getting all worked up about something that didn't have to be such a big deal?

It wasn't as though she'd never had a fuck buddy before. A casual lover. Friends with benefits. Oh, since Mick there'd been one or two serious relationships, one that had seemed destined for a white dress and a walk down the aisle, but it hadn't worked out. And because there was a curse to being self-aware, Alice had to admit it was because that although Brad had been a great guy who treated her well and they'd had a lot in common, when it came to fireworks it might as well have been rain every Fourth of July.

With Mick, it had always been fireworks.

Things had been strained between them since the fight about her trip to the beach. Nothing she could point out specifically, but a pervasive tension that left every conversation tasting slightly sour. They'd spent the night together before she'd left for Rehoboth. Dinner. A movie. He'd put air in all her tires and filled her car with gas and changed all the fluids, though she'd told him that she was only driving to Wendy's house and would make the rest of the trip with her and Raj and the kids. He'd insisted on doing it anyway, as well as updating her GPS even though it took forever and she would far rather have spent the time with him doing something more . . . fun.

They'd had sex, of course. And it had been good. Better than that, amazing, really. Mick had spent an hour getting her off, three times before she'd begged him for a break. They'd slept tangled together and woke before dawn to make love again.

When it came time for her to leave, Alice had kissed his mouth and clung to him, squeezing hard. "I'm going to miss you so much."

"Nah," Mick said. "You're going to be having too much fun. Me, too, at the lake. Before you know it, we'll both be home."

It was not the reply she'd hoped for, though she'd be damned if she told him that. It shouldn't grate at her, but it did. So much, in fact, that she'd turned off her ringer this morning and left her phone in a drawer instead of taking it with her. Too bad she couldn't turn off her brain.

Not even the sun could burn away the images of Mick in Alice's mind. The salt breeze tickling the fringes on her bikini top reminded her of his questing fingers and oh, God, his tongue. The splash of chilly water on her thighs when she got up to test the water wasn't any better. If anything, it only exacerbated the feeling of not having been touched by Mick in three long days.

"I'm going to walk up to the boardwalk and get some fries. Wanna come along?" Alice asked Wendy, who'd spent an hour or so in the water, body surfing waves with the kids.

"Hell, yes. And I think we need a beer. Or two." Dripping and slightly sunburned, Wendy gave her husband a significant look. "Hold down the fort, it's sister-bonding time."

"Can I come, Mama?"

Wendy gave Mallory a fond look and tweaked her nose. "Nope, kiddo. Me and Auntie Alice are going to eat bad food, drink some grown-up drinks, and check out the cute lifeguards."

Mallory made a face. "Okay. Gross."

"Bring me back some fries, babe," Raj said as Wendy leaned to give him a kiss. "Before you run off with a lifeguard, anyway."

Wendy laughed. "Sure thing, ding-a-ling."

Watching her sister bend to kiss her husband of nine years, Alice, for the first time, felt a pang of envy at her sister's life. Sure, Wendy and Raj had their share of arguments, but her brother-in-law clearly adored his wife. And told her so, never making her have to guess, Alice thought, barely managing not to slice herself open on her own jealousy.

"I'm glad you married Raj."

Wendy gave her a glance as they navigated the steps from the sand onto the boardwalk. "Me too, most days. But I'm glad to hear you are, too."

"He's a good guy," Alice said.

"Yes. I got lucky. Hey, I'm starving," Wendy said, pointing at a sign on one of the many restaurants lining the boardwalk. "And I think instead of a beer I'm going to have a frozen margarita. Because apparently, that's what ladies do."

"Ladies love frozen drinks." Alice read the sign aloud and laughed. "Well, I do, and I guess I'm a lady. Let's do it."

Instead of fries, they ordered a plate of nachos and some margaritas and sat under a pretty umbrella with the ocean air cooling them. People watching. Hanging out. Relaxing.

"So," Wendy said when the conversation had gone from the style of bathing suits some people really shouldn't wear to the hazards and joys of day drinking to whether or not their parents were going to insist they all go out to dinner at some crowded restaurant instead of grilling in the rented house's backyard and how they could convince them otherwise. "What's up?"

Alice sipped carefully and licked her lips, tasting salt. The flavor was too much like tears, dammit. She should've ordered something sweet, not tangy. "I think it's over with Mick."

"Why, did he stop answering your texts and stuff again? What a jerk."

Alice grimaced, appreciating her sister's outrage, though Wendy was off-base. "No. He answers my texts, at least he does that. We had a fight about me coming here. He thought I'd be going to Bernie's, but he didn't even ask me."

"You could've asked him to come along with us."

Alice shook her head. "Ugh. No. Not so last minute, and besides, it would've been super awkward for him to meet Mom and Dad here."

"Yeah. I guess so." Wendy swirled the melting

margarita in her glass. "How bad was the fight? I mean, bad enough to break up with him?"

"Not because of the fight, though it's pretty typical of the way he assumes things." Alice frowned. "I told him I was going to miss him, and once again, he gave me some lame-ass answer about how we'd both be having too much fun to miss each other. And I thought . . . really? After all this time, he still can't just tell me something so simple? It's stupid."

Wendy was silent for a few seconds. "It's not stupid if it makes you feel bad. Have you told him?"

"Yes. Of course I have. At least, I think I have." Alice shook her head. "I feel like I tell him all the time, and he doesn't listen. Or get it. Or maybe I'm not being clear, shit, I don't know anymore. All I know is that he says he wants me. But it's not enough, you know? Wanting. I want a lot of things, that doesn't mean I'm meant to have them."

"Ugh." Wendy rolled her eyes.

"I told myself I could just do the 'fun' thing. That it didn't have to mean more, or become more. But it's always been more with him, that's the problem." Alice paused. "I was doing okay, you know? Without him. I thought about him sometimes, sure, but then he swept back in my life and I'm on some kind of magic-cock carpet ride!"

For a moment, neither sister said a word. Then they both burst into hysterical laughter. Better that than hysterical tears, Alice thought. Shit.

Alice finished her margarita and let the frozen liquid settle in her belly. "He's never, ever going to give me what I want, Wendy. He's just . . . not. Maybe he can't. All I know is that he says he wants me, but he won't tell me he misses me. And he does not love me."

They both were silent for a minute. Wendy stirred her

drink, looking sad but saying nothing. Alice appreciated the silence.

"Have you asked him?" Wendy said finally. "If he loves you, I mean."

"I asked him once to tell me how he felt about me," Alice said flatly. "And he said that he loved me *on some level.* I will *never* ask him again."

"I remember," Wendy said quietly.

"I never want to go through that again. Ever. It was horrifying."

"I don't blame you."

"And now it would be worse than the first time around, because see, I already know how it felt when it ended. How the whole world turned gray. How losing him destroyed me. And I won't be that girl again, Wendy. I can't. It was too much. I can't invest myself in someone else that much again, and especially not Mick."

Alice was quiet. Wendy frowned. Alice shrugged.

"You should tell him you love him, Alice. See what he says. At least give him a chance. Then if it ends, at least you said it, and maybe . . ." Wendy cleared her throat and sat up a little bit. "Maybe it won't take you ten years to get over him. Maybe this time you could just move on."

Alice gave her sister a look of horror that hardly had to be exaggerated. "He might be shit with telling me how he feels about me, but maybe he's got the right idea about not saying anything. I don't need to make a fool out of myself over Mick McManus again."

"But . . . you do. Don't you? Love him," Wendy said.

Alice again stayed quiet. Her throat closed. Her eyes burned.

"You should tell him, Alice. Maybe he'll surprise you. And if he doesn't . . . at least you'd know for sure. You wouldn't have to wonder."

"I was stupid, wasn't I? To think that just because time had passed that it would be different this time?"

"You weren't stupid, honey. You're in love. Okay, maybe that's the same thing," Wendy said with a small laugh.

Alice shook her head. "But I don't want to be!"

"Guess what," Wendy said. "You don't have a choice. It just happens to you, and you can't do anything about it."

"I do have a choice. I can stop seeing him. End it before it's too late."

"That's not going to make you feel better, Alice!" Wendy looked sad. "You're crazy about him. You know you are."

"Yeah," Alice said bitterly, "and Mick is just having fun."

Alice to Mick

Knock Knock.

Who's there?

Nobody.

Nobody, who?

Silence

—Alice to Mick

Chapter 45

The party at Bernie's had been great, of course, lots of food and drinks and fun. But empty, for Mick at least. No Alice to sneak into his bedroom at night or greet him over coffee in the morning.

No Alice for the whole week after, either, while she was at the beach. He'd texted her several times throughout the weekend, but got no answer. He'd called and left a few messages, but with no answer to those, he'd stopped. For the first time, Mick understood why, exactly, Alice got so bent out of shape when he didn't reply to her right away. Still, the longer it went on, the more deliberate it felt, and the more irritated he got. Sure, he might've chosen to take his time responding to her messages in the past for one reason or another, and yeah, maybe once in a while he still didn't answer her immediately, but he'd never gone this long while deliberately ignoring her.

She was due home Saturday, but he didn't know what time, only that they'd have to check out of their rental house sometime in the morning. Add in summer traffic and he figured she'd be back by the afternoon. So when dinner time rolled around and he hadn't yet heard from her, Mick put on his big-boy briefs and called her again.

This time, she answered. "Hey."

"Hey! Are you home?" He didn't want to admit the feeling rushing through him was relief. That he'd started thinking maybe she simply was never going to answer him again, that it wouldn't be ten years without Alice this time, but the rest of his life.

She sounded tired. "Yeah. About an hour ago. Traffic was brutal. I rode with Wendy and her husband and kids, we stopped about a million times for the bathroom and to eat, just to break up the trip, but we were still in standstill traffic for hours. I'm wiped out. I took a shower and I'm heading for bed. So much stuff to do tomorrow before I go back to work."

"I want to see you," Mick blurted. Silence was his answer. He listened to her breathing. Certain she was going to say no, his stomach dropped.

He didn't like this, whatever was going on. Something felt off. Something wasn't right. But then she sighed.

"Sure. But you'll have to come over here. I'm not driving any more today."

"I'll be there in an hour," he promised, knowing the drive usually took at least an hour twenty.

She was quiet for a couple of seconds. "You could wait until tomorrow, Mick. It's only one more day."

"I can't wait another day to see you."

More silence. He imagined her smile, though could hear nothing of it in her voice. "Okay."

It did indeed take him only an hour to get to Alice's house. He'd brought along a bottle of wine, though it was probably too late now to drink it. A bag of chips and container of dip, because that was all he had in the kitchen. When she opened the door, all he could think about was kissing her, but instead he held out the bag.

"I brought this for you."

Alice smiled and let him in. She took the wine and peeked at the chips. "Are you hungry?"

He did kiss her then, thinking that was a better answer. She moaned when he touched her; when he dug his fingers into the hair at the back of her skull and tugged, her eyes went glazed and dreamy, and his cock got hard. He loved watching her get turned on by something so simple as his touch. No woman had ever responded to him that way.

He'd stopped wanting any other woman to.

"Upstairs," he breathed into her mouth. "Now."

Alice broke the kiss for a second, looking hesitant, but only for the second or two it took for her to lick her lips. She nodded and turned, looking over her shoulder with another inscrutable glance. Mick followed, already thinking of getting her out of the silky pj bottoms and tank top.

In her bedroom, Alice sat on the edge of the bed. Mick went to his knees in front of her. She let out a small, startled laugh.

He lifted one bare foot and held it tight so she couldn't squirm away. Making sure she was looking into his eyes, he kept her gaze as he kissed each toe. Then the other foot. By the time he was done, they were both breathing hard. Moving his hands up her legs and thighs, over the silky fabric, he found the heat of her center.

He had missed her so damned much that finally being with her was . . . overwhelming. Shit, it was strangling him, almost, this desire to make love to her. Not just that, but to make her feel good. To make her scream and moan and cry his name. To make her want him as much as he wanted her, which was all the time and in every way.

He kissed her through the fabric, first her thighs. Then the juncture between them. Her scent made him harder. He needed to taste her.

Mick hooked his fingers in the waistband of her bottoms and pulled them down. Still kneeling between her parted legs, he bent to kiss her bare flesh. Alice jerked at the touch of his tongue. At the press of his lips, she moaned. When he parted her to ease a finger inside her while he sucked gently on her clit, her hand found the top of his head.

It was too much effort to work his belt and zipper open while he made love to her with his mouth, sweet torture for his cock to press against the denim, and Mick couldn't decide which he wanted more. To make Alice come under his tongue or to get his cock in his fist while he did it.

Her pussy swelled under his kiss, the tight walls clutching at his finger when he stroked upward. She was already rolling her hips and pushing against him. Close. He could tell. Her taste flooded him, making his head spin. Urging him to moan her name, a command or a plea, he couldn't be sure, only that he wanted and needed to know he was making her feel good.

Her body tensed and twitched. She cried out, shaking. Her clit pulsed under his lips, and he eased the stroking as he slipped his finger free of her clutching flesh. With both hands free, he got himself undone, his cock leaping into his waiting fist for a few strokes before he sat back to look at her.

She wasn't looking at him. She lay back on the bed, one arm flung over her eyes. Her chest rose and fell rapidly with her breathing.

So fucking beautiful.

Mick shucked out of his jeans and briefs and T-shirt, tossing them to the side and crawling up over her. He slid his cock over her clit. Back and forth, teasing, until she moaned again. Alice opened her eyes and reached for him.

"Kiss me," she said.

He kissed her. Sweet, hard, tongues sliding. She moved her hips. She was so slick and wet he moved easily against her. And then, with a small and subtle shift of their bodies, unexpected, he was inside her.

He should hold out, he thought, but was helpless to stop. Not with her moving underneath him that way. Her fingers digging into his back. Her legs hooked behind his thighs, pushing him to fuck into her harder. Deeper. Faster.

He'd wanted this to last, this first time after more than a week without her. There was no drawing this out, no holding off. When Alice sank her teeth into his shoulder, Mick lost himself. Her body tensed around him, and he gave up trying to hold off. He was looking at her when he came, but Alice's eyes were closed.

He rolled off her, still breathing hard. Beside him, Alice was silent. She didn't roll to cuddle against him, so he turned his head.

"WHY?" Alice asked so softly he barely had to wake to mumble an answer.

"Why what?"

"Why couldn't you wait until tomorrow to see me?"

Mick smiled, half dreaming, and reached with one clumsy hand to pull her closer. When her warmth had pressed against him, he kissed her hair. "Because I wanted you."

"That's all?" Alice murmured. "You wanted me?"

Mick smiled again, nuzzling into her. Warm and sated and filled with her taste and scent and the general glory of being with her. "What more is there, other than wanting you?"

Mick to Alice

Let me paint my name upon your skin with my lips and teeth and hands and tongue, you won't regret the song we sing when we both come undone.

—Mick to Alice, unsent

Chapter 46

For once, Alice was up and about before Mick, who still snored lightly when she slipped out of bed. She had too much to do today to laze around. She had a week's worth of salty, sandy laundry to do. She had her cat to pay attention to, because Cleo would shit in Alice's shoes if she didn't. She had mail to sort through.

Yet here she sat at the kitchen table, doing none of it. She'd made coffee, but it wasn't quite right. Not as good as Mick would make it. She didn't have any food in the fridge to cook for breakfast, and no motivation to run out and get some. All she could manage to do was drink some now-tepid tea and try to think of how she was going to break up with him.

"Morning." Sleepy-eyed but with a wet head and fully dressed, looking too fucking scrumptious to stand, Mick bent to kiss her. "You're up early."

"Mick."

He paused in looking through her cupboards to glance over his shoulder. "Yeah, babe?"

The words rose up, choking her. Bitter. Sharp as glass. She coughed, but couldn't force herself to say them.

He was staring at her. "You okay?"

She was not okay. Anything but, as a matter of fact. But all she could do was nod.

"Hey, you wanna go out to a diner or something? You don't have anything to eat."

A diner. Oh, God. He wanted to take her to a diner, where they'd order eggs and hash browns and toast and coffee and maybe a pancake or maybe a whole stack, and he would hold her hand while they waited for their food and he'd hand her the cream and sugar without her having to ask because he knew how she liked her coffee, and he would give her the syrup first. He would tell her jokes and make her laugh and shake his leg up and down, rattling the silverware on the table, until she gave him a look that would make him stop. They would play tic-tac-toe on the backs of the menus.

And she would love him, Alice thought bleakly while Mick gave her a curious, confused stare. She would love him and want him and let him take her home and make love to her, any time he wanted. And she would miss him when they were not together, even if he never did.

She loved him, and there was no helping it or stopping it. She'd fallen into it deep. There was no climbing out.

Alice to Mick

You've known for a long time how I felt about you, and you just kept letting me. Just like I knew for a long time how you didn't feel about me, and I just kept letting you. So which one of us is to blame, in the end? I guess we both are, or we both are not, but either way, all I know is that I am totally and completely in love with you. I can't imagine the rest of my life without you in it. And yet all I see for us is good-bye.

—Alice to Mick, unsent

Chapter 47

"Hey," Mick said, sliding into the chair across from her to take her hand. His thumb stroked the back of it. "What's wrong, Alice? You're white as paper."

"Tired, I guess."

She sounded tired. Looked it, too. Maybe she was coming down with a post-vacation bug.

"We don't have to go out for breakfast. I can run to the store, grab some bagels." Concerned, he put a hand on her forehead to check for fever.

She leaned into his touch, her eyes closed. Her face was cool, though two bright spots of color had appeared high on her cheeks. She put her hand over his when he put it on her cheek.

She opened her eyes. "We can go to breakfast. Just let me take a shower, okay?"

"Yeah. Sure."

She hadn't convinced him she was fine. The opposite, in fact, because while normally Alice showered with the door wide open and sang show tunes, today she closed the door tight, and Mick swore he heard the muffled sound of sobs.

Shit.

Anxious, he made the bed while he waited for her to finish her shower. Noticing that her closet door had come off the track again, he tinkered with it until he got it to work. Pleased, he pointed to it when she came out of the bathroom, bundled in her robe with a towel on her hair.

"I fixed your closet door."

Alice glanced at it. "Thanks."

He demonstrated how smoothly it now opened and closed, watching her face for signs that she was happy. Or at least that she didn't look sick anymore. The circles under her eyes had faded a little, but her eyes were red-rimmed.

So she *had* been crying.

At the diner, she ordered eggs and toast. No pancakes, no potatoes. She sipped at coffee and gave him a weak smile when he tried to joke with her. But when he tried to take her hand across the table, she didn't let him.

His stomach sinking, Mick didn't have much of an appetite. Neither of them did, apparently, because when the waitress came with the check, she had to take away a bunch of plates that were mostly still full. He paid the check and left an extra-large tip, like that would make him feel better. It didn't.

In the car, Alice stared out the window in silence as he drove. The radio played one song after the other, none of which he knew the words to, but while normally he'd have made some up to make her laugh, now he stayed silent. The drive back to Alice's house took only a few minutes, but it felt like hours.

In her driveway, he didn't move to get out of the car. He twisted in his seat to look at her. "You sure you're okay?"

"I'm fine."

"You don't look fine."

She gave him a smile that looked like a lie. "Too much vacation, I guess."

They sat in silence, staring, and for the first time since they got back together, Mick wasn't sure he knew what to say to her. He wanted to reach for her hand, but didn't.

"I guess I'll get going, then," he said, hoping she'd ask him to come inside with her.

"Sure," Alice said with a fake smile that didn't reach her eyes.

When he moved to kiss her, she turned her head just enough so that his lips caught the corner of her mouth. They stayed that way for a few seconds. Then she pulled away.

She looked at him, expression inscrutable. She touched his face, traced his eyebrows with a fingertip. His chin. She kissed him, then, fully on the mouth, soft and sweet.

Then she got out of the car and went inside the house.

Mick to Alice

Alice. Answer the door. I'm not leaving until you talk to me.
—Mick to Alice, text

Chapter 48

What more is there, other than wanting you?

Alice couldn't decide if that were better or worse than Mick loving her "on some level," which she'd previously thought to be possibly the most horrifically disappointing and gut-wrenching thing anyone had ever said to her. She thought that love on any level had to be better than there being nothing more than wanting. Either way, once again she'd asked and once more she'd been given an answer.

She'd cried herself sick in the shower this morning, but she wasn't going to do that now. She wasn't sure what she was going to do. But it wasn't that.

What she'd said to her sister still felt true. Mick was never going feel about her the way she felt about him. The question was, what was Alice going to do about it.

For now, she thought, she was going to finish unpacking and doing her laundry. The rest would come later, because that was how life worked. Shit happened. You got through it. Sometimes it was easy, sometimes it was hard, she thought grimly, but one way or another, you did it.

She hadn't noticed her phone's buzzing until she came

out of the laundry room and found it on the kitchen table. Several missed texts from Mick. A call that had come in only a minute or so ago. Before she could even listen to the voice mail, her doorbell rang.

She knew it was him before she opened the door. Talk about déjà vu. What she had not expected was the look of despair on Mick's face when he came through the doorway.

"What's going on?" he demanded. "Is there someone else?"

"What?" Shocked, Alice took a step back, then another. He followed her into the kitchen, where she drew a glass of water to help calm her stomach.

"What's his name. Bob? Bill? That asshole you were seeing when we got back together. Is it him?"

A flash of guilt poked her, but Alice hadn't done more than exchange a few texts with Bill in months. The guilt lasted only seconds, replaced by a thin anger. "What the hell are you talking about? There is nobody else!"

Mick, breathing hard, a little wild-eyed, ran a hand through his hair and whirled on her. "Then what the hell is going on with you?"

"You. You're what's going on with me." The words popped out of her before she could stop them, but once they were out, she didn't even want to take them back.

Mick visibly deflated. ". . . What? What are you talking about?"

"This isn't working, Mick."

There. She'd said it. Out loud, to him, no taking it back. Just as she'd hopped on a train months ago at Bernie's house, now Alice was once more taking a ride. Only this time it was no slow-moving locomotive but the bullet train, no stops. Only one destination.

End of the line.

"I don't understand," he said.

Alice swallowed hard and shook her head. "Some things just don't work. Us. This. Second chances. Things don't change—"

"Everything's changed." He threw out his hands, then curled them into helpless fists. "I answer your calls and your texts. I'm there for you when you need me, I would never leave you sitting the way I did that other time. And I never blamed you for hating me over that, Alice, believe me, I know what an asshole I was, but even murder has a statute of limitations. How much more do I have to prove to you that things are different?"

"But they're not," Alice said, voice hard. "Not really."

"How can you say that? I've done everything for you. Everything." To her horror, his breath hitched. Mick sank into a kitchen chair and put his head in his hands for a second before giving her a look of naked confusion. "What more do you need from me?"

She blinked at him, not sure if she should be furious or desperate or numb. "What do you mean, everything?"

"I try to take care of you," Mick said in a low voice. "The best way I can. Obviously, it's not enough for you, and if that's the case, I don't know what more I can do."

She thought of coffee made the way she liked it. Of the closet door he'd fixed. Faucet he'd repaired. Tires, rotated. Alice forced away a sob, thinking of the myriad ways Mick had taken care of her. Of all the things he'd done . . . but all the things he'd never said.

Before she could say anything, Mick stood. "I showed up at your door and told you that I love you and I want to be with you, that I'd do anything to prove it—"

Finally, at this, she lost it. "Love me? You showed up at my door, all right, but you didn't say you *loved* me. You said you wanted me. 'I *want* you more than I've ever wanted any woman, Alice.' That's what you said. And whenever I asked you about us, you said . . . you said it was fun. Over and over again, just fun." Her breath hitched and choked. "So you're going to blame me for thinking that meant you just wanted to fuck me?"

"I love you!" Mick's shout echoed through the kitchen. He took a step toward her, eyes blazing, fists clenched. "I might only have said I wanted you, but I *meant* I love you!"

"On some level, right?" Alice sneered. Furious. Broken yet again by his words. She put the glass carefully in the sink even though she wanted very much to shatter it on the floor at his feet. To cut him the way he'd cut her.

"No, Alice. Not on some level. I love you." Mick shook his head and stepped closer to take her by the upper arms.

No longer shouting. No longer furious. Mick looked broken, too, and though she did not want to soften toward him, she did.

"Then you should have told me that in the first place, instead of assuming I knew." Her voice cracked, thick with tears.

Mick winced. "I thought I did. I mean, I thought everything I did was enough so that you'd know."

"Well, it wasn't. I don't read minds." Still angry, but now also aching, Alice shrugged out of his grasp. The sink behind her was too close for her to back up a step, so she went still, instead.

"I'm sorry." He didn't touch her, but the way he moved told her that he wanted to.

Alice looked him in the eyes. "You never said it. You never even *wrote* it. You said you wanted me, and I figured that would be enough. I figured it would be whatever it was. Just fun, the way you told me before. And I hoped . , , I mean, I wished, I wanted, but I couldn't let myself believe it, Mick. I didn't want to end up where I was ten years ago, curled up in a ball on the floor of my shower and sobbing my eyes out every night for the sake of wanting you. It was agony then, and it would be even more so, now."

"I never want to hurt you," Mick told her. "Ever. I'm so sorry, Alice."

Hesitantly, he pulled her close until her cheek rested on his chest. Beneath her cheek, his heart thumped in the swift but steady rhythm that had become so agonizingly familiar to her all over again. And though she didn't want to, Alice gave in to the comfort of Mick's touch. His warmth. The slow stroke of his hand down her back. And finally, his kiss.

"I love you," Mick said against her mouth. "I'm sorry I didn't say it before. I'm sorry I made you think it wasn't real, or it was only fun, or whatever it was. I'm an asshole. Forgive me."

She pushed away to look him in the eyes. "I love you, too."

"Forgive me," he asked again.

Did she have a choice? This man had been in her heart for a decade. He'd drained her dry, but he'd filled her up, too. She could live without him, if she had to, but there was no doubt in Alice's mind that without her Mick, her life was an infinitely darker place.

"Kiss me," she told him. "And take me upstairs. And love me, Mick."

"I do," he told her. "I might not always say it in the way you want me to, Alice, but I promise you, I'll always mean it."

And that was enough, she thought as the press of his lips on hers took her breath away once more, the way it always did. Always would. Finally, this love was enough.

Playlist

I could write without music, but I'm so glad I don't have to. Below is a partial playlist of the songs I listened to while writing Perfectly Reckless. Please support the artists by purchasing their music.

What Am I To You? — Norah Jones
If You Want Me — One Less Reason
From Can to Can't — Corey Taylor, Dave Grohl, Rick Nielsen & Scott Reeder
Last Love Song — ZZ Ward
Bet U Wish U Had Me Back — Halestorm
Pardon Me — Staind
Mercy — Brett Young
Without Me — Halsey
Watch — Billie Eilish

Hurt the One You Love

EXCERPT

She had no idea how stuff like that party worked, Simone would be the first to admit. Political wheelings and dealings. Currying favor. But one thing she did know was how to talk to people like they were important when they weren't, and like they were no big deal when they were. It had been her experience that a lot of people who were used to being ass-kissed kind of liked it when someone didn't treat them like they were made of spun sugar, ready to melt if you blew on them.

"How come you hate parties?" she said in the cab Elliott had flagged for them. He'd said nothing to her in the past ten minutes while they waited for the ride.

"Who says I hate parties?"

"Barry."

Elliott looked at her, finally. "Barry talks too much. I don't hate parties. I mostly just get bored, that's all. Everyone trying to impress everyone else. Like your friend from Louisiana."

"I just met the guy tonight. He's hardly a friend."

"He invited you to his party next time he's in town," Elliott said darkly.

She let her hand rest on his knee, squeezing gently. "He invited both of us. Don't worry. I'll go with you. Even if you are sort of an intolerable date."

Beneath her hand, the muscles went tight, bunching. He didn't take her hand and throw it off him, but there was no doubt from the look on his face that he was considering it. She took it away. She didn't need to chase.

They said nothing else after that. When they pulled up in front of her building, she squeezed his knee again. "Walk me upstairs."

Elliott sighed, but didn't protest. Simone couldn't stop herself from smiling, not that she let him see her, as she led him to the elevator. She was giving him a hard time about being a pain in the ass, which was true. He totally was. But she'd been on worse dates, with bigger assholes than Elliott Anderson, and the fact was that his terse attitude intrigued her more than it made her mad. Oh, yeah, he'd been a little brusque tonight. Impolite, though immediately recognizing it when she'd pointed it out. Acknowledging it, if not contritely at least sincerely. She was having a helluva time figuring him out.

She liked that.

Maybe that made her kind of sick, but that wasn't anything she didn't already know about herself. She'd always been drawn to arrogant men, the ones who thought they knew best. Those were the ones who could give her what she craved. The problem with men like that was they were also the ones who felt like they had the right to tell her what to do.

Elliott was different. She'd known that for a while, watching him bring the parade of blondes into his office.

Fucking them on his desk, sometimes without so much as a kiss beforehand. The way his hands always found their way into their hair, pulling. The roughness with which he handled them. But she'd watched him do other things in that office, too, things that had told her a lot more about his personality even than the way he fucked.

She'd seen him clean his desk phone with an antiseptic wipe and eat Chinese food from a container with chopsticks he pulled from a wooden case out of his desk drawer. She'd watched him bent over his computer, scowling, and she'd watched him with his cell phone pressed to his ear, face alight with laughter. She'd seen him working and playing. It was kind of creepy, actually, how much she knew about him from watching him after hours. What would happen if he knew everything she knew about him, she thought as she pushed the fourth-floor button and watched him lean against the interior elevator railing across from her.

"I'm at the end of the hall."

"Of course you are," Elliott said in a half-weary voice, though he followed her. "I guess you expect me to make sure you get inside okay, too."

"Yes." Simone bit back another smile.

"Do you want me to go inside with you?" He asked as she fit her key into the lock and pushed open the heavy wooden door. "Make sure there's no serial killer lurking behind the shower curtain, that sort of thing?"

He might be a pain in the ass, but that dry sense of humor was the cherry on top of the panty-dampening cake. Simone turned to face him as he came through the doorway behind her. She tossed her keys into the small bowl on the table by the door.

"I don't have a shower curtain. But tell you what," she

said, "since you came all this way, you could kiss me good night."

He'd been looking around her apartment when she said that, blatantly assessing everything from her couch to the art on her walls, and at this, his head swung slowly toward her. "Kiss. You?"

"It might surprise you to realize this," Simone said, annoyed and amused and also a little aroused, "but I don't usually have to even ask."

"No. I don't suppose you do."

The way he said it gave her a little shiver from the base of her neck all the way down her spine, where it lodged. Simone didn't move closer to him. He didn't move closer to her.

For a long few seconds she thought he wasn't actually going to kiss her, and she would have to make the first move, because there was no way in hell she was going to let him out of here without at least tasting his mouth, just once. But then she didn't have to worry, because Elliott reached for her, his fingers brushing her sleeve, then closing on her wrist.

It still ached a little from his earlier grip. More a memory of the small pain he'd inflicted than any real discomfort, but her heart skipped a beat anyway. Her nipples tightened. The shiver that had traveled down her spine now spread outward, turning electric, sending heat through her belly and between her legs.

"Come here," Elliott said.

It was never the commands that got her hot, but the promise of what might happen should she disobey. Frankly, Simone could take or leave being bossed around. Mostly leave it. But the threat of discipline, of punishment, of pain . . . that set her on fire. She let him pull her closer, step by step, as though she were hesitant when they both knew she was anything but.

In the last moment, Elliott snapped her against him in a swift movement that made her stumble, but his grip on her wrist kept her from falling. She put both hands flat on his chest. In these heels she still wasn't quite tall enough to look him in the eye, but she didn't have to crane her neck to get her mouth close to his. Elliott's free hand slipped behind her neck to cup the base of her skull, and everything inside her went liquid. Melting. She gave him her mouth, but he didn't take it.

His fingers tightened in her hair. She'd worn her hair short forever, finding it more flattering and easier to take care of, but one thing she missed about having long hair was having it pulled. Somehow, Elliott had found the perfect way to tug it, short or not. The brief pain in her scalp went right between her legs. Electric.

Her lips parted. She murmured his name. He pulled her closer, his other hand leaving her wrist to cup her ass and grind her against him.

Finally, his lips brushed hers. Soft, soft, barely a kiss at all. More like the shadow of a kiss. A murmur. At least until she opened her mouth, giving him her tongue.

At the touch of it, Elliott groaned. His grip tightened in her hair and on her ass. Pinching. He ground his mouth on her. His cock rose between them, the heat and solid length of it on her belly sending another series of shivers through her.

A moan slipped out of her. Another when his fingers dug deep into her flesh and his tongue stroked hers. At the nip of his teeth on the corner of her mouth, Simone cried out.

Elliott moved back from her, blinking. If he'd let her

go, she surely would've fallen, but he still held her tight enough to keep her steady. At least for a few seconds, and then his grip loosened.

"That was lovely," Simone said, a little dazed. "Do it again."

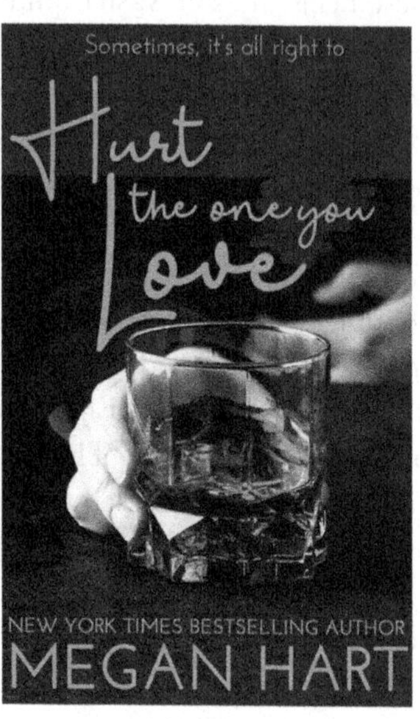

Sometimes, it's all right to
Hurt
the one you
Love
NEW YORK TIMES BESTSELLING AUTHOR
MEGAN HART

Perfectly Reckless

EXCERPT

"It shouldn't matter when I fell in love with you. Or how. All that matters is that I did." Even as Maura spoke, she knew her words wouldn't matter. She could see it in the cut of Ian's gaze from hers, the way he covered his mouth with his palm, the fingers curving over his cheek toward his ear. She knew nothing she said would make a difference, but she said it all anyway. "I am crazy in love with you, Ian. I didn't look for it, but there it is. And I don't regret it. Not a single second."

Maura paused, leaning forward across the table, smiling and hoping to urge him to return it. "Well. This part's not so great. But all the rest…"

He didn't smile, but he did look at her. At least he gave her that. "Maybe you shouldn't set yourself up to get disappointed."

Maura flinched, helpless against that blunt sting. Frowning, she warmed her hands on the mug of coffee that Ian had pushed toward her earlier. Sweet and black, exactly how she liked it. Because he knew just how much sugar she wanted, Maura thought. Because he knew everything about her.

There were plenty of words to give him, but if Ian knew her so well, Maura also understood him inside and out. He wasn't going to listen to her, no matter how pretty she made the words, how compelling her argument. She let her silence speak for her instead, and it stretched on and on until finally, Ian met her gaze.

"I can't seem to give you what you want," Ian said.

At that typical male bullshit excuse, that final slice that severed the already fragile thread of her patience with him, Maura stood. "Have you ever even asked me what I want?"

He had no answer for that.

She watched him struggle to find one for a few seconds before she leaned toward him again, both hands flat on the table. "No. Of course you haven't. You just assume you know. It's not that you can't give me what I want, Ian. It's that you don't want to give me anything."

"I'm sorry."

She shook her head. "No. You're not. You're scared. There's a difference."

That made him angry. "You're the one who always told me it wasn't going to last. This is not an exit, remember that?"

She remembered, all right. "I was wrong. I was scared, too."

"And now you're not?"

"I'm terrified," she told him in a low voice. "But at least I'm willing to try. Can't you even give me that, Ian? Can't you even try?"

She'd always been able to read his expressions, but now whatever went on behind his eyes was masked with a blankness no less impenetrable because she knew he was forcing it. Ian turned his mug in his hands, around and around and around. This was not the man who'd once made her come in the backseat of his car without ever taking off her clothes. This was someone else. A stranger, and though her heart cracked, it didn't quite break.

"I think we shouldn't see each other again," he said.

No. That was not what she'd come here for today. Not the reason she'd lined her eyes and mouth and scented her skin and curled her hair. She'd known the conversation was going to be uncomfortable and probably fraught with emotion. She hadn't been certain of the outcome, not exactly, but not seeing him again could not be it. Never that.

"How can you say that?" She asked him. "After everything, that's your answer?"

He looked at her. "You need time, Maura."

"Time. I took my time. It's been months, Ian. I waited until everything was official before I called you. I did that so there wouldn't be any reason to hold us back." She shook her head, trying to keep her voice from shaking.

"All of this is going to take time before you're ready for a relationship again. You need time to figure out what you really want."

"I know what I really want. How long do you think it would take me?"

"At least eighteen months," Ian told her, and Maura's jaw dropped.

"You think I need a year and a half to figure out that I'm in love with you and have been for the past three years, and that I can't imagine the rest of my life without you in it? Ian," Maura said, "have you ever known me to be a woman who wasn't sure about what she wanted?"

He gave her a stubborn frown. "You're asking if I can

make a go of this with you now, and the answer has to be no."

After all this time, the years, the grief, and now he was deciding he had to tell her no?

Maura straightened. Shoulders square. Chin high. Not accusing, not demanding. Not begging. "You're going to let me walk away."

"Yes."

She swallowed her anger. Made herself calm. "When we are together, everything shines."

"You'll find someone else."

"Of course I will. You think I can't walk out that door right now and find someone? A dozen someones?" It should've sounded arrogant, but it was the truth. "I don't want someone else. None of them will be you."

He tried to laugh, to make a joke. "C'mon. You'll have your pick."

Maura wasn't laughing. She moved around the table while he still sat. It gave her a little power, at least, standing over him this way. She made her face and voice cold because she wanted to be warm. "You don't get to pick who makes you shine."

And then she left him in his spotless kitchen, alone.

Perfectly Reckless

Also by Megan Hart

All the Lies We Tell

All the Secrets We Keep

A Heart Full of Stars

Always You

Broken

Castle in the Sand

Clearwater

Crossing the Line

Deeper

Dirty

Everything Changes

Flying

Hold Me Close

Hurt the One You Love

Indecent Experiment

Lovely Wild

Naked

Out of the Dark

Passion Model

Precious and Fragile Things

Reawakened Passions

Ride with the Devil

Selfish is the Heart

Stranger

Stumble into Love

Switch

Tear You Apart

Tempted

The Darkest Embrace

The Favor

The Resurrected One: First Come the Storms

The Resurrected Two: And Then the Infection

The Resurrected Three: And After That...Resurrection

Womb

The Space Between Us

Unforgivable

Vanilla

About the Author

I was born and then I lived awhile. Then I did some stuff and other things. Now, I mostly write books. Some of them use a lot of bad words, but most of the other words are okay.

I can't live without music, the internet, or the ocean, but I have kicked the Coke Zero habit. I can't stand the feeling of corduroy or velvet, and modern art leaves me cold. I write a little bit of everything from horror to romance, and I don't answer to the name "Meg."

If you liked this book, please tell everyone you love to buy it. If you hated it, please tell everyone you hate to buy it.

Find me here!

www.meganhart.com

readinbed@gmail.com

Made in United States
North Haven, CT
24 October 2023

43136155R00202